THE BUSINESS TRIP

:Subscribe to my Youtube Channel: @itsCallieTaylor

:)

THE BUSINESS TRIP

JESSIE GARCIA

ST. MARTIN'S PRESS
NEW YORK

This is a work of fiction. All of the characters, organizations, and events portrayed in this novel are either products of the author's imagination or are used fictitiously.

First published in the United States by St. Martin's Press, an imprint of St. Martin's Publishing Group

www.stmartins.com

Library of Congress Cataloging-in-Publication Data

Names: Garcia, Jessie, 1970– author.
Title: The business trip / Jessie Garcia.
Description: First edition. | New York : St. Martin's Press, 2025.
Identifiers: LCCN 2024025613 | ISBN 9781250364418 (hardcover) | ISBN 9781250364425 (ebook)
Subjects: LCGFT: Thrillers (Fiction) | Novels.
Classification: LCC PS3607.A721834 B87 2025 | DDC 813/.6—dc23/eng/20240624
LC record available at https://lccn.loc.gov/2024025613

Our books may be purchased in bulk for promotional, educational, or business use. Please contact your local bookseller or the Macmillan Corporate and Premium Sales Department at 1-800-221-7945, extension 5442, or by email at MacmillanSpecialMarkets@macmillan.com.

First Edition: 2025

10 9 8 7 6 5 4 3 2 1

Dedicated to my mom,
who gave me a love of the written word

PART ONE

CHAPTER 1

Jasmine

The Day of the Flight

I had to move carefully, quietly, grabbing only what I could in the dark without waking Glenn. He snorted and rolled to his side, and I froze, hand in midair above the suitcase, ready to abort the mission and slip back under the covers if needed. I could always lie and tell him that I had just gotten up to use the bathroom. If that happened, I was praying that he wouldn't notice I was wearing jeans.

His mouth began to gape open in a comical way, and he lightly snored. He seemed to be solidly asleep, perhaps thanks in part to Ambien, his sleeping medication. He hadn't exactly taken one by choice last night. I had crushed up a pill and put the powder into his beer can. He kept the Ambien in the bathroom cupboard. They came from a buddy on the black market and were extra strong, he told me, more than any doctor would prescribe. These would usually put him out like a light.

But even with him asleep, I couldn't risk opening a dresser drawer. That old wooden dresser creaked with every tiny move. I also couldn't take the chance of the clatter of hangers in the closet, so I would have to select from what was on the floor or in the laundry hamper to take with me. A pair of sweatpants and leggings, some underwear and a bra from the hamper, a couple of shirts of mine, and one warm red flannel button-up of Glenn's I had always liked. It was January, after all, and I was headed from Wisconsin to Denver. Giving me his flannel shirt was the least he could do.

I couldn't find any matching socks, so I took a few orphan ones and threw them in. I could buy new socks in my new city. Same with a toothbrush and other necessities. I wanted my patchouli perfume, though, and quietly I plucked the small sample bottle from the drugstore off the top of the dresser, dabbing my wrists gently with the familiar scent that so reminded me of my grandma before securing the lid tightly so it wouldn't leak in my purse.

Slowly I slipped on my tennis shoes, keeping my gaze on Glenn the entire time. His eyelids were fluttering in REM sleep. My heart seemed to be going just as fast. He usually wasn't up until around eleven a.m., six hours from now. I had tried to time it perfectly, to make my escape two hours after he fell asleep.

Glenn would never guess that I was at the airport. If he was suspicious, he would probably check the bus station in downtown Madison, maybe the train depot in nearby Columbus. More likely he would think I was at a friend's or coworker's and just pouting for a night, and he would go storming around looking for me, as he had in the past. No way he would believe that I had money for an airplane ticket, but I did. I had been squirreling away my tips at the bar for more than a year, and grabbing the occasional ten or twenty from Glenn's wallet when I thought he wouldn't notice. Paydays and lucky nights at the casino were usually prime times.

As I stood up, my eye caught the outline of my face in the

mirror above the dresser, moonlight illuminating half of it. Long blond hair, a pair of fake circular glasses from Goodwill that always reminded me of John Lennon. They didn't have real lenses, just clear plastic ones, but I liked the way I looked in them and would put them on occasionally. I was proud that at my age of forty-four I still didn't need real glasses.

Easing one of my shirtsleeves up, I winced looking at the deep bruise with the finger marks that Glenn had created a few nights ago. Our last fight. The one that broke me. He accused me of flirting with guys at the bar, called me a "fucking whore," and pushed me onto the bed, forcing sex. I turned my head away and shut my eyes. When it was over, he grabbed my arm, the one now bruised, and squeezed it until it became numb.

"What's wrong? Are you thinking about one of the guys at the bar instead of me? Huh? Don't fucking lie to me . . . bitch."

He kept the pressure on until I begged him to stop. Finally, he tossed the arm back down to the bed hard and went to shower. He liked to tell me I was dirty. I would always curl up into a ball while he was in the shower, crying softly, biting my fingernails, and plotting my escape.

I had tried twice before to leave him, but he found me, dragging me by the hair, throwing me into his pickup truck, and bringing me back to his trailer. He didn't allow me to have my own car. He would pick me up and drop me off for work, and often he spent most of his night in the bar too, ostensibly playing pool or darts, but I could feel his eyes on me, especially as I waited on other men.

How had it gone so wrong? When I first met Glenn, he was one of those bar guys. I'd had a series of jobs I never enjoyed over my life but had landed at a large, rollicking Midwestern tavern thanks to my old high school friend Anna, who worked there. It was the kind where the beer and laughs flowed freely late into every night. I was feeling like I could begin to stand on my own two feet coming off a long, tumultuous relationship. It was just three months after the breakup, in fact, and I wanted to spend time alone to heal and *then* try to meet someone decent. But my alone time didn't last nearly long enough.

Glenn was a burly guy who made an entrance wherever he went. He had broad shoulders and long hair in a ponytail, and he caught my eye right away. Before I knew it, we started flirting as I brought him his bottles of Miller High Life.

He seemed so kind at first, offering to walk me to my car after closing time so that I would be safe, politely asking me if I would share my phone number with him. On our first date, he insisted that I not get out of the pickup truck until he could walk around and open my door. It was so old-fashioned it made me giggle.

At first, I didn't know if he'd actually be into me. He wasn't even forty yet, and I felt like a much older woman next to him. But we both liked live music, so we had gone to concerts and shows, and in the dancing and sweat and heat, we had our first kiss, and I spent the night at his trailer.

For months, things were great. I thought I had found my Prince Charming. We would stay up late, sleep in, make love before breakfast and sometimes after, and take rides out to the country on weekends on his Harley. I moved out of my place and into his in short order, my original plan to be alone for a while fading at the prospect of new love.

But the first sign of things going awry was when my car broke down. Glenn insisted that we just sell it for scrap and that he would drive me wherever I needed to go. I didn't like the idea of losing my car. She had been with me for almost ten years. I nicknamed her Motoring Maeve, and I didn't relish the idea of Maeve being gone, forcing me to depend on Glenn.

But he insisted that it made the most sense since he had a flexible construction job and could come and go as he pleased. The scrapyard gave us $600 for dear Maeve. Glenn declared it would go to "household expenses" and pocketed it.

Then his jealousy started. If I talked to a salesclerk at a store, Glenn would press me for whether I found the stranger attractive. He also started telling me what not to wear at work: "That top shows too much of your tits" or "That color makes you look even older than you are."

He didn't like me to be alone, not even for a Sunday stroll. "Why would you need to go without me?" he would ask. "Aren't we in love?" He always kept his arm tightly around me the entire time. At first, it felt loving, but as time went on, it morphed into possessiveness.

The rough sex was next. He wanted to try tying me to the bed and I balked. He said I needed to please him and we would try whatever he wanted, and then he pushed me down and just did it, my arms pinned to the bedpost. After that, it was sex whenever he wanted in whatever way he wanted, no matter how exhausted I was when I got home from work.

But the worst of it happened unexpectedly in the middle of the night. I was sleeping when suddenly I felt a deep pressure around my head and an inability to breathe. Realizing with horrifying clarity that there was a pillow on my face, I heard Glenn laughing as I began to flail. Just as I tried to belt out a scream, he lifted the pillow and fell over on his side, cackling uncontrollably.

Tears came to my eyes as I coughed and sputtered, finally gaining enough breath to blurt, "What the *fuck*?"

"Oh my God, Jasmine. Your face, your face when I took the pillow off. Your eyes, holy shit, I've never seen your eyes look like that . . ."

He continued to belly laugh, clutching his side and falling over, as I reached over and pounded his arm with my fists, crying and coughing.

"That. Is. Not. Funny. Jesus Christ, Glenn."

"Come here, baby, I'm just joking around." He pulled me into his arms and started kissing my head and face.

That's when I decided to take part of my tip money each night and hide it in a tampon holder in my fringed purse. He always wanted some of my tips to go to those elusive "household expenses," but I could manage to slide a bit away without him noticing. I would then transfer the cash into a photo album I kept in a cardboard box in the storage area of his trailer. He would never look there. He didn't care about my childhood pictures or the cards and mementos I had in the box. I figured he would just trash the whole thing or throw it into a firepit once I was gone.

To make room for my ever-growing stash of cash, I removed the plastic holders from the circular metal hooks in the photo album, taking the aging pictures out of their liners and keeping those loose-leaf. With no full page holders, I had space for bills. Using a box of matches, I set the holders on fire out back while Glenn was at work, the scent of burning plastic and paper overwhelming my nose and making my eyes water, but also smelling like freedom to me.

It went on like this for over a year, me faking that things were normal with Glenn while plotting my escape. I had become a robot around him, a shell of the former lively Jasmine that I was. Jasmine Veronica was my name. What my mother was thinking I never knew. Then again, she had felt like a stranger to me for much of my life. Mom had three kids with three different men, and for some reason she decided early on that I was the bad seed. I must have been only eight or nine when I overheard her tell a friend that she *never* should have had a third, that my dad was the worst of the bunch, that I was too much like him. Rumor had it he was in jail somewhere. Not that any of our fathers were ever around. Mom resented being saddled with kids—that much was clear—or at least she resented being saddled with me.

I was five years younger than my sister and seven years younger than my brother. I grew up feeling like a constant outcast. Skinny and awkward, I needed years of braces while my siblings were blessed with near-perfect teeth. Mom complained constantly about the cost. I struggled mightily in math and science while they both seemed to find everything about school easy. It got so bad for me that I was almost held back a year. Mom told a friend, in front of me this time, how mortified she was.

Everything I did or wanted seemed like a bother, even basic needs such as food. "You're hungry *again*?" she would say with a deep sigh and a long stare, even at what felt like normal mealtimes to me. She nicknamed me "Little Piggy" and would call out "This Little Piggy went to market . . ." when I came hunting for a snack. My siblings were no help. They never seemed to find me anything but annoying, telling me to leave them alone when I tried to initiate play or talk about any emotions.

As I grew up, I had some run-ins with the police in high school. Wasn't that normal? Then I got knocked up and had an abortion that Mom had to pay for when I was eighteen. Wasn't that better than bringing an unwanted kid into this crazy world? So I didn't go to regular college like my brother and sister. I tried cosmetology school because I had always liked playing with makeup, but Mom told me that she was done paying for stuff, and I had to drop out when I couldn't afford tuition.

The truth was she just didn't like me and never had. The fact that she worked as a nurse's assistant at an old folks' home was the ultimate irony. She could care for complete strangers with tenderness, but not show an ounce of TLC for her own daughter.

Mom and I really drifted apart after the abortion and the cosmetology school mess. For some years, we exchanged perfunctory Christmas cards, the writing increasingly stilted and formal, as if we were talking to a long-lost neighbor, not a close family member.

"Have a very Merry Christmas," Mom had written on the last one. It didn't even have my name on the inside, and she had signed it "Your Mother" and not "Love, Mom." I couldn't help but mentally compare it to what I thought she would be writing to my brother and sister, and I decided then and there to stop exchanging cards, or words. When I moved to a new apartment in town, I didn't give her my address. We hadn't talked since. Last I heard, my brother lived in Chicago and my sister somewhere in upstate New York. He did something with computers, and she was one of those businesswomen who worked as a pharmaceutical rep and who I imagined jetting around the country to important meetings and stuff. I hadn't shared my new address with them either. The same year I moved on from Mom, I moved on from them as well. It was just easier for me all around to harden my heart.

I tried not to think of them or Mom very often. It made me angry and sad. I was mostly OK being away from all of them now, but sometimes I wished I had a family to lean on. This was one of those times. Instead, I would have to rely on my own smarts. I might not have been book-smart, but I was street-smart, I knew that.

It was my time.

The city of Denver sounded attractive to me. I didn't know why, didn't know anyone there, had never been, but a place with mountains and a bunch of laid-back outdoorsy people seemed glorious. Why not make a new start there? I didn't have much of a plan beyond getting to Denver with enough money to live until I found a job. I just needed to leave Glenn safely first. I had my cell phone, the huge wad of cash that I had retrieved from the photo album after Glenn had fallen asleep, some clothes, and a plan to fly that afternoon.

My big dilemma was how to get from our trailer to the airport without a car. Having never used Uber before, I asked Anna, the high school friend who had secured me the job at the bar, to show me how to install the app. We did it in the women's restroom after we were done cleaning up the night before. Anna was good at this sort of stuff, always had been. Back at Madison North High School, she liked to show us all kinds of technology that kind of blew our minds. At first it was stuff on a desktop computer. Now it was iPhone tricks, AI art, and what types of questions you could ask ChatGPT.

In the darkness of the trailer now, I nervously slipped my phone from my purse and cupped my hand around it so the light would not be too bright for Glenn. I was trying to summon a ride to the end of the drive where Glenn's trailer was parked. If this Uber app didn't work, I wasn't sure what I would do. Maybe abandon the plan for another day or week until I could get Anna to show me what I had done wrong. But as I searched for nearby cars, it seemed to function perfectly. It put a dot on my exact location and said a car driven by someone named Carlos was fifteen minutes away.

Fifteen minutes. *Breathe, Jasmine, breathe.* Confirming the pickup, I looked over at Glenn. He was naked, the way he always slept, with a thin sheet haphazardly flung over him. I was always cold and needed warm pajamas and sometimes two blankets, especially in January in Wisconsin. He called me an "old fucking lady" and tried to get me to sleep naked too, but I would shiver all night if I tried.

Bending down, I pushed the bulk of my cash into the suitcase and started to carefully zip it closed. This might be the trickiest part, other than actually sneaking out the front door without making too much noise. Carefully, I inched the zipper a centimeter and waited to see if he had any reaction. Another centimeter and I waited again. I tried an inch the next time, but he flipped onto his back, his arm going up over his head, and I stopped and waited until he fully settled into sleep again.

I glanced at my side of the bed, and a fantasy flashed into my head: What if I grabbed my pillow and smothered *his* face while he slept? What if I didn't release it as he had to me? I could just leave him there, dead. But I wasn't sure I could overpower him, and the prospect of a life in jail was too much. Everyone would know it was me.

No, just pure escape was best. Back to the centimeter plan with my suitcase. It took me over five minutes to get it fully zipped. Picking it up in my arms so as not to roll it, I backed out of the bedroom like a thief, eyes trained on Glenn the entire time.

The front door was next. It had a heavy main door and a squeaky screen door, but I had played a trick on Glenn a few days ago, taking a box cutter from his toolbox and slashing a gash into the screen that I said was from the recent winter windstorm knocking it open. That forced Glenn to take it to his buddy at Monona Storm and Screen for repair. With the screen door out of the picture, the front door wouldn't be as bad to open.

And I was the stupid one? I'd show him, my family, everybody.

Suddenly, I thought of the coming Uber and wondered if I

needed to hurry. Would the driver honk if I wasn't there right at the appointed time? My heart went even faster, and my hands began to sweat, causing the suitcase in my arms to slip for a moment. I righted it, wiping each palm quickly on my jeans as the other arm held the suitcase.

I could still hear Glenn's rhythmic breathing down the hall of the trailer, the rasp of air in and out of his lungs. He was such a heavy breather. My right hand went to the door handle and turned it a millimeter at a time, listening for that final click as it yielded open.

An owl hooted in a nearby tree, and the sound both startled and calmed me. With renewed purpose, I pulled the door open and stepped outside the trailer. Breathing in the cold air, I shut the door behind me as carefully as I could. A blast of winter shouldn't be the thing to wake Glenn.

It was so frigid outside that my breath crystallized, but it would be quiet weather for flying. A snowstorm would have foiled my plans. I had been watching the forecast on the local CBS affiliate for a week to be sure. Their main meteorologist was my favorite. He was good-looking and funny. Glenn had once asked me if I thought the meteorologist was sexy. I lied and said no.

There was the sound of a car rolling along the gravel in the distance, and I saw a sweep of headlights. Glenn didn't like full-blown RV places—too many people, he said—so he had gotten a small plot of land and set up his trailer there. We had some neighbors within walking distance but not close enough to see on a daily basis.

Cocking my head to listen for any movement from Glenn over the gravel sound, I was filled with relief that the trailer remained silent. Wrapping my arms around my suitcase, I straightened up to walk as upright and confidently as I could toward this waiting Uber. I had to look in control, not like a madwoman on the run. Taking deep gulps of air and composing my face into a bright smile, I made my way to the car.

I planned to tell the driver I was going on a business trip if he asked. I thought of my sister with what I imagined to be fancy clothes and all the makeup she wanted and expensive shoes on her feet. I could act like I was important and fantasize that I would be wowing some room with my business savvy later in the day. Maybe it wasn't too late for that life for real. Maybe I could take some business classes in Denver and eventually find my way to a job like that. This was the new me.

Carlos was a heavyset guy whose unkempt hair made me wonder if he had just woken up, but he was chatty, asking me lots of questions. I started in on the lies. Why was I flying? "Business trip." What did I do? Channeling my sister: "I work for a pharmaceutical company." Where was the trip? I didn't want to say Denver, just in case Glenn somehow tracked this man down, so I picked my sister's state too: "New York." I figured there had to be plenty of conventions and meetings there.

Deftly, I turned the conversation to him, and he started droning on about his kids and their extracurriculars. Perfect. Zoning out, I stared out the window, making only small comments of affirmation when I felt I should be responding.

Carlos pulled up to Delta departures. As he was retrieving my bag from the trunk, I had a sudden flash of fear. What if I saw someone I knew at the airport who happened to be flying the same day? Someone from the bar or from my other previous jobs around town, including gas station attendant and maid at several places? I had a plan, but it didn't feel very foolproof.

A blue Los Angeles Dodgers baseball cap from a thrift shop sat in my purse. That, plus those fake round glasses, would be my partial disguise. I could also hide in a corner chair or even in the women's bathroom for as long as I needed to before the flight took off.

Quickly, I slipped on the cap and tucked my hair up into it as best I could, keeping my eyes low as I made my way to the ticket counter. A perky woman with a flawless bob and way too much eyeshadow greeted me.

"Good morning! Checking in today?"

How could she be *this* awake at 5:30 a.m.?

"Yes, I actually have to buy my ticket. It's OK to pay cash, right?"

"Sure is," she answered, but I thought I could also feel her eyeing me. What woman shows up in a baseball cap and pays cash? "And where are we headed today?"

"Denver," I replied and mustered up fake enthusiasm. "Bachelorette party. Girls just want to have fun, right?"

"Yes, they do," she said, taking my driver's license and typing in the information as I carefully reached into my purse and removed some of the cash. Not enough for her to see the wad that remained, of course. I didn't want her to get suspicious. I set the bills on the counter and added, "I've been saving up tip money for this. I can't wait!"

"Do you need a return ticket too?" she asked.

I hadn't anticipated that question. I had to think fast.

"Uh, no . . . I'm driving back with one of my girlfriends Monday."

She nodded and counted the bills, then hit a few buttons and a ticket started spitting out, the whir of electronic printing sounding like further freedom to me. My shoulders began to relax just a touch.

"You're here awfully early." She cocked her head slightly to the side. "Your flight doesn't leave until this afternoon."

My shoulders tensed again. I tried to act as if I were laughing it off.

"Oh. I have some work to do, so I thought I would just do it here." I gestured toward the carry-on. "My laptop is in my bag. And another girlfriend is joining me for lunch before we board."

She handed me the boarding pass. "Terrific. I hope you have a great girls' weekend!"

"Thanks." I smiled and wheeled my carry-on filled with mismatched socks and dirty clothes to the security area, picturing Glenn, still deeply asleep. But what would happen when he woke up? Nervous energy began to settle in, and I started to chew my fingernail. He might or might not report me as missing. I was pretty sure he wouldn't because he wouldn't want to be the center of a police probe. They could find out he never paid taxes and got paid mostly in cash from his construction buddies. Nor would he want the feds to see the pot plants he kept in the window by the sink. Marijuana was still illegal in Wisconsin. Would he care enough about me to file a missing person's report? Or would he chalk it up to "oh well, the bitch is gone" and move on to find someone new? I guessed the latter.

I figured I had maybe a week before he would do anything too big. In the meantime, he would be calling me, texting me, trying to track me down across town, threatening me, telling me I had better fucking get home. But after a week, I could imagine him reaching a decision point. Would he inform the police, or would he think that was too risky on himself? Continuing to mull this over as I got through security and found the gate, I slid into one of the black vinyl chairs and found a different nail to chew.

Squeezing my eyes tight, I thought of my grandma, the one person in life who I had felt truly close to. Grandma had died right before I hit high school. Mom later said that Grandma would roll over in her grave if she saw how I had turned out, but I didn't believe that. The Grandma I remembered brought me presents and candy and let me sit on her lap as long as I wanted as a young child, the smell of her patchouli perfume comforting me. She used to tell me I was smart and pretty, in that order, and not to confuse the order. That was even after my struggles with schoolwork, and those words meant so much to me. Now I needed her to look down from heaven and help guide me. I wasn't the praying type, but I shut my eyes and sent one up to Grandma anyway.

CHAPTER 2

Stephanie

The Night Before the Flight

Packing was one of my least favorite activities. Ironic, given how much I traveled. Oh, sure, I always had a small bag of toiletries ready, travel-size shampoo and conditioner from my favorite brand, a bar of moisturizing soap in a pink plastic container, a sample of my favorite perfume (floral and airy), but it was the organizing of clothes that had always been a chore for me. Now it was 10:30 p.m. and I couldn't put it off any longer.

I had promised my team I would work a half day the next morning before leaving for the conference. You know, get them going on the right foot before the boss was gone. It was going to be a long travel day: Madison to Denver. Denver to San Diego. The News Coverage Summit started Thursday morning.

In attendance would be a hundred news directors, none of whom had ever met each other, all coming together to hear from experts and share opinions. Television stations across the country were trying to make local TV news better than it was. Viewers wanted something different—declining ratings proved that—and we were all attempting to figure out exactly what.

When I looked over the clothes in my closet, a dark green

silky blouse caught my eye, and I slid it off the hanger, pairing it with some tan work pants; that would work for outfit number one for the first day.

Now for outfit number two. My eyes scanned the rows of professional clothes. I had tried to organize my closet by work and play, half on one side and half on the other. The play side was a mess: yoga pants and sweatshirts haphazardly strewn about, jeans discarded on the floor. But the work side I kept fairly well organized. Had even arranged it by color. Green was taken care of with the blouse, so how about a pop of something else? I spotted a bright pink blazer and found a fitted black shirt to go under it with some black pants. Those could go with black pumps. For outfit number three, I dialed it back a bit and chose a navy blue sweater and houndstooth pants with shoes that looked like sneakers with a heel.

Now that the main outfits were taken care of, I could add the supplementary ones. A long floral dress and a shorter black one, pajamas, workout shorts, running shoes, my favorite pairs of underwear, several bras ranging from practical to lacy, Spanx of various configurations, and a mix of socks.

Adding my prescription sleeping medicine, Ambien, and a flat iron and curling iron for options, I packed up a travel jewelry box with short and long earrings and a selection of necklaces. Finally, around 11:15, the duty was done. Heaving a sigh as fatigue started to creep up behind my eyes, I was zipping the suitcase closed when Fred came and rubbed against my leg, purring softly.

"Hey, Freddie boy." I picked him up and cradled him on his back like a baby in the crook of my left arm. He blinked at me approvingly and purred more as I continued to pet his belly with my other hand. "Yes, Mama is going away, but I'll be back soon. And Robert will feed you."

Mama had to go away too often. My boss, Dave, was always asking me to represent the station at conferences, seminars, workshops, and our quarterly meetings at corporate headquarters in Cleveland. I had been feeling for a long time like he probably thought I was the easy button to push. Maybe I was. A divorced woman with a grown child and only a cat, I could drop everything and go, that much was true, but the travel was wearing on me. None of it was fun travel. It was work, and I had to be "on" all the time, schmoozing with others and talking corporate-speak. This was the fourth work trip in the past six months I had been asked to go on.

Kissing Fred on the top of his head, I put him back on all fours. He sniffed the suitcase, rubbed his cheek against it twice, and jumped on my bed, walking in a slow circle to find his spot, ready for sleep.

Changing into flannel pajamas and pulling on some slippers to combat the relentless January cold, I headed down to the kitchen, took out several cans of wet cat food and a bag of dry food, and put them on the counter, scribbling a note for Robert.

Hi Neighbor. Thanks again for feeding F. I'll get you a present from CA. Good luck on your date! Also, I decided to get that alarm clock that wakes you up with light, the one you told me about. It's coming Friday. Can you bring it in?

I was so thankful for Robert. We had become good friends since he moved into the townhouse next door to me two and a half years prior. Our relationship started on a summer day when he was unpacking. We both had windows open, and I heard him blasting the soundtrack to *Fiddler on the Roof*. As a former high school theater kid myself, I started humming along and smiling. Later that afternoon, I was out front watering the plants on my side when he came out with a load of folded cardboard moving boxes in his arms.

"Oh, hey there. Are you my neighbor?" he asked cheerily. Quickly, I sized him up. Silver hair, black-rimmed glasses, and a smile that was slightly crooked. He was wearing a T-shirt that said "Gay and Gray. Wanna Stay?"

"Yes, hi, I'm Stephanie," I said, trying to put on my best cheery-neighbor voice. "Stephanie Monroe. Welcome."

As I extended my hand, he put the boxes down and took it. The grip was firm and confident, and his eyes sparkled as he pumped my arm.

"Thank you. Happy to be here. I'm Robert Tayburn, the new and obviously obnoxiously loud person next door to you. I hope you don't mind. The first thing I do in a new place is hook up the Bluetooth. I can't unpack without a little fun music to bop around to."

"No, I don't mind. In fact, I love *Fiddler*," I said and then added some of the lyrics for good measure in a singsongy tone: "*To life! To life! L'chaim!*"

"Oh. My. God. You know the words!" He threw his head back and laughed.

"I was in the cast in high school." I smiled. "Just the ensemble, but I loved it."

"I may have died and gone to neighbor heaven!" Robert cried out.

From there, we just kept talking. Since we were a pair of self-professed musical connoisseurs, Robert suggested "Broadway and Bubbly" nights, and we took turns at each other's townhouse, eating from charcuterie boards, drinking champagne, and singing along. He also had a cat, and soon Evita and Fred were a shared conversation topic.

Robert had never been married. He told me about dates he went on and new men he met, and he encouraged me to get out there more. I told him about my time-sucking job and the crazy television news business I was in. He never watched the news unless there was a storm coming and he needed to see the weather. The rest he considered too negative or too fluff. More than once, he chided me for my profession in a joking way. Eventually, though, he became my confidant. Because he didn't care that our anchors or reporters were locally famous and because he was a good listener, I found myself downloading things that happened at work.

"So you're telling me this anchor was acting like the evil stepmother in *Cinderella*?" he would ask. "Just turn 'em into a pumpkin and move on, sister! You're the boss!"

He helped when I complained about the still male-dominated field. Sometimes at awards banquets or events, other news directors in town, who happened to all be male, would sit together in what appeared to be a good old boys' club.

"They're jealous," Robert would counsel. "Because you're kicking their ass and they feel threatened."

At least I had a good boss. Dave treated me with nothing but respect, and Robert liked him for that.

"But don't tell Dave that you don't watch local TV news," I had laughed one night during Broadway and Bubbly. "You're part of the problem that every station is trying to fix."

"Don't worry, I'm an excellent liar," he said, giving me his full crooked smile. "He'll think I'm the biggest Channel 3 fan out there."

Robert felt like a brother. He worked from home for a local tech company, so he was happy to feed Fred when I was out of town. I could trust him with a key to my place, which was why he always had one on his side of the townhouse.

Back upstairs after writing the note for this latest trip, I brushed my teeth, washed my face with an apricot scrub, wiped it with exfoliating pads dabbed in witch hazel toner, applied under-eye night eye cream, and put on way-too-expensive face moisturizer that Gwyneth Paltrow claimed in an Instagram ad was a miracle product. I had clicked on it in a moment of weakness when my forty-five-year-old face looked closer to fifty than forty to me. It smelled like roses but had done nothing so far to tighten my skin.

Spritzing my pillow with lavender sleep spray that also smelled nice but didn't seem to induce instant sleep very often, I climbed into bed next to Fred and reached for my phone on the bedside table. Yes, I knew the blue light was bad for me. Yes, I knew I should be reading a book instead, but the lure of a digital hit before bed was too great.

My order of checking items was always the same: texts, Teams messages, work email, personal email, Facebook, Twitter (I refused to call it X), Instagram, Threads, TikTok, and my news app. As news director, I had to be constantly up on what was happening both here in Madison and also across the country.

Thankfully, there were no texts. You never knew what you might get when you oversaw a newsroom full of young journalists. People were always asking questions, feeling the need to text me or my assistant news director at any time of day or night, especially the overnight crew, who arrived at ten p.m. and worked to produce the morning show. They were fresh out of college and fearful of making mistakes, so they asked a lot of questions.

I was glad to see that it appeared to be a quiet night in Madison. That was one of the reasons I liked being a smaller-market news director. Shootings were rare. Our biggest events were tied to the university or state politics. We still covered things like the opening of the RV show or the Little League tournament that brought out thousands.

I had done the big-city thing, had gone to college at DePaul and worked in Chicago, moving up the ladder from intern to executive producer. The long commute from our suburb to the NBC affiliate in downtown Chicago was just about killing me, though, ninety minutes each way on a good day, so when an assistant news director job opened in Madison, my then husband Jason, our son Evan, and I packed up and decided to give smaller-town living a try. Two years in, the news director left and Dave promoted me. I had been in the role ever since.

Evan was just out of college now and working his first career job doing marketing for a soccer team in Minneapolis. Jason and I had lasted only a year past Evan's empty-nest departure for college. We found we just didn't have much to say to each other without the hustle of a shared child, and we drifted further apart, watching our favorite TV shows in separate rooms, finding excuses to stay late at work, and exercising, shopping, and eating at different times.

I would steal glances at Jason around the house and try to find the young guy I met at DePaul, but everything seemed to have changed. His face was older, of course, as was mine, but I couldn't identify the handsome kid I had fallen in love with. Instead, things he did annoyed me: the way he never rinsed out his coffee cup but instead left it sitting next to the sink so that a dark brown film hardened on the bottom; his obsession with football and how he seemed to think he was part of the game himself as he rocked and swayed with each play; the way he not only snored but snorted when he fell asleep on the couch; the way he always left the grocery shopping and laundry to me, even though I worked longer hours. When we took walks, we walked at different paces. His stride was much longer than mine, and I noticed he didn't slow down like he used to in order to let me keep up. Even a simple walk showed how out of sync we were. We were so young when we had Evan, and Jason had been a good father, but I was just bored and increasingly irked by him.

Finally, one night, I built up the courage to ask him if he thought we were still compatible. He sat up from his reclined position on the couch, looked at me without speaking for a solid thirty seconds, and then said, "I guess we've both been feeling the same thing, huh?" My stomach dropped. When he added, "Maybe we should try living apart," I felt an equal amount of relief, hurt that he had been the one to propose it, and sadness that a partnership that had raised such a solid kid was coming to an end. We never even tried counseling. It was an amicable divorce and it was fast. Thankfully, he told me he had no problem with me keeping Fred. I would have fought hard for my Freddie boy.

Jason remarried sooner than I would have thought, which gave me a few pangs when I saw the wedding pictures with his new wife and her daughters, plus Evan, looking so dapper in his suit, but a part of me was happy for Jason. Truth was, I just wanted the same. I liked my life, but I longed for the sort of easy companionship I had with Robert, just with someone who found me physically attractive. Maybe I'd meet a guy this weekend—dark and handsome came to mind. A new romance would be so exciting. I longed for adventure, change, a vacation, and a life partner. None of it had been happening in my life for way too long. When I suggested to Dave that my assistant news director, Bruce, be sent to this conference, Dave said that Bruce would have a hard time getting away because he had two younger children still at home. I tossed a few other names from the newsroom out to Dave, saying that they might enjoy a conference, but Dave shut them all down. They either also had families, or they were too young and inexperienced to represent the station. So I just kept going on a hamster wheel I seemingly had no control of. It was long past time to step off, even briefly.

If someone looked at my life from the outside, they might be impressed. I had money and a career and a healthy adult son. I had never had a major disease, and while my body could stand to tighten up a bit—the little bat wings under my arms especially bothered me—I was still in decent shape. My brown hair had a slight natural wave. Grays were creeping in, but I went to the salon to have it dyed every other month and wore it in a professional cut below my ears and above my shoulders. I had my eyebrows microbladed twice per year and my fingernails and toenails gel-polished every three weeks. This month both were a soft pink. I had a Peloton that I didn't use nearly as much as I used to, a treadmill, yoga mats, bricks and bolsters, Pilates balls, and a home weight set, all in a spare room in my townhouse. Clothing arrived in a box from Stitch Fix, meals in a box from Hello Fresh, anything else I wanted in a box delivered within twenty-four hours from Amazon. Sometimes I felt as if my life was a series of boxes. Robert joked that I was "boxed in." He preferred shopping in actual stores.

I guess I was just a normal American female executive. But I felt a sameness to my days, a lack of camaraderie outside of Robert. Even my relationship with Evan seemed like it was slipping out of my control. He appeared to be upset with me, not Jason, over the divorce, for reasons I couldn't fathom, and now he usually said he was too busy to talk. Our once-per-week conversations were becoming more like every other week or even less frequent. He had chosen Jason's house for both Thanksgiving and Christmas this past year, saying it was more fun with his stepsisters in the house. I practically had to beg just to get him to meet me for lunch the day after Christmas.

At night, when I lay awake staring at the ceiling, I would sometimes wonder if all the times I had missed school events when I was working nightside or pulling a double in television news had hurt our relationship too. Jason's normal day job let him be there for everything. Could Evan harbor resentment about me pulling those late hours and not being able to slip away to all of the band concerts and soccer games of his youth? Or taking a phone call from a young staffer during dinner, stepping away and telling Evan I'd be right back as I answered some urgent plea about something? He had never said so, but the thought gnawed at me. The thing was, we had needed the money, and those were my hours and duties in a 24/7 business, so I didn't regret it from that standpoint, but my son's recent coldness had ripped a small seam in my soul that seemed to be expanding.

Sometimes I thought that Evan might need a reminder of how important I was to him. Nothing tragic, of course, but if I were diagnosed with a disease that would scare him just enough but I would recover from, maybe he'd feel some sympathy for me and get back into my corner. Or if I got lost in the woods for a few nights and returned as the conquering hero—would that make him respect me again? Would he come running into my arms like he did when he was a toddler? Maybe that would be the kick in the butt he needed. I had been a good mother, damn it, and launched him into full adulthood with every tool he needed, and now he largely ignored me. I vented about it to Robert one night, and he chuckled.

"So . . . are you telling me you'd be willing to be kidnapped?"

"I mean, maybe, as long as I'm not hurt in the process."

"A kindhearted kidnapper, got it," he said. "I'll put an ad on Indeed for you."

I punched him in the arm.

But truly, Evan wasn't my only issue. I longed for the old me when I used to be a rebel in college. I had been the one willing to skip class or use a fake ID to get into a bar. I was known for playing pranks on others in the dorm, or dressing up as a professor and doing an imitation of their style. Sadly, those days seemed another lifetime ago. I was a professional woman now and had appearances to keep up. Secretly, though, I ached for something fun and rebellious.

At least I would be meeting Diana, a new friend, in San Diego. We had a lot in common. I had just recently connected with her, and she seemed as interested in having an adventure as I was. She didn't work in news, but she would be a good help to me in having just a little bit of excitement this weekend.

I had been dreaming of just running off, starting a whole fresh and invigorating world for myself in Mexico, getting out of the news business and retiring to a life of wine and good books. Maybe that would make Evan want to visit me just to be living at my beach shack, checking out the girls down at the surf. This life-as-an-expat fantasy came more and more often lately. I found myself watching *House Hunters International* and making a list of places I could move to in Mexico due to its warmth and easy proximity to the US. What was keeping me in this cold northland other than Robert? He was a great neighbor, but I couldn't pin my whole world around that, could I?

I sighed as I put my phone back on the bedside table. My long-term future was too much to ponder at 11:45 at night. I just needed sleep. Clicking the light off and closing my eyes, I tried deep breathing to slow my heart rate. In for four counts, hold for seven, out for eight. The lavender scent from my pillow drifted into my nostrils, and I focused on letting it wash over me.

But it wasn't working.

As I lay there with my fluffy flowered comforter surrounding my body, and Fred by my legs, I felt myself becoming more alert instead of more tired. The fatigued feeling I'd had just forty-five minutes prior was disappearing. I felt like I had missed my window of sleep. There was anxiety poking at me about the trip ahead.

Opening one eye and peeking at the clock, I saw that it was almost 12:30. I had to be fully functional as the boss of a TV newsroom in less than eight hours, up in six and a half. Fuck. This wasn't good. *Go to sleep*, I told myself. *Go. To. Sleep.* But my mind fired back and said no.

At 12:45, I gave up. Heaving myself out of bed, to the annoyance of Fred, who lifted his head and gave a meow, I zipped open my suitcase, dug around in the dark until I found the bottle of Ambien, twisted the cap off, and swallowed one pill whole, washing it down with the water in a glass at my bedside table. My doctor had warned that I shouldn't drive within eight hours of consuming Ambien, and now I would have to be on the road in just over seven, but I needed to sleep. Sorry, Doc.

I hated nights like this, and they came too often, my mind whirring with a variety of worries—personnel issues, viewer hate mail, viewer love mail for some of our anchors and reporters that bordered on stalking, declining ratings, social media shenanigans by our staff. The list went on and on.

Crawling back under the flowered comforter and fumbling for my phone, I typed "ASMR" into the search bar. One of my girlfriends from an annual girls' weekend had turned me on to this years ago, and when I really needed sleep, I leaned into it. There were thousands of videos to choose from, mostly women but also some men. They did things like role plays where you were visiting a doctor or getting a facial. The soothing sound of their low talking promised to give you an autonomous sensory meridian response (ASMR)—or, in other words, a tingle in your head. It was my secret weapon for relaxation. I dialed up an oldie but goodie: a woman pretending she's giving you a consultation in a tattoo shop. Between that and the Ambien, I was finally getting sleepy a little after 1:15 a.m. As I drifted off, I kept thinking that maybe a change of scenery this weekend would be just what I needed. Maybe I'd actually have fun. Or have a fling. Maybe my life would never be the same again.

CHAPTER 3

Jasmine

The Day of the Flight

It was a long morning waiting at the airport. First, I grabbed a breakfast sandwich and some coffee and tried to catnap in my seat for a while, but the caffeine plus adrenaline made it impossible. Checking my phone over and over, I waited to see when that first text from Glenn would come in. As predicted, it was shortly after eleven.

Where the hell are you?

My stomach tensed up to the size and density of a golf ball, but I had a plan for this. Figuring I could buy myself a little time, I texted back.

We were out of milk and a few other things. I walked to the store

He didn't know that I had dumped the milk down the drain the day before in case he opened the fridge to check.

That's a fucking long way. It's cold. You know I don't like you walking alone. I'll come get you

No, I need the exercise. You told me to lose a few pounds, remember? I'll pick up stuff and make dinner. I'll see you after work around 5:30. I'll make steak

Medium rare. And potatoes too

This lie about walking to the store would buy me some crucial time, really all day, before he got home at 5:30 and saw I wasn't there.

I pictured him throwing off the sheet now, standing up and letting out one of his giant yawns, maybe adding in a belch or a fart too, then walking naked to the bathroom to take what he liked to call "my morning pisser." Shuddering at the image, I distracted myself by looking around at the other passengers in the airport. Such a mix of humanity, so many of them appearing happy. It wasn't fair that they got to experience joy and a carefree trip while my stomach was in shambles, my head jumbled with images of a boyfriend I was trying desperately to get away from.

Keep your breathing steady, Jasmine, I told myself. *Don't look nervous.* My hand went to the baseball cap on my head. It felt reassuring now, but I decided I would take it off when I walked down the jetway to the plane. That would be the moment the new, confident me was boarding, not the old, meek me. I wanted to present to the world a woman on a trip, flying with confidence and spark, a twinkle in her eye. A woman who fully knew herself and her place in the world, not the truth, a woman running from a tattered past that extended all the way to childhood.

Instead, I let the fantasies zip through my head. I could be going on a girls' trip *or* a business trip, depending on who I was talking to. I had already fooled the Uber driver and the double-eyeshadowed woman at the ticket counter.

But even as I tried to inject my body with self-confidence, seeds of doubt prickled at the corners. I was the stupid one of my mom's three kids, the dumb waitress who needed a man to support her, a chick in her forties who had never really done anything in her life, never had a chance to be truly free, to get outside of Madison and experience life—real, vibrant, exciting, adventurous life.

I felt myself teetering between joy at getting away on my own terms, fear of the unknown, and depression over how little I had accomplished in my years. My hands felt cold, and I stuffed them into my jean pockets, wiggling my toes in my tennis shoes. My toes were chilled too.

Deciding I needed to take a walk, I pulled a premade sandwich from one of those grab-and-go coolers in the gift store, glancing briefly at the MADISON mugs, hats, and sweatshirts they sold and promising myself I would never return, ever.

There had been no other texts from Glenn. I pictured him at the job site—he was helping to tear out carpet and move furniture for a big corporation that had relocated its headquarters. He had to be there for about five hours and would then be home, expecting the steak dinner I'd told him I was making.

It was the start of my normal midweek break from the bar, which I had planned so that I could have at least two days before anyone at work questioned where I was. When I didn't show up Friday, they would wonder—maybe get worried—but Anna would soon help my cause and buy me some time. She was the only one I trusted. Heck, she had even loaned me extra getaway money when I knew I didn't have enough. She promised she would lie to protect my whereabouts, and I promised I would repay her the $500. Anna had smiled in a sympathetic way when I had asked her to help me figure out Uber the previous night. She patted my arm. "You know I have a couch you can crash on if you want for a few days. Are you leaving anytime soon?" she whispered.

"I don't know yet," I lied. Some things needed to remain secret. The flight and Denver were things I held close to my heart. I would tell her soon, once I was established and had a job with money to repay her. For now, it was enough that she knew I was going somewhere at some undetermined time in the future to escape Glenn.

Everyone at the bar was aware that he had a temper. He had been in several fights, and his previous girlfriend left him when he pushed her so hard against his pickup truck that she broke a rib. Months later, she took out a restraining order. Of course no one bothered to tell me any of this when I started working there. Maybe that's because he also had a charming side, the side I first saw when he began walking me to my car at night. He could make the whole bar laugh, and he had a way of getting people to loosen up. I had seen him break up fights too. That was the enigma. His protective side and destructive side co-habitating. It was the unpredictability of the latter that finally broke me.

Now, as they called us to board, I was mere steps from full freedom. Letting my hand slip down into my fringed purse, I just wanted to touch the wad of cash that was wrapped in rubber bands. A lot of twenties, some fives and tens. Nothing larger than that. A year's worth of escape money. Feeling it there comforted me. There was close to $2,000 even after paying for the flight. Tightening my grip on both the handle of the rolling bag and my boarding pass, I pulled my elbow in to my side to keep my purse firmly in place. The line moved slowly ahead.

"Welcome," the gate agent said as I handed her my boarding pass. She had no idea how that one word was like a salve to my soul.

Entering the jetway, I felt a rush of excitement. About halfway down the ramp, I took the baseball cap off, shook out my long blond hair, and put the cap in my purse. I was the new me.

CHAPTER 4

Stephanie

The Day of the Flight

Coming out of Ambien sleep was never easy. Groaning, I shut my eyes again. The drug was trying hard to pull me back to slumber. Fighting it with all of my willpower, I fumbled for my phone.

The first duty I had every day was to see who might have texted me to say they were calling in sick. It was a rare day when no one had. Between lingering bouts of COVID, normal colds and flus, mental health days, and people who I suspected were lying just to get a free day, we had a lot of sick calls. The business we had all chosen was not an easy one. There was heightened stress making sure we didn't get beat by the other TV stations in the city, and extra pressure to triple-check that everything we put on the air was fair and factual.

I took a look at Teams messages and turned my attention to emails. In a news station, you can get hundreds of emails each day, maybe even thousands, story pitches and press releases and statements from politicians and internal notes from reporters and producers and viewer feedback. It was a never-ending sea of things to look through. Scrolling my overnight and early-morning emails, I dismissed 90 percent of them as unimportant but flagged some to respond to later.

My bladder was urgently calling me out of bed, so I put the phone down and attended to business, washing up and putting on some work clothes that would also be OK for the plane: a stretchy pair of yoga-type pants that looked like work pants, low boots that were comfortable to walk in, and a baggy but professional sweater with a cowl neck.

My work makeup was next. I would take a full shower the next day. Today was my "day two" hair anyway, and I liked how it flattened just a bit after a night of sleep. I chose a pair of simple fake-pearl earrings that went with anything. Amazon always had a wide selection of fakes.

Making coffee and a quick breakfast, I turned on our morning newscast, standing by the kitchen counter assessing our show. The anchors really didn't like each other much in real life. They did a good job of faking it most days on the air, but I felt like there were times when I could see one side-eyeing the other or even borderline rolling their eyes. It was on my to-do list for the next week to check in with each of them to see how things were going, and maybe to give them a little kick in the pants. They might need a stern reminder that viewers want to like the people they're watching on TV, especially in the morning.

Throwing back the coffee, I rinsed the cup and put it in the dishwasher. Next came Fred's breakfast, and I was ready to leave for the TV station by just after eight. The morning meeting for managers started at 8:30. Luckily, I lived ten minutes away. Stopping at the thermostat, I turned it down to 62 to save some money on heat. Just as I was grabbing my light blue Kate Spade purse off its hook, Fred came lumbering down the stairs.

"Freddie, my favorite beast." I knelt down to scoop him up. "Will you miss me? I will miss you. I'll see you soon."

Kissing the extra soft spot on the top of his head, I plopped him next to his bowl and left through the attached garage door.

The day was cold but sunny, good for flying. Traffic in Madison was nearly nonexistent, and my view on the way to work was a mix of suburban houses, mature oak trees, and upscale strip malls, nearly all of them having a Starbucks and a Panera.

I always flipped between NPR and our local talk radio station in the morning to make sure I had a handle on the news of the day. This time there was coverage of an earthquake in Egypt and a strike at a local construction company. I made a note to assign a reporter to the strike story and pulled into the parking lot at the TV station.

The effects of the Ambien were still there as I turned off the car. Sleeping drugs were weird. Sometimes I woke up feeling sharp and completely rested; other days I would be moving in slow motion or swimming underwater. This was somewhere in between. I shook my head to clear it before going in, vowing to grab a second cup of coffee. I would try to catch some sleep on the plane. I would need plenty of energy later.

As I got out of the car, I looked at my longtime workplace. Something about those big satellite dishes and the call letters on the side of the building with the CBS eyeball still got me jazzed after all of these years. One of my former bosses used to say that television had the biggest megaphone of anyone, and I believed it to be true. We had a power and a responsibility, neither of which I took lightly. I had fallen in love with TV when my dad would watch the evening news. The names of that era—Diane Sawyer, Barbara Walters, Peter Jennings—still had meaning to me.

"Good morning, Steph!" our receptionist called as I walked

into the main lobby. Bernie had been there for over twenty-five years and was as happy as ever every single day.

"Good morning, Bernie! How are you?" I started to key my way into the secondary door that led to the newsroom.

"Great. I hear you're flying somewhere *faaancy* today. Have a safe trip!"

"Thank you, B!"

I suppose it did sound fancy to fly to San Diego. But I knew the truth: Not only was I fed up with this kind of travel, there wasn't a drop of glamour to it. I was flying coach. The time difference would make it hard to adjust and sleep well, and I needed to give my boss, Dave, a full report when I got back. I had a plan for that.

The newsroom was only slightly buzzing at this hour. The two anchors I had seen on the morning show were talking and joking with different people on opposite sides of the room, as they usually were. Sometimes I felt as if they were in competition to see who could make a coworker laugh the loudest.

The overnight producers were either gone or packing up, and I waved to two of them. The assignment desk manager was just arriving and setting down his coffee mug for the day. My assistant news director had a dentist appointment that morning and would be coming in about an hour late, so it was on me to get the dayside reporters going.

My office was set off to the side of the newsroom. It wasn't large and had no windows, but I had done my best to make it feel cozy with a throw rug, some accent lighting to offset the fluorescent overhead, a few framed pictures on the wall, and some knickknacks on the bookshelf.

Slipping off my coat, I settled into the computer. Already I had more than a dozen new emails just since I had left the house. It didn't take long to go through those and hit the coffee room for one more blast of caffeine. I was slowly starting to wake up.

Walking to the conference room where my other news managers were assembling for our meeting at 8:30, I set my laptop on the table.

"Good morning, happy Wednesday! Let's get going." Our team included the dayside executive producer, the assignment desk manager, the head of digital, a special projects producer, and our chief photographer. "Just a reminder I have to fly out this afternoon, but Bruce will be here after his dentist appointment."

Three hours later, the reporters were all on their stories, Bruce was back in the saddle, and it was time for me to head to the airport. I made it a point to stop and see all of my managers, checking in on various projects and setting up a few meetings for when I returned. As I closed my office door, people in the newsroom started calling out:

"Have a good time!"

"Lucky! So jealous!"

"You won't decide to stay in sunny California, will you?"

"You never know!" I said. "No, I'm pretty sure you'll be stuck with me next week!"

I was feeling annoyed again about always being the one to pick up the slack in these travel situations, but tried to cover my irritation with joking. They had no idea how much effort these trips took. Everyone seemed to think it was all fun and games. At least on this trip I would make it so.

At the airport parking lot, my phone pinged just as I was unloading my suitcase from the back of the car. Fumbling for it in my pocket, I saw that it was my sister, Renee. She lived in Indianapolis near our childhood home and worked as a schoolteacher. She must be on her lunch break.

Hey, Little, be safe flying today.

She always called me Little because I was five years younger, Mom and Dad's "oopsie baby." I was touched that Renee had taken a moment to reach out so I texted her back.

Thanks, Big. Flight is on time. I'll text you when I land.

I threw in a heart emoji. Renee had been like a surrogate mother to me when Mom died of breast cancer while I was still in college. Dad had done his best in her absence, but now he was gone too, a heart attack taking him not long after Jason, Evan, and I moved to Madison. The absence of my parents left a crater of sadness in me. At least I had Renee.

The suitcase bumped along through the quiet of the parking lot. I checked my Apple Watch: perfect timing as long as security lines weren't unusually long. They almost never were in Madison, so I was fairly confident it would be fine, and I was right. I was in and out quickly and at my gate with over forty-five minutes to spare.

Airport food was insanely expensive, of course, and tricky to find for a budding vegetarian. I had been trying to be one ever since Robert, a longtime vegan, made me watch a documentary on a slaughterhouse. I grabbed myself a basic salad for lunch at one of the kiosks and figured I could get something else to eat in Denver before the second flight. I didn't have much of an appetite anyway.

My fellow passengers in the boarding area were the usual mix of work types buried in their laptops, a few older couples who I guessed to be on retirement trips, a guy at the counter trying to gate-check a snowboard, a woman with a baseball cap so low I couldn't see her face, a group of middle schoolers jostling one another as chaperones kept shushing them, and moms and dads laden with diaper bags and strollers and looking stressed. *Please don't let there be a screaming baby*, I thought. An uneventful flight would be a perfect flight.

PART TWO

CHAPTER 5

Anna

The Day After the Flight

I woke up to see three new voicemails, all from Glenn. Still lying in bed, I hit play on the first one and his voice blared like a tornado siren.

"Anna—where the fuck is Jasmine? She pulls this shit too often. I need her to come home, so *fucking tell me where she's at* so I can go get her."

Wow, that was a hell of a way to wake up. I rubbed my eyes. I really hadn't expected Jasmine to just up and leave right after I showed her how to use Uber. I thought she'd give me a heads-up, maybe ask for my couch.

I didn't even bother listening to the next two messages. Instead, I texted Jasmine.

Are you OK? Glenn is calling looking for you.

No response.

Pushing the blankets off, I pulled on some thick socks and stood up. My golden retriever, Rocky, jumped off the bed, eager to get outside and do his business. While I let him out the back door into the cold and stood shivering, waiting, I contemplated what to do about Glenn.

I could never tell him that I had helped Jasmine, that was for sure. I would lie to protect my friend. Maybe it would help assuage some of the guilt I still felt at not alerting her to his behaviors when they had first started dating. I rationalized that I had thought maybe Glenn might *finally* rise to be the kind of guy who took care of a woman. Yet it didn't take long before I saw the way he stared her down as she waited on others and heard the bossy tone in which he spoke to her. I recognized the sad look Jasmine had as she told me that Glenn instructed her on what to wear and what not to wear to the bar. It made me both sorry for her and happy that I was single. But the guilt still bothered me so much I had loaned her $500 to help her escape.

Letting Rocky back in and pulling the storm door tightly, I looked at my phone again. Still no response from Jasmine. Was she OK? Maybe she'd show up at my door late tonight.

Poor girl. Jasmine had never had an easy lot in life. Not that I had either, but hers seemed even worse. We met in seventh grade, when my mom moved us to Madison. My parents were divorced, and I lived with my mother and two younger brothers in a tiny house with leaky faucets and spotty heat in Jasmine's neighborhood. As Jasmine and I grew closer, I saw the way her mom treated her. One time, Jasmine invited me over, and after talking and listening to music in her room, we went to the kitchen to find a snack. Her mom was at the sink doing dishes. She turned and said, "Oh, I see we have two little piggies at the trough today. Who's your friend, and who's going to pay for all of these groceries, Jasmine?"

Jasmine's face turned beet red as we grabbed one crumpled

bag of potato chips that was nearly empty anyway and disappeared. An hour later, as we were hanging out in Jasmine's room, her mom opened the door and said, "Jasmine wore her hair in pigtails all through elementary school for a reason, right, Jasmine?"

After that, I didn't like to be at their house.

Freshman year of high school, Jasmine and I became friends with Raven, another girl without much money but with a knack for getting things that she needed. The three of us had an area we called "the secret spot" behind the high school in a dark corner by the tennis courts, and we would spend hours there bitching about school, our families, and how other girls had so much more money than us. We shared candy bars and cigarettes Raven stole from the corner store and her mom. Since our first names started with *J*, *A*, and *R*, we called ourselves JAR for a while, but then Raven had the idea to flip it and add an *E* so we became RAJE. It fit. We were mad at the world.

Junior year, Jasmine and Raven got into an argument. It happened before Drake's Halloween party. I was out of town that weekend, my mom forcing us to go to Milwaukee for my grandma's birthday, so I only heard about the fight from each of them later. Everyone in Madison knew about the Halloween party, though. It was all over the news because Drake raped and strangled his girlfriend, Allison, right in his backyard. Jasmine had been there. She never wanted to talk about it. Neither did anyone else. The whole school was in shock for what felt like the rest of high school. Drake and Allison had been in the super popular group, a clique that called themselves "the Fun Bunch." After the tragedy, I think the group dropped the moniker.

Jasmine and Raven made up, much to my relief, and we stayed close, all of us continuing to run with the hardscrabble group of high schoolers. We did a lot of stupid things, from shoplifting to "skeeching" (holding on to the back bumper of someone's car in the winter and getting a ride along the snowy streets). We were busted for underage drinking multiple times, and once, we vandalized a neighboring school and had to clean it up and do community service.

The three of us kept in touch even after high school. Raven split time between Madison and Atlanta after she met a guy from the South. Jasmine and I stayed around Madison. I knew Jasmine had tried cosmetology school and had to drop out. I had never been the college type and didn't want a bunch of debt, so I never went that route. Instead, I jumped into the working world. Jasmine and I got together for drinks every now and again through the years. She had jobs around town and so did I, but we had never worked in the same place until she called me saying she was leaving her boyfriend and needed a job. Was the bar I worked at looking for any help? It was perfect timing. A waitress had just up and left. Jasmine fit right in, and the guys all flirted with her. She was pretty, with her long hair and trim figure. Why she drifted to Glenn, of all the choices, I never knew. I didn't find him attractive at all.

Now I went back to my phone and texted Glenn to get him off my back:

Got your voicemails. No idea. She never said anything to me. How long has she been gone?

She said she was making dinner last night but when I got home she wasn't here and some of her shit was gone. One of my flannel shirts too.

It's only one night, Glenn. Give it some time, maybe she'll come home.

She won't call me back. She never said nothing to you?

We worked together but that was it.

If you hear anything you better tell me.

Asshole. Trying to intimidate me. But to keep him off my trail, I decided to act like I was all in.

Sure, will do.

Then I texted Jasmine one more time.

Glenn is getting pissed. Let me know if you need anything, or at least just let me know you're OK.

There was no response.

CHAPTER 6

Glenn

The Day After the Flight

Where the *fuck* was Jasmine? I had known something was up the second I turned into our gravel driveway the night before. Starving for that steak after an afternoon of ripping carpet, I couldn't wait for dinner, a few beers, some fooling around if I felt like it, and bed.

But the trailer was dark. Slamming the car into park, I stormed inside, where it was cold and silent and obvious that no cooking had been done. Looking around the bedroom, I suddenly noticed a rolling suitcase was gone and some of her clothes too. My red flannel was also missing. I hadn't paid attention to see if anything was amiss in the morning. I had believed her texts. How could I be so stupid? There was no note now, no text, no call, nothing.

The bitch couldn't be far. She had no money. If it wasn't for me, she wouldn't even have a roof over her head. I paid for groceries, gas, heat, water, electricity, everything. She gave me money for household expenses, but she didn't make shit at the bar. Plus, she didn't have a car. There was no way she was too far gone.

I started by calling her. She didn't pick up, so I left a voicemail. If she was still pissed because I had squeezed her arm hard the night before, maybe she would come right back and make that steak if I sweet-talked her, so my first message was nice. I told her I'd change my ways and I loved her. Sometimes I truly thought I *would* change. I had tried a few times, but it never lasted long because she always pissed me off with something she did or said, and that little devil in me would come out. It wasn't my fault. In fact, it was *her* fault for making me angry and bringing out the devil.

When she didn't respond to the first voicemail, I started leaving more. I had to make a frozen pizza and eat that, not at all satisfied with my dinner. The devil was rising in my chest with each minute. I downed some vodka, smoked some pot, left more messages—each getting nastier—and eventually passed out on the couch.

In the morning, I had a pounding headache and was doubly pissed. A person doesn't disappear. It had to be Anna helping her. There was no other explanation. I knew Anna and Jasmine had been friends for a long time. I think they even went to high school together, although which high school, I had no idea. I didn't pay attention to ancient history like that.

So I started leaving voicemails for Anna too. Now she was texting me back saying she didn't know where Jasmine was. Maybe she did or maybe she didn't, I couldn't tell, but what if Jasmine was right there, peeking at my texts over Anna's shoulder and laughing? The thought of the two of them laughing at me made me so infuriated that I picked up a water glass and hurled it across the room, watching with glee as it smashed against the wall, right next to the hunting rifle that was hanging on two hooks. The pieces of glass shattered all over the floor. I wasn't planning to clean it up unless I had to, though. I'd rather step over glass than get a broom and sweep.

The hunting rifle caught my eye. It was a classic piece my dad had given me and his dad had given him, and it seemed to be calling me over to it. Walking to the wall and crunching my boots on the glass, I lifted it off and blew air on it to get the dust off. I used to hunt a lot, but it had been some years. The barrel felt strong and solid. Bringing it to my eye, I looked down the sight line and pointed it around my trailer, enjoying the power I felt with it in my hands, the dominance, the control. The same feeling I had when I bagged a buck or a pheasant.

Anna and Jasmine lying to me came to mind again. The thought of me regaining power over these two bitches filled me with elation. No female was going to outsmart me. I also had a handgun under the seat of my pickup truck. Jasmine didn't know about that one. I had never told her. Some things were better as my little secret. But maybe it was time she found out. Depending on how this all went down, perhaps Jasmine and Anna would become very familiar with both of my guns.

CHAPTER 7

Robert

Two Days After the Flight

Friday morning dawned cold and dreary, typical for a Wisconsin winter. Steph had been gone for two days, and Fred was waiting for me. I threw a red-and-white Wisconsin Badgers baseball cap over my unshowered head, grabbed her house key from the drawer where I kept it, and strolled over to her side of the townhouse. The package with the alarm clock she had ordered was leaning against the front door.

I called for Fred, he came down, and we completed our morning ritual. He was happily munching his food as I walked over to inspect the plants Steph kept lined up by the window. My neighbor was a lot of things, but a nurturer of plants, definitely not. I sighed as I saw how they needed to be pruned, watered, and, in one case, repotted. Poor plant, it was bursting at the seams of the way-too-small terra-cotta pot it sat in.

"I'm sorry, buddy," I whispered to the plant. "I'll get you some help when your mama gets home tomorrow."

Filling the watering can Steph kept under the kitchen sink, I did what I could, watering and plucking, then glanced around the rest of her lower level.

Steph's style was a bit too Pottery Barn for my taste. I preferred eclectic, my townhouse a mix of posters from musicals, brightly colored vases from Mexico, rugs from a market in Jordan, and masks from Africa, remnants of travels with boyfriends of the past. I tried to block out the boyfriends and focus on the travel memorabilia. The pieces reminded me of some of the exotic locales I was able to frequent thanks to my tech salary and me being a SINK (single income, no kids). I went on long trips once or twice per year, and Steph repaid my cat kindness by taking care of Evita.

She really was the best neighbor. I was thrilled to have met her. Moving to Madison for this new job had felt scary, even at my age of fifty. You never knew how people would treat you as a gay man, but I had heard it was a progressive city, so I decided to test the waters by wearing my "Gay and Gray. Wanna Stay?" T-shirt that an ex had given me for a birthday.

When Steph not only wasn't scared away but seemed to genuinely find it, and me, to be funny, I knew I had a friend for life.

Although I had never been into women, I had a hard time understanding how she remained single. She seemed like such a darn good catch. Pretty, successful, smart, funny. It bothered me how her TV station took advantage of her being single and sent her on so many trips, always asking her to stand in for those who didn't want to jump on a plane or represent the company at meetings. I wondered if she would meet a guy on one of these journeys. I knew someone would eventually scoop her up. It made me happy to think of her feeling fulfilled with a new man but also sentimental to think of a guy who might mean the end of Broadway and Bubbly one day.

Fred jumped on the chair next to where I was standing, plopping down in a ball of fur, licking his paw and looking so cute that I had to take my phone out and snap a picture to text to Steph.

Hi Mama, I miss you. I'll see you tomorrow! Love Freddie (and your favorite cat-sitter)

It was eight a.m. in Madison, which meant only six a.m. in San Diego, but I sent it off anyway, figuring Steph would appreciate the text when she woke up. She had already posted a picture from the conference on Facebook. It was a sign outside of a ballroom that said "Welcome to the News Coverage Summit." I liked it and added a comment wishing her a good trip. I certainly hoped she was getting out for some sun and warm weather too. That would make one of us.

Opening the drawer where I knew Steph kept scissors, I went back to the Amazon box and extracted a large alarm clock that had a decorative wooden base and a globe on top. There were a multitude of buttons for setting the time and level of light you wanted, and you could sync it up to your phone. Turning it over in my hands a few times to see it from all angles, I picked up my phone again and texted.

Opened your package. It's bigger than I thought. Lots of options and settings. I think you'll love it. It will make you feel great. Would you like me to put it next to your bed?

Kneeling to pet Fred for another minute and enjoying his deep purr, I told him I'd be back before my date that night and went out the front door, locking it softly behind me.

As I walked back to my place, I wondered what Steph would get me from California. Her gifts were usually silly little trinkets. I suspected she bought many in airport gift shops, but I tried to keep in mind the old adage that it was the thought that counted. My cupboard had four mugs with city names plastered across them, my bar area contained cheesy WELCOME TO LAS VEGAS shot glasses, and my refrigerator was sprinkled with magnets from cities across the US.

I didn't want to hurt her feelings, but none of these things were items I would have spent money on, nor had any need for. She could have saved herself the trouble. I would have fed Fred for nothing. In fact, I probably would have done just about anything she asked of me.

Back home, I made a Nespresso and fed Evita. She settled on the kitty condo in her favorite spot at the window as I sat down to begin my workday. Just as I got through emails, my phone pinged with a text. Glancing down, I saw it was Steph and I smiled.

Thanks for the pic! So cute. Hey—I know this is super unexpected but I met an amazing guy at the conference and I'm actually going back to his place with him! Can you watch Fred for a little longer? I'll be back in touch to let you know when I'm returning. Thank you so much! And regarding the package, go ahead and put it

in the bedroom. Maybe I won't
need it anymore now that I met
this guy, ha ha! Thanks.

"What the heck?" I almost dropped the phone. She met a *guy* and was going to travel home with him after just being there since Wednesday? And what did she mean about the alarm clock? Was she implying that she might just sleep in for the rest of her life? Or that she would move in with this guy and use his alarm clock? Regardless, this was amazing news. I couldn't even believe it. I typed back as quickly as I could.

Girlfriend, you call me right
now. I want every detail.

Five minutes ticked by, then ten. I texted again.

Don't you dare ignore me
when you have news like
that!

Another fifteen minutes. I couldn't focus on my work. I got up and paced, then tried calling her. It went right to voicemail. I couldn't stop myself from texting one more time.

You can't drop a bomb on
me and then ghost, uh-uh,
ain't fair. Who is this guy??
Is he cute? Is he a news
director? Does he have a
nice tush? At least tell me
his name and where he's
from.

It wasn't until that afternoon that she finally wrote back. By then, I had called twice more.

Hey! Sorry I didn't get back to you. Really busy day here at the conference. He's amazing. His name is Trent McCarthy and he's from Atlanta. We really hit it off and I just need to roll with this. Can you give me a week? I'm going to go back to Atlanta with him. I'll send you some pictures!

A week?! Cavorting with Trent from Atlanta? My mind was trying to process all of this new information. Sure, I could take care of Fred, although she had never been gone this long from him. He might get lonely, I thought, and mentally planned to structure my days so I could pop over at lunch too. The bigger question was my dear friend *who had found a new guy at a conference and was jetting back home with him*!!! I wrote back:

Well, aren't you just the Queen of the Nile?! Of course I'll take care of Fred. Have an amazing time and call me when Trent is out of earshot. I want to talk to you! Every. Single. Damn. Detail.

CHAPTER 8

Anna

Two Days After the Flight

Glenn was in the parking lot leaning against his pickup truck smoking a cigarette when I pulled up for my Friday night shift. I could almost see the anger seeping off him. If there were a heat map of his body, it would have been all dark red and burnt orange. He caught my eye, threw the cigarette to the pavement, and ground it out with the toe of one boot. Heaving a deep sigh, I turned off the ignition as he strode quickly toward me. I unrolled my window just a crack.

"What, Glenn? I told you I don't know anything."

"She can't just disappear, Anna. She has *no* money and *no* car. Somebody knows something or is helping her. Where the fuck is she?"

"The last I saw her was Tuesday night. We don't hang out outside of work. Lay off, man. I'm not hiding her. Why don't you ask some other people?"

"I've asked everyone. Let me borrow your phone and I'll text her as if I'm you. Maybe she'll answer."

"I don't give my phone to other people, Glenn, and for your information, I did text her and she never wrote back. I don't know shit. Deal with your own business. I have to go to work."

I rolled up my window, pushed the door open, and stepped out.

"Anna, I swear to God, if you're lying . . ."

"You'll do what, Glenn? I'm not lying."

I walked past him and into the bar, trying to look confident as I went, but feeling nervous and a bit unsteady. That look in his eye unnerved me. He was unpredictable and furious, a bad combination. Going to the restroom to get ready, I took some deep breaths to steady myself. *Be cool, Anna, be cool.*

I had a strong feeling Jasmine wasn't coming back to Madison anytime soon. It gave me a mix of sadness at losing her at the bar, curiosity over where she was, and anger that she had put me in a situation where I had to deal with her boyfriend without telling me the exact day she was leaving. But twenty years working in a bar had given me all kinds of experiences, and I reminded myself I could handle it. I would deny helping her in any way until he finally shut up and moved on, and if Jasmine suddenly showed up at my doorstep unexpectedly, well, I guess I would deal with that too.

In the bathroom, I changed into my work clothes and tied on my apron, then slipped my phone from my purse. Holy crap.

There was a text from Jasmine.

Hey Anna—I'm more than OK.
I met a great guy named Trent
McCarthy. He makes me feel
safe and beautiful. More details
when I can!

I read the text twice and felt a strange mix of emotions. Relief met a bit of jealousy over her meeting a great guy so soon, and there was still anger over the situation she had put me in, but I tried to be the supportive friend as I texted her back.

OMG, Jasmine, that's awesome. I'm so excited for you!

As soon as I sent my response, I deleted the text exchange. No need to have any evidence for Glenn just in case he somehow managed to get his hands on my phone and hacked his way in.

When I came out of the bathroom, Glenn was seated at the end of the bar. He looked at me with a hard stare. I glared back as best I could, but my heart was pounding.

Lifting his right hand, he put his index finger out and thumb up in a shooting motion, aiming it directly at me. Narrowing his eyes, he lowered his head toward his hand, looking as if he were staring down the sight line of a gun.

"Bang bang, Anna," he called out. A couple of other guys at the bar chuckled. Ice water traveled the entire length of my spine. Pretending I hadn't noticed, I turned away and grabbed a bar rag, going to wipe a table.

I was able to distract myself most of my shift, but that night I couldn't sleep. The vision of Glenn pointing at me with his finger gun kept me tossing and turning. I was pretty sure he was a hunter and had an actual gun, maybe more than one. Getting up twice to check the locks, I contemplated staying up all night until dawn broke. But I was tired. When I crawled into bed, it was Rocky who finally helped me to calm down. His warm golden fur provided the comfort I needed. Snuggling my body next to his and throwing one arm over him, I forced myself not to think about Glenn and finally fell into a fitful rest.

I would usually sleep late after a night at the bar, but I woke up at 7:45 and rubbed my eyes. Opening the curtain of the window next to my bed to check the weather, I almost screamed but clamped my hand over my mouth so as not to scare Rocky. There sat Glenn's truck, idling. Slowly he began driving away. My heart was hammering like a metronome on steroids.

CHAPTER 9

Robert

The Weekend After the Flight

I couldn't stop myself from texting Steph Saturday. I was just aching for details about this new guy she'd met. It took three texts from me pressing for any nuggets at all for her to finally write:

> Conference is over, heading
> to the airport. Going to Atlanta
> with Trent!

That night, after I had badgered her for more, she said:

> Landed, heading to his place.

I left her alone after that, imagining her having drinks with Trent. My mind tried to conjure up an apartment that might fit this guy. Big-city news director. I pictured a lot of chrome and black in the space, kind of dull, maybe designed by a decorator, with boring but tasteful art on the walls and nothing personal or inviting. Not like my place. Thoughts drifted to the two of them in bed together, and I shook the image free. It was early—maybe they were still in the courting stage.

The next morning, I waited until eleven a.m. (noon in Atlanta, so plenty of time for them to have had a leisurely breakfast) before texting again.

Inquiring minds want to know, how was the first night with Trent?? Do tell all, please.

I put in an emoji of a questioning face. Her response came quickly.

So far, so good. He wants us to stay in all day today to get to know each other.

I wrote back with some hearts.

Va, va, voom!

Going back to Fred three times that day, I even brushed him, to his delight. I couldn't wait to hear more details from Steph about Trent, but I forced myself to be patient.

It was back to work for me Monday, but Steph was obviously having a blast. She started texting early and kept up the pace all day.

The first one had an address and a picture of what appeared to be an upscale white stucco condo building.

This is Trent's place. Check it out on Zillow, it's gorgeous inside

It looked nice enough, some trees and bushes cleanly landscaped. Popping open my laptop, I did what she suggested, eager to get a glimpse of how his place looked, but it really wasn't that gorgeous at all. It was much like I had pictured. Basic walls in a medium gray, dark wood cabinets in the kitchen, track lighting. It had an imposing and domineering feel, very masculine.

Still, I wrote back with one of my snappy comments:

Ahh, the love nest. Very nice

A few hours later, she sent a picture of two lattes on a café table. The mugs were distinctive, brightly colored with big pictures of peaches on the side.

Checking out the local places
in Trent's neighborhood,
Peachtree Village. It's an area
just full of life

That comment made me think of *Fiddler on the Roof*, so I wrote back:

L'chaim, l'chaim, to life!

I thought she'd enjoy that reference, but she didn't respond.

It wasn't until that afternoon that she sent three more pictures. In one, she was standing looking out over Centennial Olympic Park, fountains dancing in front of her. It was a head-and-shoulders shot from behind. She was wearing a cream-colored hat that I knew was one of her favorites, and her hair hung below it.

He's such a good tour guide,
he's taking me all over the city

Before I could even answer, another text came in, this time the exterior of a TV station, satellite dishes and microwave live trucks visible behind a chain-link fence, an NBC logo and the well-known peacock design on the side of the building. This time, it wasn't a text but a voice memo. I hit play, excited to hear her voice. It rang out:

"Last stop: Trent's station! He's the boss here and he's very bossy with me—tells me exactly where we should go and what we should do and I just follow. Talk soon!"

Out of jokes by then, I just wrote:

Great to hear your voice.
Have an amazing time. Fred
is doing fine.

I was so torn over how I felt about this whole thing. If she found true love, wasn't that wonderful for my dear friend? But if she found true love, then our Broadway and Bubbly days might be over. She could move to Atlanta. I shuddered at the thought of losing her and gaining a different neighbor in the townhouse. What if we didn't get along? What if they were even homophobic?

The final text pinged twenty minutes later. It was a picture of a white mug with a bright yellow sun and outlines of buildings on it with a saying scrolled across it in cursive: ***Greetings from Hot-lanta.***

Your gift from my trip

I was touched that she was thinking of my gift during the early fog of love, but it was so gaudy I really didn't like it and imagined hiding it behind others in my cupboard. Just to make her feel better, I wrote back:

How fun! Thanks.

Then I forced myself to turn back to my work. I mean, I couldn't obsess about my friend's love life all day, could I?

CHAPTER 10

Glenn

The Weekend After the Flight

Jasmine had been gone since Wednesday. I knew people at the bar were whispering about it. I could see them stop talking when I approached, and it made the little devil in me expand. Every hair on my head was angry. My devil had a pitchfork in his hand and flames behind him and was taunting me to do something about her pulling one over on me. I wasn't sleeping well. I was eating only McDonald's because I despised cooking. The one thing that made me feel better was target practice.

I took a bunch of empty beer cans out back and set them up on some stumps. Then I got the hunting rifle and handgun and alternated between the two, varying the distances from the targets and trying different angles. I was getting to be a good shot, and every time a can was punctured with a loud bang and fell over, glee would overtake rage for one satisfying moment.

Saturday I spent most of the day shooting, but Sunday I had an even better idea. I went into the storage area of the trailer to find some pictures of Jasmine in the cardboard box I remembered she kept there. I was surprised to see the state of the photo albums. Pictures were taken out of their holders and stuffed randomly inside. Where the holders were, I had no idea. But then again, maybe it had always been like this. I had never taken the time to look at these albums. Now I perused through a bunch of the loose-leaf photos, setting some of her aside.

There was a stack of old birthday and Christmas cards in there too, still in their envelopes. Randomly I picked one up.

"Have a very Merry Christmas," the card said inside, and was signed "Your Mother." I had never met Jasmine's mom. Jasmine barely spoke of her family. Pitching the card to the side, I picked up a birthday card from someone named Raven. It had a return address from Atlanta.

> *Jazzy—Happy Birthday! I'm so glad we met in high school. You, me and Anna. RAJE against the machine, right? I guess we still have a lot to be raging about. I can't believe what you told me about that guy, Glenn, you're living with. What an asshole. If I can be of help, you let me know! I have a way with people, if you know what I mean. Love ya lots!*

My hand froze. I went back to the envelope to see the postmark. It was sent just five months ago, her most recent birthday.

"You fucking bitches," I said aloud, reading it again and feeling the devil start a bonfire in my chest. He was throwing wood on as fast as he could. Jasmine was talking to other women about me and calling me an asshole?! After all I did for her?? And who was this Raven chick in Atlanta? She clearly went to high school with Jasmine and Anna. They *had* to be in this escape plan together—there was no other way. Raven had even said, "If I can be of help . . ."

Grabbing the card and a fistful of photos, I went back into the trailer, got some scissors out, and started haphazardly cutting and discarding all others from the photos except Jasmine. Then I taped the photos of her to my beer cans. Perfect. Now I would have a target, extra motivation. There was even one photo of Jasmine, Anna, and a third girl I guessed to be Raven, all looking much younger, and I put each picture on its own beer can. I didn't care that I was ruining Jasmine's entire photo collection. *Too fucking bad, bitch. That's what you get when you leave me.*

I returned to shooting, which felt great for a while, until I realized that this wasn't wholly satisfying. I wanted to share the feeling of power with someone who needed to be on the receiving end of it. I texted Anna:

Tell Jasmine that I will stop at nothing to find her. You better not be lying to me and helping her too. BTW, I'm having fun with target practice this weekend

I attached two pictures: one a beer can with Jasmine's photo taped to it, and a second with Anna's. In Jasmine's picture, she had braces, and her hair was in two weird side rubber bands that I think girls called pigtails. In Anna's photo, she looked to be in high school and was standing with a tennis court behind her and a cigarette in her hand.

I imagined shooting a bullet right through both of their faces and watching it come out cleanly on the other side of the can, and I smirked, then added one more text to Anna just to double down:

Bang, bang

CHAPTER 11

Anna

The Monday After the Flight

I had been nervous at work, feeling Glenn watching me. I asked one of the cooks to escort me to the car every night after my shift. In fact, it wasn't just work. I was nervous all the time.

Barely sleeping, I was startled by every sound, getting up to double-check the locks at least once per night. I didn't own a gun, but I had put my old softball bat next to my bed. The problem was that Glenn could easily overpower me; plus, a bat wouldn't do me much good in a gunfight. But the texts to me with pictures of his target practice were the last straw. I couldn't stand this shit anymore.

Who could possibly help? My mind scrolled through my entire list of friends and family. Certainly not Jasmine. She was God knew where with this guy she met. Not my mom. She would freak out with worry. My two younger brothers were more pacifist types and would never stand up to a guy like Glenn. My coworkers at the bar and other friends around town were busy with their own worlds and would want to stay away from this. There was only one person who came to mind: Raven.

Raven could handle any situation. I had never seen her back

down from anyone or anything, and she had connections everywhere. If you were in jail, Raven would be the one to get you a pocketknife, contraband food, cigarettes, drugs, condoms, or booze. Somehow, she would bribe a guard or do whatever she had to do. I picked up my phone that morning and called her.

"Anna!" she cried out as a greeting.

"Raven, it's good to hear your voice." I told her of my predicament, of how Jasmine had left and Glenn was now making threats against me and I didn't know what to do. It all came out in a rush. I barely took a breath as I spoke, the words tumbling over one another. She was quiet until I finished.

"Jasmine told me about this super dickhead Glenn some months ago. I've got you covered, girl. Just text me his address and it will be dealt with."

"What will you do?" I asked, suddenly thinking of some of the more nefarious possibilities and feeling jittery.

"Don't worry, Anna. He will never bother you again. I know lots of people in Madison. If I could hop on a flight right now, I would, but I've got a lot of things going on here in Hot-lanta at the moment. But you're my girl and so is Jasmine. I protect my girls, and of course I *always* take care of myself."

"What do I owe you for doing this?" I asked, thinking that I didn't have a lot of extra cash after loaning that $500 to Jasmine. And when would I get that back?

"Free," she said. "I have some buddies who owe me a favor. Just text me his address."

Thanking her profusely, I hung up. I didn't know Glenn's address off the top of my head, but I remembered a card Jasmine had sent me for Christmas less than a month ago. I kept all of my cards in a cigar box. Retrieving the envelope, I found their address, plain as day. I hesitated for only a moment. Would I regret sending this to Raven? Nahh. I needed her, and as she said, she always took care of her girls. Herself too, of course, but in this case she was protecting us.

I texted Jasmine:

Glenn is getting weird but Raven is going to help out.

She wrote back:

Really? She's helping me with something too

That was odd. Raven hadn't said anything. I replied:

What is she helping with?

But Jasmine did not respond.

CHAPTER 12

Bruce

The Monday After the Flight

I was looking forward to Steph returning to work today. It was always extra on me as assistant news director when she was gone. I could be faced with any number of decisions to make, from legal issues about whether we could run an image or a piece of music, to factual issues and whether we were being fair to both sides, to basic HR things—someone needed to take bereavement, someone else was having back surgery, two employees were sniping about each other and needed an intervention, things like that.

My days were nonstop anyway, what with a pair of teenagers at home, which meant running a shuttle service to practices, rehearsals, and hangout times, but then add in Stephanie being gone—and she was kind of gone a lot, in my opinion—and I had my hands full at work too.

I'd see her for the 8:30 manager meeting and fill her in on the stuff I had dealt with: We had a reporter who was complaining that she didn't like to do live shots in the cold, and our chief meteorologist, who was so popular with the public, was being difficult again. He had retweeted something political that he shouldn't have. We had an election to plan for and Black History Month coming up in just a week that we needed to finalize stories for. But there were no major issues while she was gone. No one had walked into my office and said they were quitting; no one had complained that they absolutely couldn't work with so-and-so. All things considered, it was a good week.

I said goodbye to my wife, Ellen, and son, Will, but took my daughter, Claire, her giant cello, and the dog with me in the car. Driving Claire to middle school and dragging her cello out of the back of the minivan, I nearly dropped it in the process.

"Daaaad," she moaned, but scooped it into her skinny arms and ran off without so much as a goodbye. Next I left Barkley at the way-too-expensive doggie daycare that Ellen insisted on so he wouldn't get bored. Barkley also left me without so much as a proverbial dog wave.

The final stop before work was the McDonald's drive-through for coffee. It was cheaper than Starbucks and, in my opinion, better. Taking my mega-cup into the station with me, I gave a hello to Bernie at the reception desk and went into the newsroom, where the place was just coming alive.

Glancing at my watch, I saw that it was 8:23. The manager meeting started in seven minutes. Steph's door was closed and the light was off. She was usually here by this time, but maybe she got stopped by a train or something. Continuing to look over my emails, I evaluated our reporter-photographer pairings and story selections for the day.

At 8:29, her door remained shut. The other managers were gathering in the conference room across the newsroom. A tinge of annoyance surged through me. If she was going to be late, couldn't she have the decency to let me know? Double-checking my phone in case I'd missed anything, and seeing that I hadn't, I shot her a quick text:

> Are you running late? Do you need me to start the meeting?

No response. The clock moved to 8:30 and I sighed, picking up my laptop and walking into the conference room. The rest of the managers looked at me quizzically.

"Where's Stephanie?" our digital director, Lucy, asked. "Isn't she back today?"

"I'm not sure. Let's get started and we'll bring her up to speed when she gets here," I replied.

Running a meeting was bad enough. Running one when you weren't expecting to was worse. I felt out of sorts and screwed up the order of people I needed to call on, even though I had done it many times.

When we broke at 8:50, I checked my phone again. Nothing. Now I felt a prickle of worry. This was really unlike Steph. Had something happened? A car accident on the way to work? No, it couldn't be that. One thing about working in a TV station: You knew of every accident, shooting, stabbing, heart attack, fire, and train derailment in a five-county area. Police scanners were on 24/7, and those who were monitoring them at the assignment desk would have alerted us if anything big happened.

The dayside executive producer, Nora, must have sensed my feelings because she lingered in the conference room after the others had left.

"Is everything OK with Steph?" she whispered. "Wasn't she supposed to come back today?"

"Yeah, I thought so too, unless I missed a memo or something," I said, walking back to my desk to make sure that wasn't the case. But no, the last correspondence from Steph was a "yes" response to an election meeting I had set up. It had come late Wednesday afternoon. She had probably done it from the Denver airport on the layover.

Picking up my phone, I called her. It went immediately to voicemail. I tried texting again.

Everything OK? We're getting a little worried. People are asking about you. Aren't you supposed to be back today?

Nothing.

In the meantime, I had a newsroom to run. Reporters and photojournalists had to be assigned; producers had to know what to put in their shows. The nine a.m. newsroom meeting was coming right up.

I pushed any thoughts of something terrible out of my head and went to work, running the meeting as well as I could in my still-foggy, not-prepared-to-do-this mode.

I told the team Steph was coming in later; after all, no need to worry them too. We got reporters out the door on their stories, and I was just considering whether to alert our GM about the situation when my phone pinged with a text.

It was her!

I pounced at it, eager to see what excuse she had. I really couldn't imagine a good one unless she told me she was in the hospital with appendicitis.

Hi, sorry for the late notice. Something very unexpected happened at the conference and it required me to go to Atlanta. I will need to be off this entire week. Maybe more but I'll keep you posted. Thank you in advance.

I had to read the text three times. She was in Atlanta and asking for the entire week off? Maybe more? And she was springing this on me now? I must have had a shocked look on my face because Nora came over to me.

"Did you find out something? Is she all right?"

"She's in Atlanta," I said in a low voice so no one would hear. "For a week . . . or more." I passed her my phone and her eyes skimmed the words.

"What the *heck*?" she asked. "What do you think happened at the conference?"

"I don't know." I felt myself running my hands through my hair in a nervous habit that always annoyed Ellen. My mind was already racing ahead to the week—we had the election planning meeting she had RSVP'd for, a reporter-candidate interview, and I was supposed to be off Thursday and Friday. Now would I even be able to do that?

"Well, answer her and maybe she'll tell you more," Nora whispered. We were both trying not to bring attention to our situation. The rest of the newsroom was in normal busy mode, though, and no one seemed to be paying attention to us. I took my phone back and quickly typed.

This is really sudden news, Stephanie. Can you tell

me more? I can run the newsroom but we have a lot on our plates this week and I'm off Thursday and Friday, remember? Did you want to reschedule the election meeting too?

I watched as the typing bubbles were going.

Don't worry, I'm fine. I know it's sudden but sometimes things pop up. Please reschedule the meeting.

Taking a deep breath, I wrote back.

OK. Do you have a second to talk on the phone? If you're going to be out all week there are some things we should touch base on.

It took twenty minutes before she responded. This time it wasn't a text but a voice memo. I hit play, and her voice said:

"No, I really don't have a moment. Please don't check in with me until next week. I will be very busy."

Now the anger surged. This was how she was going to treat me? I wasn't sure what else to say.

My fingers hovered over the phone as my mind whirred for a proper reaction to my direct supervisor. In the end, I just hit the thumbs-up button because I felt anything else I tried would be either too nice or too snarky for the moment. I needed to collect my thoughts.

After I passed Nora the phone, she read the rest of the text exchange and listened to the voice memo.

"Well, that's just a shitty thing for her to do," she said. "She had better have a damn good reason."

"I know," I responded. "I just don't know what it could be."

The only thing I could think of was that maybe she was looking for a new job. Perhaps someone at the conference had started courting her to move to Atlanta, and she was down there interviewing. That made the most sense, but I had never heard of a job interview going an entire week.

One thing was for sure, the general manager of our station needed to know that his news director was out. I sent him a direct message on our Teams platform asking to see him, and he told me to come right down.

I wasn't used to going to the GM's office. That was largely Steph's duty, and she reported back to me anything critical. I felt a little nervous walking up there but also felt that he would definitely want this info, perhaps for more reasons than one. If she was looking for a new job, it was not my duty to protect that info. She hadn't asked me to either. But it *was* my duty to let him know that his news director was unexpectedly out.

Dave's office had a huge bank of windows overlooking a sloping drive that led to the parking lot. He was seated in a leather office chair looking through some papers when I reached his doorway. He didn't turn his head but must have seen me out of his peripheral vision because he said:

"Bruce, come on in. What can I do for you?"

I ran my hand through my hair again and stepped forward.

"Hi, Dave, sorry to bother you." I sat down across from him nervously. "I just . . . I just wanted to let you know that I got a text from Stephanie. It appears she's planning to take the whole week off. Maybe you're already aware, apologies if you are, but if not . . ."

Dave had a habit of stroking his mustache when he spoke and started doing so now.

"She's out this week? She was just in San Diego last week. I did not know about this. Did she say why? Or where she is?"

"Well, sir, uh." I hesitated. "Do you want to read the texts?" It seemed better than me trying to explain. He could decide for himself. I slid my phone across the wide dark oak desk. As he read, his bushy eyebrows went up.

"This is unlike Stephanie. I have never known her to leave the newsroom without a lot of advance notice. Let me try to reach her. She always answers my calls."

He opened a desk drawer and pulled out his own phone, pushing a single button and holding it to his ear. I could hear voicemail picking up. He looked annoyed.

"Stephanie, Dave Jenssen. Call me the minute you get this. I need to know what's going on."

He hung up and said, "I'm sure she'll be getting right back to me. I'll be in touch when I do talk to her, Bruce, and thank you for bringing this to my attention."

Nodding, I walked back to the newsroom, confident that Dave would get the full story. She couldn't lie to her boss.

The day went by as a news day does. The noon show needed attention, then lunch and the two o'clock afternoon meeting to get nightside crews going, then the four o'clock show and the rest of the evening shows were on tap. It was 4:30 and I was just looking over final scripts from reporters when Dave sent me a Teams message asking me to come back down to his office. Relief and curiosity flooded me. At least we would have some real answers.

"Bruce, Stephanie has not responded to me all day. I left

three messages. I am extremely upset with her. If you hear from her again, even in the form of a text, let me know. And Bruce—let's not get others involved right now. Keep this between us."

"Will do, sir," I said, the pit of anger suddenly resettling into my stomach, replacing the emotions that had been there just moments prior. How could she not respond to Dave?

As I walked back to the newsroom, a sudden thought hit me: Dave asked me not to say anything to anyone, but I had already told Nora. Now I would have to make sure she kept it quiet. Butterflies flew into my stomach.

Then a different thought came to mind.

What if Steph got fired and I was promoted? It was something I had wanted for a long time, never thinking it was possible at this station. As much as I liked Steph and enjoyed working for her, if she dug her own career grave, that was on her. The thought of more money for the big chair made my eyes glisten. I didn't know what Steph made, but it had to be at least $20K more than me. Oh, that would help with two growing kids and looming college tuitions. I would have to keep in Dave's good graces, just in case.

Back in the newsroom, Nora was talking with a producer. I made eye contact and motioned her to the back conference room.

"Do you have any news about Steph?" she hissed.

"No," I replied. "But I'm going to have to ask you not to say anything to anyone about this. Keep it between us. Until we find out what's going on, it's best that we not gossip about anything."

Her face blanched, and her eyes shot to the floor.

"I'm so sorry," she stammered. "A few people asked me if I

had heard anything and I told them about her texts . . . I didn't know it was a secret."

Damn it. I cursed at myself for telling her in the first place.

"If it's any help," she went on, barely lifting her eyes to look at me, "I know Lucy texted Steph and Steph texted back."

CHAPTER 13

Dave

The Monday After the Flight

"What the *hell* is going on?" I said aloud to an empty room as I packed my briefcase and clicked the metal tabs before heading home.

Alone in my office, the newsroom down a long hallway, no one could hear me, but I was so pissed I couldn't help but talk to myself. I was the general manager, and my news director had gone rogue and wasn't answering my calls. And this was Stephanie! The woman I had worked with for ten years! How could she treat me like this?

Firing up the remote ignition for my BMW, I took out my bewilderment and frustration on the light switch (extra hard flick with my hand) and the door (slammed it for the satisfying feeling it gave me), then stomped my way through the January early darkness of the parking lot, seething.

If she didn't call me back tomorrow . . . I would . . . I would . . . Truth be told, I didn't know what I would do. Would I fire her? I guess eventually, but this was a trusted employee who had done good work for a long time. I felt at ease when she ran the newsroom. It wasn't that Bruce wasn't a solid guy or a good journalist, but my nerves were always just a bit more on edge when he was in charge. I would casually "swing by" the newsroom just a little more often.

If Stephanie left the station or I fired her, would Bruce get the job? I would have to open it up to outside candidates just for the Equal Employment Opportunity Commission requirements. Maybe someone better might come along—we'd see.

Throwing my briefcase across the driver's seat to the passenger side, climbing in, and slamming the door, I cranked the radio to a local country station and steered in the direction of home, thumping my hand on the steering wheel to the beat. Halfway there, I calmed down enough to mute the radio and command the car:

"Call Lisa."

It responded in a soothing woman's voice: "Calling Lisa."

"Dave?" my wife's voice answered, even more soothing to my ears. After decades of marriage, I still got a tiny flutter talking to her. She remained drop-dead gorgeous to me.

"Lees," I sighed. Before I could say another word, she had my mood pegged.

"What's wrong?"

My wife did know me well, that was for sure.

"Well, you're not going to believe this, but Stephanie was a no-show at work today. She texted Bruce that she would be out all week, but she refused to answer any of my calls."

"What do you mean, a no-show? Is she sick?" Lisa had always been a fan of Stephanie's. They got along famously.

"I don't think so," I said, putting my blinker on and changing lanes on the Beltline Highway. "She apparently went straight from the conference in San Diego to Atlanta. That's what she told Bruce anyway. She only said that something came up. Lees—she absolutely refused to answer my phone calls or call me back. This is so unlike Stephanie."

"She never even sent you an email?"

"Nope, not a thing. I checked my inbox and spam at least a dozen times. She just bailed on us."

"I'm baffled," Lisa stammered. "Did you call Evan?"

"Her son?"

"Yes, maybe he knows something."

God, my wife was so smart. That thought hadn't even occurred to me. Of course I could call Evan. Emergency contacts were listed in our computer system. Stephanie must have him on there.

"Good idea. I'll try him when I get home."

Forty-five minutes later, I had changed into lounge pants and an old college sweatshirt. I had a scotch on the rocks in my hand, and I sat in our den with my laptop, looking up the emergency contact information for Stephanie.

Sure enough, there was Evan. She talked of him often, so I knew he was living in Minneapolis and working for some sort of team. He seemed like a good kid—I had met him a few times when he came through the TV station when he was younger. Maybe he would have some information.

But what if he didn't? I didn't want to freak him out by alarming him about his mother either. I sat there, my hand over my phone, wondering what to do. How would I phrase a call?

Hi, Evan, this is Dave, your mom's boss. Do you have any idea why she went to Atlanta? or maybe just *Have you heard from your mom recently?* It seemed a rather awkward thing to say, and I couldn't imagine being on the receiving end of that call. No, it didn't feel right.

Looking at the emergency contact list again, I saw that Stephanie had two others listed: a sister, whose address was in Indianapolis—I had never met her—and a guy named Robert whose address was just two digits different from Stephanie's. At first, I couldn't place who he was or what he looked like, but as I lifted my eyes to the ceiling to think, it came back to me.

A Fourth of July barbecue Steph hosted the summer before in her backyard. Robert, with a bottle of craft beer in his hand, coming over to introduce himself as her neighbor. Gray hair, glasses, an awkward smile. He told me that he watched Channel 3 every day and loved it. That sort of compliment always made me happy. We chatted for a minute, and he said he took care of Steph's cat when she was out of town. The conversation had ended shortly after when Lisa summoned me over to say hello to another group of people over by the red, white, and blue cupcakes.

Yes, I knew who he was. And as the cat-sitter, maybe he did know a thing or two. Glancing at the clock, I saw that it wasn't even seven p.m., not too late for a phone call, right? I picked up my cell and punched in Robert's number.

CHAPTER 14

Robert

The Monday After the Flight

The townhouse felt extra cold. I had already turned the heat up to 70 degrees, two notches higher than I ever kept it. The electric fireplace was more for show than heat, but I put it on for the ambience and even grabbed some fingerless gloves in my mudroom drawer. Powering up the teakettle, I prepared a cup of chamomile, always a calming and warming favorite, especially with honey and lemon.

I thought of Steph's side of the place, even colder. She had turned her thermostat down for the trip, as she always did. Poor Fred. I had gone over three times already that day and was contemplating one more. Was it my imagination, or did he look forlorn when I was there to feed him dinner? He seemed to be moving extra slowly, and his meow was plaintive.

Settling on my couch with a favorite Mexican blanket I had gotten in the streets of Tijuana, I was just about to turn on my TV and start flipping mindlessly through a thousand channels when my phone rang.

Steph? No. I didn't recognize the number, but the area code was Madison.

"Hello?"

"Is this Robert? Are you Stephanie Monroe's neighbor?"

"Yes." I sat up straighter and the blanket slid off one leg. "Who is this?"

"This is Dave Jenssen, the general manager from Channel 3. I'm sorry to bother you in the evening. I met you at Stephanie's barbecue on the Fourth last year."

"Oh, yes, I remember. Is everything OK, Dave?"

"Well, actually, Robert, this is kind of awkward, but Stephanie didn't show up to work today and sent us some texts that quite frankly were a little out of character for her. I thought if you were watching her cat, maybe she told you more?"

"What did she tell you?" I asked, grabbing the remote control and clicking the TV off.

"She didn't actually talk to me. She told Bruce, our assistant news director, that something had come up and she needed to go to Atlanta for at least a week. She wouldn't explain and didn't even give us a heads-up before the workday started. Do you by chance know anything more? We just want to make sure everything is OK."

My mind flashed to Trent and his white condo with the perfectly plucked trees outside of it, to the two of them sharing a latte and a stroll through the sites of Atlanta, maybe hand in hand. To the imaginary bed I had conjured in my mind, bodies perhaps tousling in sheets. To how excited she had seemed in her first text to me that was so filled with exclamation points about this new guy.

Should I share all of that with her boss? She clearly didn't want her workplace to know all of the things that I knew or she would have told them herself. But they were worried too—I could see that. For a moment, all I could do was to take a deep sigh as I contemplated it all.

"Dave, ummm . . . I do know a bit more. Not a lot." I hesitated. This whole conversation felt like trying to open a car door with a pinky. Not impossible, but awkward and a little painful nonetheless.

"Go on," said Dave, and I took a deep breath.

"I believe . . . I believe she met someone in San Diego. That's all she shared with me. I don't know anything else, not a name or an occupation or an address . . ." I don't know why I said all of that. Why would he expect an occupation or address? I had diarrhea of the mouth and had to tell myself to stop talking.

Dave was silent and then let out a low whistle.

"She met a *man* in San Diego?"

"Yes . . . she's been divorced for three years," I added, as if to justify the whole thing.

"I am aware of that, but this is certainly unexpected," Dave said. His voice sounded annoyed. "I can't believe she would shirk her work duties. She wouldn't answer my phone calls. I called *three times*, Robert."

"I'm sorry, Dave, I don't know what to say. I'm only the cat-sitter." That seemed to snap Dave back into professional mode. His voice changed.

"Yes, of course. You've been very helpful and I appreciate it. Does her son know about any of this?"

And that's when I realized that I had no idea. It didn't seem like something I needed to tell him now. His mom was off having a fling. Would any kid want to know that?

CHAPTER 15

Lucy

The Monday After the Flight

As the digital manager of the station, I was in charge of finding fun content in both Madison and nationally to share with viewers across our website, TikTok, Twitter/X, Instagram, Facebook, and YouTube accounts. I loved it when I could take a fun little thing—like a new exhibit of sloths at the zoo—and make it so TikTok-friendly that people would share it. The zoo itself had even reposted one of my latest ones, and I walked around with a glow in my cheeks all afternoon.

Since I spent my whole day in the social media and website space, I would also share interesting things I came across with those in the newsroom. And I was the tech wizard. Anyone who needed help with their phones or computers came to me rather than corporate IT.

Steph had always been like a mentor to me. She seemed so calm and natural. I could turn to her with questions I had. She was also just a nice boss. She bought us little gifts at Christmas and praised our work often. I had never heard her yell at anyone.

Despite a fifteen-year age difference, she and I had several things in common. We were both lefties and coffee drinkers, and had a shared affection for certain celebrities, especially Wisconsin native Mark Ruffalo.

It started in one of our editorial meetings when someone pitched a story about famous people from Wisconsin. Ruffalo's name came up. The actor hailed from Kenosha, forty-five minutes south of Milwaukee, and we all thought that was incredibly cool.

"He's hot, even though he's kind of old," I added, and Steph laughed and replied, "I agree that he's good-looking—and he's closer to my age."

It became a running joke between us. If I told her I had a date, she would say, "Are his initials M.R. by chance?" and if she was going on a trip, I would sometimes quip, "Tell Mark R. we said hello."

So when Steph didn't show up to work and our dayside executive producer, Nora, pulled me aside as I was getting my afternoon cup of pick-me-up and told me about the texts Steph had sent Bruce, I immediately thought that I might try to get Steph back to herself through humor. When I returned to my desk, I picked up my phone and texted her.

> I hear you're out this week. Should I reschedule that meeting with Mark R.? He'll be very disappointed but I'm sure he'll get over it

It took over an hour as I distractedly worked on some web stories for our site, but finally my phone pinged.

> Yes, please reschedule with Mark R.

I knitted my brows together. So formal? I tried again.

Mark R. says to call him as soon as you can, he misses you

Silence. I followed that up with another.

Are you dissing Mark R.? You know he'll turn into the Hulk

I thought the reference to one of Ruffalo's famous movie characters might make her smile.

It wasn't until that night when I was home doing yoga with a YouTube video in the living room that my phone pinged. Hitting stop on the video, I came out of a cross-legged twist pose to see her name and a text.

I am very busy this week, I asked you to reschedule the meeting. I should be back next week

I'm sure the shock I felt would have been obvious in my slack-jawed face, if there were anyone around to see it.

I didn't know how to react or what to say, so I didn't reply at all. But as I hit play on the yoga video again and moved into downward dog, something started gnawing at my gut. This situation felt off. I vowed to pull Bruce aside the next day and ask him what he thought.

CHAPTER 16

Bruce

The Tuesday After the Flight

There had been no further word from Stephanie since the texts yesterday saying she was out for the week. I was resigned to running the newsroom.

A part of me enjoyed being the full boss when Steph was gone. It gave me practice in case I wanted to be a full-time news director. But another part of me felt the weight of responsibility. I was the final gatekeeper on anything that went on our air. There was no one else above me to lean on. General managers usually came up through the sales side and didn't have newsroom editorial experience, so they stayed out of day-to-day decisions.

At the manager meeting, we did the usual whip-around to each person to hear what was happening in their departments—staffing for the day, story ideas, what was trending on digital, what special projects we were working on. I felt a lot more in my groove today. I was prepared to run the meeting, unlike yesterday. *You got this*, I told myself. My McDonald's coffee was next to me. The daily cup of joe was like an old friend; it comforted me.

We wrapped the meeting and had about ten minutes before the nine a.m. one with the whole newsroom. I stayed in the conference room to check some of the relentless emails that were always rolling in. I noticed Lucy, the digital manager, seemed to be taking a long time to pack up while everyone else walked out. When they all departed, she softly closed the door and turned to me, a worried look on her face.

"Bruce, can I talk to you about something?"

"Sure." It came back to me that she had been texting with Steph. Did she have news? And how would I tell her to not talk about this with Dave or anyone else? I really couldn't get into trouble with Dave. Not now, not when the spotlight was possibly on me for the news director seat. I gulped a bit, thinking that I had violated what he had asked of me.

"It's about Steph," Lucy began. She sat down and started jiggling her leg up and down.

"Yes?" I knew Steph and Lucy were pretty close, and had seen them laughing together over stuff that I was pretty sure was entirely female-centric, so I had stayed out of it.

"You know about the running joke I have with Steph regarding Mark Ruffalo, right?"

I didn't, but nodded anyway.

"Well, yesterday Nora told me that Steph was acting loony tunes, so I texted Steph about Ruffalo in a joking way. You know, said she had a meeting with him and should I push it back, that kind of thing."

"Uh-huh."

"So she texted me back," Lucy continued, "as if 'Mark R.' was a real person in our newsroom. She told me to reschedule the meeting and then started kind of blowing me off. I don't know, Bruce, it felt super odd. Like creepy *Dateline* odd."

"*Dateline* odd?" I asked. I wasn't fully following.

"Yes," she said with an urgency in her voice. "Like someone-has-her-phone odd."

I cocked my head, considering her words.

"Can I see the texts you're referring to, Lucy?" She passed me her phone, and I looked them over twice, then passed it back.

"I'm sure it's fine, really, Lucy. She's probably just messing with you, like reverse sarcasm. Or maybe she's blanking on your joke. How would anyone have her phone? And if they did, why would they be texting us about meetings and stuff? It doesn't make sense. She posted on Facebook from the conference last week. She sent me a voice memo yesterday."

Lucy leaned across the table toward me, narrowed her eyes a bit, and whispered.

"Bruce, I have a gut feeling. My Reiki coach told me gut feelings are what guide us. What can we do to find out?"

"Listen," I said in my best dad voice. "If something bad happened to her, why would the person have her cell phone? They would know it could be traced. Police could probably find it in minutes."

There was commotion outside of the conference room door, and we both looked over to see people beginning to gather for the newsroom-wide meeting.

"I'd like to do some more digging, Bruce," Lucy said. "I'm going to find out if it's truly her. I'll send some bad information and see how she responds."

"Well, uh . . ." I didn't know what to say, but now the conference room door was swinging open and people were starting to walk in, so I had to respond.

"I guess," I whispered. "Keep me posted."

"I will," she responded with a determined look on her face.

CHAPTER 17

Anna

The Tuesday After the Flight

Glenn hadn't been at the bar the night before. Rumors were swirling that there had been a robbery at his trailer and he was beaten up pretty badly and had to go to the hospital with a broken arm. One of my fellow waitresses said she heard he had teeth knocked out too and that these robbers threatened him about something.

I kept my mouth shut and head down, but I was feeling an immense amount of relief. He would be out of the mix for a while if he was in the hospital. I could sleep easily.

Now it was an hour before work and I was just unloading the dishwasher when my phone pinged with a text. Glancing over at the phone resting on the counter, I saw that it was Jasmine. The dishes were still warm and slightly damp as the cycle had just finished, so I had to wipe my hands on a dish towel first, but then I opened her text.

This guy Trent is super sexy but he has a temper. Don't worry, I can handle myself. Don't tell Glenn.

I typed a fast reply.

Things have been crazy here. Glenn is in the hospital.

Glenn's in the hospital? I promise I will send your money soon. Thanks for everything.

Yeah, robbery at the trailer if you know what I mean. He got beat up pretty badly. You're good though? You don't need anything else?

I'm good

CHAPTER 18

Lucy

The Tuesday After the Flight

It was a busy news day, but my mind was elsewhere. After Bruce gave me the green light, I kept formulating texts in my head. What could I say that might put a person into a trap? If it was Steph and she was just being weird, we could all laugh it off later. But if it wasn't . . .

At lunch, I saw Nora in the break room. I needed a co-conspirator, so I pulled her aside and quickly briefed her on everything.

"Help me think of some trappy texts," I whispered.

"What if you made up some names?" Nora asked. "Like tell her Susan and Frank called and need to speak with her and you have to know what to tell them, or something like that."

"That's a good idea," I said. "Let's try it."

I typed those exact words into a text to Steph and hit send, then waited for a reply. There was nothing for over an hour, but as I was walking across the newsroom to talk to the assignment desk manager, her reply came in.

Tell them I'm out of town.

I felt as if the blood all drained from my body at that moment into a pool on the floor. I had to grab the back of a nearby chair to steady myself. I really thought for a moment I might faint. Nora came up next to me.

"Did you get something?" she asked in an urgent whisper. Hand shaking, I handed her the phone. Her eyes grew wide and she grabbed my arm.

"Come with me. We're getting Bruce and going to Dave's office."

We motioned for Bruce and pulled him into the back conference room. When we briefed him and showed him the texts, he blanched.

"Listen, guys," he said. "There's another problem. Dave asked me not to say anything about this, but I didn't know that at first. If he thinks the whole newsroom is talking about it, he'll blow a gasket."

"The whole newsroom is not talking about it," said Lucy. "It's just the three of us. I haven't said a word about this text thread to anyone but you two. I know how fast gossip spreads in a newsroom."

"Bruce, I'll fall on the sword if need be," said Nora. "Dave can't be mad at us for this. It's information he's going to want."

CHAPTER 19

Dave

The Tuesday After the Flight

I had called Steph again that morning just in case she was finally in the mood to answer, but there was nothing but voicemail. I was thinking about her being with some guy in Atlanta and completely ignoring her very important job, and I was just contemplating my next move—should I call HR?—when Bruce, Nora, and Lucy burst in. Lucy was talking very fast.

"Dave, we're sorry to bug you, but we think something bad may have happened to Stephanie. There is no way this is her responding to my text." She shoved her phone my way and I tried to absorb the information. All three were staring at me.

I scanned their faces and stopped my eyes harshly on Bruce, who had clearly disobeyed my orders not to say anything. He knew exactly what I was thinking and looked down. Nora jumped in.

"Dave, it's my fault. I told Lucy. We're only trying to help, though. Please look at the texts."

"And who told you, Nora?" I couldn't help but unpeel this onion to see who had violated my orders.

Bruce gulped but stepped forward and said, "I mentioned

it to Nora when it first happened, sir. I didn't know at the time that we wanted to keep things quiet."

"Things like this always need to stay quiet," I scolded them. "Some things are private, the entire newsroom doesn't need to know. Bruce—we'll talk more about this later. Now what am I supposed to be looking at?"

"This text, about Susan and Frank," Lucy said, pointing.

"Who are Susan and Frank?" I asked, my hand starting to stroke my mustache.

"Those are my parents' names," replied Nora. "But Steph doesn't know that. We just threw names into a text to try and trap her. We think someone else might be controlling her phone."

"I'm sorry, what?" I asked. "Controlling her phone? Like acting like they are her?"

"Yes," Lucy and Nora said almost in unison. Bruce was very quiet.

"Stay calm," I said, channeling the voice I used with my three-year-old grandson. "Sit down and let's talk this out."

The three of them perched nervously on the edges of their chairs and looked at me expectantly.

"Let's think rationally," I began. "Maybe Stephanie knows a Susan and Frank that we don't know, so it makes sense to her. She was obviously at the conference, so are you saying something has happened to her since then?"

"Yes, that's what I'm saying," said Lucy.

"Hmmm . . ." My mind was whirling. Could someone actually have her phone? I couldn't show my worry to Nora, Bruce, and Lucy, though, so I tried to think of another plan. "If you truly believe that someone else has her phone, we need a bit more evidence."

"Wait a minute, I have an idea!" Lucy called out. "She only

has one sister, right? What if we texted something about a brother and see what she says?"

We all looked at one another, eyes flicking back and forth. Bruce gave a slight nod, Nora a more enthusiastic one. They turned to me. I realized I had a big decision to make. I had more information than they did. I had talked to Robert. I knew she was shacked up with some guy. Maybe she just needed space, or maybe the new boyfriend was texting on her behalf as she was sleeping or in the shower. But what if he was controlling her? Keeping her trapped somewhere and using her phone? I gulped at the thought. This was Steph, a trusted employee, someone I cared about.

"OK, I guess," I said. "Try it and see what happens."

Lucy eagerly took the phone and started typing. When she was done, she read it aloud.

Your brother stopped by to invite you to lunch. Since you're out, he said he would call you to schedule a time.

She looked at all of us anxiously. "How does that sound? If it's really her, she'll be like, 'You know I don't have a brother! What are you talking about?'"

"Fine, hit send," I told her. She took a deep breath, her finger hovering over her phone, then pushed it down. We all reflexively leaned forward, trying for a better view. Lucy was staring at the screen, waiting.

"Nothing yet," she said. "It might take a while."

I sighed. This seemed like a fruitless exercise. How long could I have these three in my office away from the newsroom? I was just about to usher them back when Lucy jumped.

"Wait! The typing bubbles are going," she cried out. We all sat, collective breath held. The room got very quiet, and the sound of a car driving past was the only noise. Lucy's hand began to shake a little bit.

"It's taking a long time to write back," she said in a loud whisper. Nora leaned over to watch the bubbles. My throat felt dry.

Lucy's face and Nora's simultaneously contorted into shapes I couldn't make out. Nora made a guttural moan.

"What does it say, Lucy?" I asked.

"It says, 'OK, thanks,'" she squeaked out.

Bruce slumped in his chair and ran his hands through his hair. Nora's eyes filled with tears. A prickle overtook my spine.

Lucy began typing something back, but we were all too preoccupied for the moment to stop her. I saw her hit send.

"What did you say back?" I asked. She passed me the phone and I read the text out loud.

I know you have a couple
of brothers. This was the
youngest one—I forgot his
name, what is it again?

"Since she has zero brothers, I want to see how she responds," said Lucy. "I know she saw it, the read receipt is up."

We waited for a full five minutes, but there was no return text.

"Let me try again," she said, typing quickly and then reading:

Something with an A, right?
I just can't recall

"The real Steph would think I was nuts at this point and say something snarky back. She read this one too. Why is she not saying anything?" Lucy said.

A few more minutes passed. We all looked at one another with worry.

"Something is really wrong here," said Lucy. "I'm going to just ask her straight up."

Steph—are you OK?

Lucy's voice shook a little as she read it aloud and hit send. I felt a twitch in my right thumb, something that always started up when I was nervous. We stared at one another. There was no response, and somehow we knew, we all knew, that this was very, very bad.

CHAPTER 20

Robert

The Tuesday After the Flight

It was snowing when I woke up, kind of a sleety snow, not very pretty. Instant slush all over the place.

Ugh. Given that it was supposed to hit a deep freeze later that night, I knew I would have to put some salt down on the front walk or it would be a skating rink. Guess I'd need to do Steph's side too.

I sighed just thinking about her. She was acting like a giddy schoolgirl. I was further torn between being happy for her and finding this whole thing completely distasteful. Reaching for my glasses and the phone on the bedside table, I saw I had a new text from Steph. Immediately, I opened it, thinking it would be some love-filled soliloquy. Instead, I saw this . . .

I'm typing this while Trent is sleeping. I think I might come home earlier than expected. Remember how I said he was bossy? Well he actually yelled at me. It scared me. His anger came out of nowhere. He

doesn't like it when I contact
people from home. I'll call you
when I can

My heart seemed to quite literally stop for a moment and my throat closed up. Frantically, I started typing.

Oh my god, are you OK?
What's happening? Do you
need help?

I waited for the read receipt to pop up on the text chain, but it just said "Delivered." I tried again:

Steph, please answer

And again:

If you don't text me back
soon, I'm calling 911

Ten minutes later, I was seriously contemplating doing just that when she finally responded.

I'm OK. It's OK for now, he
seems to have settled down
this morning. I'm going to book
a flight though. I'll be in touch

I typed back, my mind still shocked into a state of panic:

Come home now!!

Can I call you? Can I talk to
you?

No, not right now. I have to go.
He's coming

Primal fear was not a feeling I had experienced many times in my life, but I recognized it right away. It burst into my pores. Those words "He's coming" felt like something out of a horror movie. Leaping out of bed, I started pacing frantically in my bedroom. But I was over eight hundred miles away. What could I realistically do?

I couldn't eat, I couldn't concentrate, I wasted the entire morning thinking of nothing but Steph and this controlling guy. Pacing my entire townhouse, I finally got restless and went to Steph's to feed Fred and pace her home too.

As I was walking past her row of plants for the tenth time, I had the sudden thought to look around the place more. I didn't know why or what good it would do. If she was with some nutjob in Atlanta, how would snooping around her house help? But it felt like something productive. To what end, I wasn't sure.

The first floor was tidy and organized. Not much to see. In the kitchen, I opened a few cabinet doors but saw nothing other than plates and cups and bowls. Her refrigerator had a few magnets with the logo of the station on them but was fairly bland otherwise. The cat food she had left out for me to feed Fred was getting low, and I made a mental note to bring some from Evita's stash when I came back later.

Walking up the stairs to the second floor, I started in the guest room and poked around a bit. A basic bed and nightstand, extra sheets and towels in the closet. In between the guest room and her room was a bathroom, and I opened the medicine cabinet to see the usual: makeup wipes and Q-tips, some aspirin. A tube of Vagisil made me shut the cabinet quickly.

Into her room I went. The bed was hastily made, but the

only thing out of place were a few dresser drawers not shut all the way. I took the time to shut them.

In her walk-in closet, jeans and sweatshirts were all over one side, a sports bra hanging on the back of the door handle, socks strewn about. The other side had her work clothes, neatly arranged by color. I reached out and touched a blue shirt I had always liked her in. My phone vibrated in my pocket.

Looking down, I saw that it was her.

Robert—he hit me, he hit me hard. I'm scared. I think he's going to kill me

Never have I both run and stumbled so quickly.

I twisted my knee trying to get down the stairs and dropped my phone because my hands were shaking so badly. It crashed to the wood floor, and I had a horrid fear that I had just broken it. Neither Steph nor I owned a landline, and I had to call 9-1-1. Now. What would I do if it was broken?

Urgently, I picked it back up with hands that were into full-blown tremors now. Oh, thank goodness, it seemed to be OK, just a crack on the cover.

Beads of sweat were forming on my forehead. My throat felt hoarse. I wondered if I would be able to talk to the 9-1-1 operator. Forcing my fingers to function, I pushed those dreaded three buttons that no one wants to use and held the phone to my ear, my heart thumping so loudly I could hear it, blood pulsing at my ears.

"9-1-1, what's your emergency?"

"My friend is in trouble. She texted me that a man is trying to kill her. Someone she has been seeing. His name is Trent . . ."

"Sir, calm down, where is her last known location?"

"She's in Atlanta." I felt like I was slurring, like I was drunk. "It was a work trip and she met this guy and . . ."

"Sir, do you have any idea where in Atlanta she is?"

"No . . . I . . ." But then, suddenly, I realized I did know. What she said about Zillow. "Wait, yes, she texted me his address. Hold on."

Putting her on speakerphone and with hands that continued to violently shake, I called up my text chain with Steph. Seeing her most recent text and the words "He's going to kill me" made my body go cold, but I forced myself to breathe, muttering under my breath, "Come on, Robert, where is it? Where is it?" Scrolling backward, the text with the photo of the outside of his condo popped up. There it was, her words, with his address.

"4240 Horizon Lane," I said. "She told me the neighborhood too. Um, wait, here it is . . . Peachtree Village."

"Sir, we will get in contact with Atlanta police and send a dispatch right away. What is your name?"

"Robert . . . Robert Tayburn."

"OK, Robert. We have your number. Someone will call you back if needed."

"Thank you, oh, thank you. Hurry, please. Please hurry." We hung up and tears sprang into my eyes. I sank down onto Steph's bottom stair, gulping air into my lungs and trying to steady my breath.

Wiping my eyes, I suddenly realized I had not responded directly to Steph. I was so busy calling 9-1-1 I hadn't even given a second to her. Instead of texting, I tried calling. It went right to voicemail. I tried again, and again.

"Oh, Steph, oh no," I moaned, then frantically texted:

I called 911. They are on
their way. CALL ME

There was no reply. Bolting back to my place, I felt fear and confusion now overtaking me.

"What the hell??" I yelled.

I wanted to throw the phone but knew that wasn't wise, so I picked up a couple of pillows from the couch and started hurling them around, screaming. Evita got frightened, jumped down off the kitty condo, and scurried upstairs, probably to a closet. I would have to make amends with her later.

My fit lasted a few minutes. When the rage started to subside, I curled onto the couch in a fetal position and began to bawl. I felt like a child and didn't care.

My phone rang. Standing and lunging for it, I hoped it was Steph, but instead it was her boss. I now recognized his number.

"Dave?" I cried into the receiver, skipping the hellos.

"Robert, are you OK?"

"I don't know, I don't know what's happening. I got texts from Steph and I called 9-1-1 and now she's not answering me."

"9-1-1? What did the texts say?" Dave's tone turned to worry.

"She said she thought this Trent guy she met was going to kill her. She was scared. I didn't know what to do. I called 9-1-1 and they sent the Atlanta police over."

"Robert, I think we need to get our heads together. I also have some information. Can you get to Channel 3 and meet me in my office?"

"Um, yes, yes, sure. I can . . . but what do you mean, you have information?"

"Robert—I need you to sit down now. Are you sitting?"

I wasn't, but I lied. "Yes."

"OK, Robert—we have some reason to believe that the person texting might not be Stephanie. Have you actually spoken to her since she got to Atlanta?"

Now I sat involuntarily, more collapsed, in fact, back onto the couch.

"What do you mean? Of course it's her. She texted me a ton and left me a voice memo. She sent me a photo. Of her in Atlanta. Sightseeing."

"Where was she?" Dave asked.

"Centennial Olympic Park. Do you think someone is impersonating her? I'm so confused. She sent me a picture of a gift she was getting me. It's her."

"I don't know, Robert, but please come to Channel 3 right away. We need to talk and I think we need to compare notes."

"On my way," I said, and I grabbed a coat and was out the door within ten seconds.

CHAPTER 21

Lucy

The Tuesday After the Flight

Dave had sent us back to work after our chat in his office, but how could any of us work?

I sat at my desk googling famous *Dateline* cases involving stolen phones and sending links to Bruce and Nora. My work duties of posting videos to the website and hoping for clicks had gone completely by the wayside, and if any Madison, Wisconsin, viewers were looking for cute, fun content on our website, they would be sorely disappointed.

Dave pinged the three of us to come back to his office. We raced down. There was a strange man sitting in a chair in front of Dave's desk and I thought for a moment that he could be a private investigator, but he didn't look the part. His hair was wild, eyes bloodshot, and he had on a sweatshirt and jeans.

"Team, this is Robert, Steph's neighbor," Dave said and motioned for us all to sit. A feeling of dread began to creep up on me. Was the neighbor here to deliver bad news? I glanced at Nora, and she looked the same way. Slowly, we lowered our bodies into chairs and gazed at Robert warily.

"OK," Dave said. "Time to compare notes. Robert is here to tell us what he knows and vice versa."

Robert took out his phone and started passing it around, describing how Steph told him she had met this amazing man and how she texted him various pictures and a voice memo from Atlanta, but then things had taken a dark turn. He said he had called 9-1-1, and dispatch had called him back on his way to Channel 3 to say they searched the address he gave them and saw no signs of anything wrong. When he got to the parking lot, he texted Steph one more time but there had been no answer thus far.

Bruce got his phone out and showed us how she said she simply needed time off and to reschedule a bunch of meetings. He also played the voice memo. Then I took mine out and explained the Mark Ruffalo texts and the Susan-and-Frank and brother traps and how someone had fallen into them.

"What's next?" Nora asked. "What can we do?"

"I think I might get on a plane to Atlanta tomorrow, whatever the earliest available flight is," said Robert. "I'm going crazy here being so far away. At least there I can keep an eye on that condo and see if I can figure out what's going on."

"And I'm going to call her sister and her son tonight," said Dave. "They deserve to know what we know. Maybe they'll have new information."

We all nodded solemnly, lost in our own thoughts. I couldn't stop thinking about Robert going to Atlanta, what he might learn by being there. How proactive that felt. Bruce looked down at the floor, Dave stroked his mustache and stared at the ceiling, Nora bit her fingernails, I jiggled my leg, and Robert twisted his hands over and over. It stayed like that for a solid two minutes before Dave said, "OK, everyone can go now. We'll be in touch."

We filed out like a zombie apocalypse.

CHAPTER 22

Robert

One Week After the Flight

I booked the 6:30 a.m. flight, threw everything into a hippie-inspired duffel bag I had gotten at a market in Ecuador, and left for the airport four hours early because I simply couldn't stand the wait anymore. Sleep wasn't even a thought.

Dave's wife, Lisa, had offered to watch both Evita and Fred, so I rescued Fred from his side of the townhouse and brought him, and his favorite sleeping pillow, to my side so at least they could be together. It gave me hope that perhaps Stephanie and I would be reunited soon, sitting on the couch drinking champagne and singing our hearts out to *My Fair Lady*.

At the airport, I paced the gate and stalked the one coffee shop until it opened at five. It dawned on me suddenly that I hadn't eaten in a full twenty-four hours. The only thing I felt I could stomach was a muffin. I added some coffee, but wound up dumping both after two sips and three bites.

Just as we were about to board, I heard a woman's voice call my name and I turned around.

Lucy, Steph's coworker, was walking quickly toward me.

"Robert, I decided to go with you. I bought my ticket at three a.m."

"Lucy! Wow, thank you." A rush of relief and affection for this near stranger came over me. She obviously felt as strongly as I did about finding Stephanie and figuring out what was happening.

"I have some new information from Stephanie's sister. Here, come sit." She motioned to chairs in the boarding area. "Dave texted me that he spoke to Steph's sister, Renee, who spoke to her son, Evan. Evan was able to do 'Find My iPhone.' Robert—I don't know if this is good or bad news, but it pinged at the address you told us about: 4240 Horizon Lane."

"Oh dear God," I said, clutching my heart.

"That will be our first stop when we land," said Lucy. "Let's see if we can sit together on the plane. I want to go over the entire timeline and put it on a spreadsheet. My brain works like that. Nothing else new from you?"

"Nothing," I said. "No response to the approximately ten thousand texts I have sent her. That's what scares me. Why is she not responding if she's in his house? And police didn't find anything. Unless. Unless he has her locked up elsewhere." My whole body shuddered at the thought.

"If she's anywhere at or near that house, we'll find her and we'll set her free," Lucy reassured me. I marveled at her confidence. "Let's just get our boots on the ground and see."

On the plane, we managed to convince an urban-hipster type to switch seats so that Lucy and I could sit together, and as soon as we reached cruising altitude, she popped open her laptop on the tray table.

Lucy wanted to make a list of every day since Steph had left and the corresponding information we had gathered. She began typing and reading aloud.

—Thursday: Stephanie posted a picture on Facebook from the News Coverage Summit.

—Friday: Robert texted her a picture of Fred sitting on the chair licking his paw. That was when she said she met a guy and would be going to Atlanta with him.

—Saturday: She texted Robert to say that they were at the airport.

—Sunday: She reported that he wanted to stay in all day so they could get to know each other.

—Monday: Bruce texted her about work, and she wrote back asking him to cancel all meetings and then became snarky with him. She sent him a voice memo too.

—Monday: She texted Robert pictures and the voice memo, starting with Trent's condo, then the lattes, Centennial Park, his station, and the Hot-lanta mug.

—Monday: She asked Lucy to change the meeting with "Mark R." and then got a bit nasty about it.

—Monday night: For the first time, she expressed fear about Trent in a text to Robert.

—Tuesday: She was texting about a brother she didn't have and just a short time later told Robert Trent was going to kill her. Then silence, the 9-1-1 call Robert had made, which, according to the police, had yielded absolutely nothing.

—Wednesday: Her phone pinged at Trent's house.

It was all just mind-bogglingly strange and horrifyingly scary. But as we sat there staring at it, a new thought came into my mind.

That night at my place when Steph told me that she would be willing to endure a disease, a few nights in the woods, or a friendly kidnapper to get her son back in her corner. This wasn't some giant cat and mouse game, was it? Was Trent the friendly kidnapper? Could she possibly have staged this to make Evan worry for a while and then return triumphantly?

Glancing over at Lucy, I wondered if I should tell her, but this tidbit felt too personal for a coworker. Lucy was so young and she was on Steph's staff. She would be shocked to hear it. Yet as I turned my head to look out the window at the clouds, I wondered if I wasn't being played for a fool here.

CHAPTER 23

Robert

One Week After the Flight

We landed and headed to ground transportation. I called up an Uber and punched in the dreaded address: 4240 Horizon Lane. The condo was just twenty minutes from the airport. We waited inside the terminal for the Uber to arrive.

Lucy was looking at her phone and stepped away to take a phone call. When she hung up, she walked back to me and opened her mouth to talk, but nothing came out. Fear began to climb my neck.

"What, Lucy, what?"

Still without speaking, she motioned for me to sit. I kept my eyes on her face the entire time as I did so.

"Robert," she finally stammered. "That was Dave. He said a GM friend of his called him. Apparently, word is getting out in the news community that a news director named Trent in Atlanta is in jail. For something awful. And Dave's friend said it involves another news director, a female."

Lucy's eyes filled with tears. I felt mine instinctively do the same. Jail? That sounded a lot more serious than staging a fake kidnapping with someone.

I gulped and looked down at the airport floor, the noise of the busy terminal around me. There was a din of voices, a child cried, a couple was reuniting and sharing kisses, the carousels were moving at a mechanical churn, and a robotic woman's voice came over the loudspeaker directing people to the right baggage pickup for their flight.

"Come on, Robert," she said finally. "It's not over until it's over. I won't believe it until someone proves it. And Dave's friend didn't have the name of the victim yet. Let's get over to Horizon Lane."

I stood up in a trancelike state and followed her. Our Uber was only two minutes out now, so we stood in silence on the curb waiting. Luckily the driver was quiet and serious, without any music on. It was just what we needed. Complete and total silence. As we got closer, the driver finally spoke up.

"Lots of cop cars, I can only get a block away."

"That's fine," Lucy said. I was glad she seemed to be taking the lead in getting things done. I still had not spoken a word since the airport.

We climbed out to find two squad cars blocking the street and a bunch of neighbors milling about whispering to one another. We set our bags on the ground and stood there, trying to assess what we could.

It was hard to see that far down the block, but I craned my neck and thought I could make out the top of the white stucco building that matched what Steph had texted me. The neighborhood was clearly for wealthy people, lots of modern loft-type places and expensive SUVs along the street. The bushes were well tended, and neatly planted flowers adorned some nearby lawns. I overheard three women who looked like they were in their seventies talking to one another near us.

"I heard he's some big shot at a local TV station," one hissed.

"Like an anchor?" another asked. "What a scandal!"

"You know what I heard?" said the third. "There was some kind of drug overdose, or sex game gone wrong. That's what the word on the street is."

The word on the street? From these grandmas? I had to stop myself from charging at them and wringing their sagging necks. There was no way Steph would do drugs or play sex games with a relative stranger.

Or would she? I mean, you know your neighbors, but how well really? But no, not my Steph. Impossible.

A man walked up with a poodle in his arms. He was wearing all purple and looked like a poor man's Prince.

"Y'all," he said in a Southern drawl, "there's a press conference coming up in thirty minutes. They're holding it in front of the condo, but y'all can stream it on your phones if you want to. That's what me and Poo-Poo plan to do, isn't that right, Poo-Poo?" He kissed the poodle's head and took a paw and did a fake little wave. She sat there with a dumb look on her face. The guy turned to us. His eyes traveled downward to our bags.

"Y'all from out of town?"

"Yes, just got in," said Lucy.

"And you came right here? Lord, child, isn't there a better tourist attraction? You can go to that giant waste of taxpayer money Centennial Olympic Park, can't you?"

I finally found my voice.

"We just want to find out what happened," I said, and the guy with the poodle raised his eyebrows.

"Don't we all, sugar child? I dare say murder is not common in these parts, you know what I mean? I keep an eye on the neighborhood and take pictures of strangers. I got a friend with the po-po, that's the police, as opposed to Poo-Poo, that's her." He stroked the dog's head. "And they told me they ain't got no actual body yet but a lot of evidence is pointing to someone's demise. You know, hair, blood, DNA-type stuff, plus I guess they found like a phone and some other shit in the backyard. This dude's in deep doo-doo, right, Poo-Poo?"

He waved and turned, the purple cape flowing behind him. "We're going to my condo to watch the press conference. Have a blessed day, y'all!"

A blessed day? I couldn't imagine ever having another one in my life.

"Come on, let's find a place to sit and watch the press conference," Lucy said. "A coffee shop or something."

One of the seventy-year-old women who had been whispering overheard us and chimed in: "There's one just down that block and over. Peaches and Cream. Really good lattes. Wait until you see their fun mugs."

It hit me between the eyes. That could be the shop where Steph and Trent went, the one with the picture of the two lattes on a table.

"Yes, let's go," I said to Lucy, grabbing her arm so hard I startled her. Anything to see where Steph had been, to walk in her shoes around Atlanta. We took off at a fast clip.

Sure enough, the moment we got to the place and I saw the dark brown tables and brightly colored mugs with peaches on the side, I knew it was the same shop. I remembered the angle of the table against a window, and that very table was vacant. I felt as if Steph herself were calling me to it.

"There." I pointed. "Let's sit there."

Sliding into the chair she would have been in when she took the picture of the mugs and letting Lucy have the one Trent would have sat in, I ran my hands over the edge of the table, back and forth several times, just trying to be close to anything she would have been close to.

Lucy took charge again, going to the counter and returning with two black coffees. Plucking her laptop from her travel bag, she called up one of the local TV stations to watch the live stream of the press conference.

It hadn't started yet, and we sipped our coffees and waited, both of us staring at the screen. I wanted desperately for the Atlanta police chief to come out and say this was a horrible mistake and really nothing bad had happened and they apologized and we could all go home now. If not that, my second choice was that he name some unfamiliar person as the victim. If I heard Steph's name, I thought I might combust right there in the coffee shop.

I leaned forward in my chair, eyes glued to the laptop screen. A muscular Black man with glasses and a police chief's hat approached a makeshift podium peppered with hastily assembled microphones. He cleared his throat.

"Good afternoon, I'm Chief Newman of the Atlanta PD. I will share the information that I can, but this is an active investigation and I will not be taking any questions. Atlanta police were dispatched to the residence behind me overnight for a welfare check on an individual after that individual called 9-1-1 asking for help. Police entered the residence. Enough evidence was found to take a Trent J. McCarthy, age fifty-two, who is employed at NBC6, into custody on suspicion of two homicides. We are not releasing names of the victims yet. Again, this remains an active investigation and we will provide further updates when we can."

He started to step away from the microphone, but reporters began shouting questions.

"Chief, Chief . . . what else do we know?"

"Chief Newman, is Trent McCarthy married?"

"Chief, did you find the bodies?"

The chief half turned his head and scowled.

"I told you, no questions. This press conference is adjourned."

Lucy slowly shut her laptop and looked at me. We didn't say anything; we didn't have to. Even though there was no name of the victim given, somehow we knew. We both knew. I put my head into my hands. Even if Steph had started out working with this Trent guy to stage a kidnapping, it seemed that it had gone horribly wrong.

CHAPTER 24

Bruce

One Week After the Flight

None of us could work after the Atlanta police chief held his press conference. Hell, we could barely function. I still had to be in charge, though, and I told everyone to go down to bare-bones mode. Only the most critical stories in Madison would get coverage that day. We could fill the shows with national news—there was always plenty of that available on the feeds. Yet the biggest story at the moment nationally was a news director in Atlanta who was arrested for a possible double murder.

Now Lucy was out for the day. Bernie, the receptionist, had gabbed to a few people that she thought Lucy was in Atlanta. We all moved around in robot mode, whispering to one another. By now, the whole newsroom was clued in that something was amiss with Steph, and they knew about this big national story. They were certain to put two and two together, if they hadn't already. We were journalists; we were not ones to let something just go past us without a ton of questions. And the business was small enough that gossip whipped around quickly.

At six p.m. Eastern time, police in Atlanta called another press conference. It was five our time, the start of our five o'clock news, so the anchors had to be on set and the director and producer in the booth, but the rest of us gathered around Nora's computer to see what the latest was coming out of Atlanta. I'm sure the director and producer—probably the anchors too—were sneaking peeks at their phones for updates when they could.

"Good evening, I'm Chief Newman again, Atlanta PD," said the man in glasses and a chief's hat, his badge glistening in the TV lights. "I'm here to provide an update on the unfortunate tragedy that occurred in the residence behind me. Trent McCarthy remains in custody. We can now confirm two names of potential victims. Only one of them is confirmed with DNA at this time, though."

He cleared his throat and looked down at a paper in front of him.

"That one is a Jasmine V. Littleton. The second potential victim is a Stephanie H. Monroe. Personal items from both were found buried in the backyard. We know that Mr. McCarthy and at least one of the victims attended a conference together in La Jolla, California, last week. This remains a very active investigation and we ask anyone with information to come forward. There will be no questions, and I mean it this time: *No. Questions.*"

He turned on his heel and walked away.

I felt a darkness creeping up behind my eyes. Nora screamed and someone else groaned. This couldn't possibly be real life, could it?

CHAPTER 25

Anna

One Week After the Flight

In my mailbox was a padded envelope addressed to me with no return address. The postmark said Atlanta. To my shock, $500 in cash was inside. I knew then it was from Jasmine. She had come through! How she got that much money, I had no idea, but she was true to her word and had paid me back. I tucked the money into a drawer until I could get to the bank and texted her a thank-you. She did not respond.

It was my day off, and I was just settling in on the couch, scrolling through TikTok, when my cell phone rang. It was Ed, the bar manager.

Hesitating with my finger over the answer button, I decided not to pick up. I really didn't want to be called to fill in for someone tonight. I was beat from a long week, especially the stress over Glenn and stepping up at work to take on extra duties for Jasmine.

A few minutes later Ed called again. Ignoring it a second time, I turned my ringer off and flipped the phone upside down. I needed space. I deserved it. I was exhausted.

With my phone out of the mix, I popped on Netflix and

settled in to binge-watch. When the first episode of my new series was done, I got up to make some popcorn for the rest of the marathon, and while it popped, I returned to the couch and finally flipped my phone back right side up.

There were twelve texts and ten calls, all from people at the bar. My body tensed up. What was going on?

Quickly, I opened Ed's text first.

> Have you been watching the news? Something happened to Jasmine. In Atlanta of all places. Call me. Where the hell are you?

The news? What did he mean? Frantically, I scanned the other texts I had from coworkers, which essentially said a variation of the same thing. Glancing at the clock, I saw that it was in between the six and ten o'clock newscasts. The news? I called Ed.

"Jesus Christ, Anna. Where have you been? This is bad, really fucking bad. Sit down. Are you sitting down?"

"No."

"Well, sit the hell down."

"What are you talking about, Ed? Just tell me what happened to Jasmine."

"Anna . . ." He took a deep breath. "Police in Atlanta just held a press conference. I'm sorry to be the one to tell you this, but Jasmine . . . is dead. Killed by some guy down there that she met."

I was conscious that Rocky jumped off the couch and came to my side instinctively, but I was not conscious of much else. I couldn't compute anything. "Ed, what did you just say?"

He laid it out for me as best he could, the little he knew,

adding that he was closing the bar early and all coworkers were invited over together to talk and grieve.

We hung up, and I sank to the floor next to Rocky, burying my face in his soft fur. He began to lick my hand. I started to cry.

Oh, Jasmine, how could this happen? My thoughts went back to her first text to me about how she felt safe and beautiful, and then to her last text to me when she said this guy, Trent, was super sexy, but had a bit of a temper. Yet she insisted she was OK and didn't need anything. That was just a few days ago. And he had killed her since then? My stomach roiled and I cried harder.

No, Jasmine, no. This just wasn't fair. You weren't dealt a fair hand in life. Your mom, Glenn, this. It was so unjust.

I should share what I knew with the police, I reasoned; maybe it would help them. But I'd deleted the texts. I wasn't sure if police could pull up things that were deleted. I guess I assumed so. They were probably on a hard drive in my phone somewhere.

I reached for the phone to look up the number of the Madison police, hand shaking. Something stopped me, though. No, I shouldn't go to the police. What new info would I be telling them anyway? And if they dug too deep, would I be implicated for Glenn being beaten up? I had to protect myself and Rocky. I would do what I could to honor Jasmine in other ways, a funeral, a memorial, keeping her memory alive. If the media asked me to talk about the Jasmine I knew from the bar, I would do that. But I couldn't jeopardize my own safety.

Hugging Rocky tighter, I squinted my eyes shut, willing this whole nasty mess to go away. What kind of a monster was this guy Trent? He meets Jasmine, takes her to Atlanta, and kills her and some other woman within a week of knowing them? Was he a serial killer? Did my friend fall victim to a serial killer? Or did Trent maybe finance her trip and they knew each other already? Was that possible? Jasmine didn't have a lot of money. How could she have gotten to Atlanta otherwise? Maybe he did bankroll her. Maybe that's how she was able to pay me back.

Regardless, I couldn't stop imagining Jasmine's last moments with Trent. What did she experience at the end? How horrible was it? What was her last thought on this earth?

I hoped this monster Trent would rot in hell.

PART THREE

CHAPTER 26

Trent

The First Day of the Conference

A line of treadmills overlooked a bank of windows, but the view wasn't very inspiring. Just a hospital parking lot and a highway. At least there were a few palm trees.

It was 6:30 a.m., and I had forced myself out of bed to get the ol' ticker thumping before the News Coverage Summit kicked off. My doctor had warned me that my blood pressure was creeping up, and I was committed to taking off a few pounds this year. It was my New Year's resolution. Granted, it was only the third week of January, but I had been pretty good. Couldn't let a conference get in the way.

Pearl Jam provided the soundtrack as I pumped my legs on the tread, feeling beads of sweat starting to form. The long flight from Atlanta had done a number on my body yesterday, but I had gotten to the hotel by late afternoon and even had time for a massive NY strip dinner with two double-baked potatoes and dessert, followed by a few cocktails in the bar. Met some fellow news directors from around the country who were in for the same thing. We all had a couple of laughs. I felt energized and was looking forward to meeting more people. Those of us in charge of newsrooms tended to be in our own little orbits; we didn't socialize much in our cities, mostly for fear of sharing information that shouldn't be shared. It was a competitive and secretive society. This conference felt like a chance to mix and mingle. Given that I was newly single, I was itching for a one-night stand too, and I couldn't wait to scout the chicks just in case something could develop. It had been way too long since I had a good one-night stand.

As I cranked up the incline and the music pulsed in my ears, my thoughts jerked back to one of the last things Katrina had said before she left me: that I should give her wedding ring to the TV station because I was married to it and not her. That still pissed me off.

True, I put in marathon-long days, but it was to help us as a family as much as anything. Would she be able to afford the private school for the kids and her "me days" of pedicures and shopping if I weren't working so much? I didn't think so. Now she would receive child support for Brittany and Brett and get her own house.

My fists balled up as I increased the speed on the treadmill, thinking of her dating some new guy but still living off *my* money. We had our differences. I might have cheated on her a few times, but who could possibly be loyal to one person their whole life when the world was filled with so many tempting possibilities? And, frankly, who was to say she hadn't cheated on me?

We had a few fights too, but was it my fault she could be so hotheaded? Sure, I'd pushed her a few times. That wasn't a big deal. She threatened a restraining order but thankfully hadn't gone through with it. That sort of thing could kill my career. I think she knew it would stop her flow of income too, which was why she didn't do it. She just left me instead.

I had the kids on weekends just once per month by my choice. Kids were a pain in the ass. *Daddy, I want juice. Daddy, I'm tired. Daddy, I'm hungry. Daddy, I hurt my knee.* Katrina was the woman; she could deal with that sort of crap. I even cut the hours I was with the kids so that I didn't pick them up until late afternoon on a Saturday and returned them Sunday right after breakfast. Even twenty-four hours as a single parent would have been too much.

To be honest, I was thrilled to have my freedom almost entirely back. Freedom to date, to sleep in when I wanted, to drink as much as I felt like without her checking the recycling bin to see how many beer cans were in it. Screw her. I had bigger things to think about than stupid Katrina or the kids.

Turning the incline down, I looked at the clock on the wall. Time to get ready for the conference. Slowing to a fast walk, I changed the music to Coldplay for the cooldown, and my thoughts drifted to what the hotel restaurant might offer for breakfast. My secretary had said I should do avocado toast given that I was in California, but that sounded awful. No thanks. Eggs, hash browns, toast, and bacon for me. I needed to feel full after every meal.

Grabbing a stiff, bleachy-smelling towel from the stack by the door, I wiped sweat off my forehead and looked at myself in the wall of mirrors opposite the windows. I tried to suck in my stomach. That gut had been inching out for the past five years. I was fifty-two years old, still had a boyish face, people told me, but I felt every ache and pain too. Would probably be sore from this running. I should stretch, but who had time for that? I gave it a cursory fingers-to-toes followed by a twist in each direction and decided that was enough. Stretching was for ballerinas. Dropping the towel in the laundry hamper and leaving the gym, I strode back to the elevator to get to my room.

The shower had a rainforest head and side jets, and the hotel provided bodywash and two options for shampoo and conditioner in pump containers in the shower stall. I emerged smelling like eucalyptus. Standing naked in front of the massive bathroom mirror, I thought about how good I looked, minus that extra belly fat I was working on. But my arms were toned and my face was damn handsome. My hair, barely gray or thinning yet, was my calling card, and if I ever started to lose it, I had plans to pay whatever it took for hair plugs.

Reaching for the shaving cream, I did my full shaving process, then plucked a few nose hairs from my nostrils and clipped my sideburns with tiny scissors I always brought along. Briefly, I contemplated texting my assistant news director to see how everything was going back in the A-T-L, as I liked to call Atlanta, but then thought, fuck it. I could view this as a vacation as much as anything, right? Why be bogged down with the minutiae of the newsroom? Married to my work? I'd show Katrina. I even avoided the San Diego morning news shows and instead turned on ESPN.

My clothes were zipped into travel bags, pressed and ready to go, thanks to my secretary. This first day I would wear a suit coat that was monogrammed with my initials, as were all of my work clothes. I paired that with a Ralph Lauren V-neck T-shirt, pressed slacks, and Hugo Boss shoes. Fastening my chunky silver watch, adding gel to my hair and smoothing it down, I grabbed the leather over-the-shoulder messenger bag I had gotten from one of the best tanneries in Rome and headed down for breakfast.

The eggs were a bit overdone, but the hash browns, toast, and bacon were good. I downed it all with two cups of black coffee—no milk, no sugar (sugar was for little girls, my dad had always said)—and I was feeling jacked up and powerful as

I strode into the ballroom ready for the conference. A table was set up to the left with name tags strewn across it.

"Good morning, can I help you find your name?" asked a young woman with short hair who I guessed to be an intern. She had a mega-busty chest but wasn't that attractive. Anyone wearing a nose ring always turned me off, but I put on my best news director voice and bellowed:

"You sure can. Trent McCarthy, reporting for duty."

"McCarthy . . . *M* . . ." She scanned the sea of tags. "Oh, here you go. It has your assigned table on it. Can you sign in, please?"

She pointed to a sheet. I scribbled my name in a bold cursive that had a giant *T* and an even bigger *M*. It overtook the little box I was supposed to sign in and bled into the boxes above and below me.

"10-4, done and done. You've been very helpful. Thank you . . ." I looked at her name tag as an excuse to get my eyes from her nose ring to that chest again. "Willow. You have a great day now, and if I see your boss, I'll tell him . . . or *her* . . . that you deserve a raise."

I gave her a wink and a smile to show her that by saying "or her" I was not sexist.

"My boss is a gender nonconformist and goes by 'them,' but thank you," Willow replied. I thought I saw her smirk.

I turned quickly on my heel, muttering: "You've got to be fucking kidding me." All this lib-tard BS. Boys were boys and girls were girls. You couldn't mess with nature. I would never call anyone "them" or share a bathroom with a person who couldn't decide what sex they were. Screw Willow and her whole generation.

The room in front of me was already buzzing with people in a get-to-know-you mode. There was a lot of handshaking and plenty of "nice to meet yous." The outfit of choice was work professional, women mostly in smart-looking pants outfits, men in suit coats or button-down shirts. No one wore jeans. Not a lot of color variation either—mostly muted tans, grays, darker greens, and navy blues. I fit right in, just the way I liked it. The space smelled of aftershave, perfume, and coffee. A good number of people still had disposable cups from the Starbucks in the lobby in their hands.

Glancing at my name tag for my table assignment, I made my way to table four. It had four chairs around it, all set in a semicircle facing a stage. Only one person was already there, a tall Black woman wearing small gold earrings and a dark blue pantsuit. I extended my hand.

"Trent McCarthy, NBC6, Atlanta. You are?" I stole a look at her name tag, but it was truly just for the name tag. Her chest didn't interest me at all. She had to be at least sixty years old.

"Dorothy Robinson, Boston," she replied in a voice so deep that it surprised me. "I'm a former investigative journalist. I've been at the ABC affiliate for over thirty years, news director for the past eight."

"Very nice," I replied. We made a little small talk. Something in the way Dorothy spoke seemed as if she thought I should be impressed by her. I wasn't. Instead, I was eager for new company, and I got it as another person arrived. This time it was a guy. He was small and wiry, with curly hair and glasses.

"Hello, my name is Alan Kozinski, WNJT, Kalamazoo."

I sized him up immediately to be a small-market geek who would probably live in Kalamazoo forever. He was the kind of guy I would never be friends with. I was a Sigma Tau. We weeded out dudes like him every year. But wanting to be nice, I did what I always did when I met a new guy, clapping him on the back and talking sports.

"Michigan, huh? You think they'll make it to the Big Dance?"

"The what?"

"*The N-C-Double-A tournament.*" What moron didn't know the Big Dance? "Michigan is solid this year, Al."

"Oh, basketball, yeah. The University of Michigan is in Ann Arbor," he said. "It's on the other side of the state."

"Is it?" I had gone to school at Illinois, a place I had chosen for its frat and party scene, but aside from a few trips to Chicago, that was the extent of my Midwest knowledge.

"Well, trust me, Al, my pal. Michigan has a chance this year. You keep an eye on them. That center is built like Kareem Abdul-Jabbar." I fake dribbled and took a hook shot to emphasize my point. "You *do know* who Kareem is, don't you?"

He nodded but turned and started talking to Dorothy. I couldn't think of anything else to say.

Glancing around, I spotted a woman headed our way, and my eyes stayed on her, hoping she might be our final tablemate. She stood out right away because she had on a bright pink blazer in the sea of monotones, and a shorter black dress that showed her knees and calves. Her shoes kind of looked like weird sneakers. Her hair was brown, slightly wavy, and hung past her ears and just down onto her neck; she had a pretty face. Sure as shit, she was beelining right for our table. My lucky day.

"Are you the fourth person at table four?" I asked in what I considered my "welcome to the party" voice. She hooked a light blue purse on the back of the chair. I could smell a flowery perfume.

"Yes," she said. "My name is Stephanie Monroe."

Immediately I decided she was the one I would hit on at this conference. I hadn't seen anyone hotter than her in the room.

"Trent McCarthy, NBC6, Atlanta, and it certainly is nice to meet *you*, Stephanie," I said, scanning her entire body head to toe. That was always a good opener with hot women; it made them feel sexy.

After introductions all the way around, Stephanie, Alan, Dorothy, and I settled into our seats, and the emcee walked up to the stage and clinked a fork on a glass.

"Welcome, one and all," she bellowed. "We are so excited to have you at the News Coverage Summit. I hope you all had a good trip to beautiful San Diego. We have a jam-packed few days for you, so let's get going!"

We spent the next two hours hearing from speakers who shared all kinds of data and PowerPoints. Dorothy and Alan took scrupulous notes. Stephanie and I didn't. I started to get bored and pulled my phone out a few times, trying not to look like I was checking feeds. I noticed Stephanie also did the same twice but quickly placed her phone back in her purse.

I fiddled with my watch; I daydreamed a little. Most of what the speakers were saying was not computing with me anyway. I liked the way we did things in our newsroom. Some speaker was not going to change me.

For the final stretch before lunch, we were instructed to turn to our tablemates and share some things that were working in our own newsrooms. I cleared my throat and decided that naturally I would be the one to start. I was clearly the leader at table four.

"Dorothy . . . Alan . . . Stephanie." I took a moment to point at each and look them in the eye. "In Atlanta, I run a tight ship. I've learned over the years that if you give an inch, most will take a mile. It's also important for the boss to be decisive, so I choose what we're covering each day and stick to it. Crime is rampant, and we're known as the breaking news station. People turn to us for that, and we have to live up to it. It bleeds, it leads. You know what I mean, right, Al? How about you, how do you run things up there in the Zoo?"

I was proud of myself for coming up with a nickname for Alan's home city so quickly and grinned at him. Alan pushed his glasses up on his nose and gave me a long look.

"Well, we actually take the opposite approach from your style," he said in a voice that I could only describe as wimpy. "We try to hear all viewpoints in the newsroom about what we should cover. I think that makes for the best newsroom atmosphere. It should be a democracy, not a dictatorship."

I tried to suppress my disgust. That tactic would never work or get him to a larger market. No wonder he was stuck there in Podunkville. Next Dorothy chimed in.

"We're trying community journalism in Boston. We have assigned reporters to specific neighborhoods and they are embedded there. Some even live in those neighborhoods. We do what we call 'hometown stories' and profile restaurants and people in addition to breaking news, politics, and, yes, crime. But crime is not our focus. I think people want solutions-based journalism, not just an amplification of problems. We're actually trying *not* to run out breathlessly to every breaking news scene. Just because crime happens and is the low-hanging fruit doesn't mean it automatically gets anointed to the top spot."

A second pussy station, I thought, and turned to fully face Stephanie. Her cleavage was peeking out of the black dress, and I tried not to be obvious, but I thought I saw a hint of a lacy bra. Damn. It had been too long, an escort for a few hours in my room in Vegas six months ago notwithstanding.

"So what about you, Steph? How do you do it in Madtown?"

"Umm," she said. "We kind of do a little bit of everything

you all said. You know, we just do our best to cover the news every single day."

"Uh-huh," I replied. "But like, what is your style?" I wouldn't let her get away with an answer like that. I was a journalist, damn it. I would dig deeper.

"My style?"

"Yeah, as a news director," I added, taking a swig of water from my glass and staring her down. She would give me a decent answer if I had to wait all day. "Are you someone who likes to . . . punish others? Or do you prefer, you know, a softer touch?"

I winked at her, wondering if she would get my subtle hints, if she'd flirt back. After all, she clearly had to think I was the hottest thing in this room too.

"Oh, ummm." She shifted in her seat. "Well, my style is to be nice to everyone—but tough when I need to. I can do it all."

We all just kind of looked at her. She didn't have much of a way with words, that was for sure, but she was definitely cute in a room filled with dudes, Dorothy, Willow, and a bunch of other aging or pudgy women.

"Excuse me," Stephanie said. "I have to run to the restroom."

Grabbing her light blue purse from the chair, she strode across the room and out the door by the name tag table. I watched her go. Long legs, tight rear. She really was sexy. If I could just get her to loosen up a bit. Maybe at lunch.

CHAPTER 27

Trent

After Lunch

Ninety minutes later we were back in the ballroom.

I looked around as people began finding their seats. This conference was at least 70 percent men, and I nodded to myself in approval. I mean, come on, could you blame the GMs out there for hiring male news directors? We all knew men made better leaders. I would never say that out loud, of course, or the woke mafia would come after me, but everyone knew it was the damn truth. Men got shit done and didn't let emotions come into play. Women were too wishy-washy. I had seen them cry in front of their own employees. You could burn my condo down and I still wouldn't cry in front of coworkers. I couldn't think of a single scenario in which I would. I hadn't cried since third grade when I got pushed on the playground by Tommy Reece. My teacher had called Mom, and when she didn't answer, she called my dad. He came to get me and chided me in the car for crying and being a pussy and, above all, not shoving Tommy back. That about ended my public crying.

Settling into my seat at the conference, I glanced at the program for the afternoon. More bullshit. A slew of speakers talking fluff, including a panel who was supposed to speak to us about mental health in the newsroom. I hated buzzwords like that. "Mental health"? What did that even mean? You're in a good mood some days; you're in a bad mood others. Period, the end. Why was it so fucking hard?

This conference was a snoozefest. I started to plan my escape. Maybe I could cut out early, grab an Uber to some hip part of San Diego, and start cocktail hour. Convince Stephanie to come with me. Speaking of Stephanie, where was she? I looked around for that pink blazer, but it was nowhere to be found.

Dorothy and Alan were headed my way, though, walking together and talking, Dorothy's hands gesturing about something while Alan nodded. I had seen them sit next to each other at lunch too. Luckily I had avoided their table and had just outfoxed someone else to slide into the seat next to Stephanie. It was almost like musical chairs when you had to pounce on the available spot. It was a good move, and I thought I had made some headway with Steph at lunch. She answered my questions when I asked her where she went to college (DePaul), where she was from (Indiana), and if she had any kids (a son named Evan). I didn't ask about a hubby or a boyfriend, but she didn't have a ring on her finger, which meant she was open for business, as far as I was concerned.

She asked me some questions back, and I told her about my divorce and how my ex was bilking me for money. I had sidled up to her as we took a group picture, and I pushed against her behind, just to give her a hint of the fun we could have together. I think she loved it. It was a start. Get some cocktails in her and see where we might go.

"Hi, Trent, did you enjoy your lunch? What did you have?"

Dorothy asked as she reached our table and sat down. Alan said nothing and simply took his seat.

"Stephanie and I both had chicken. Delicious," I responded, and then did the polite thing by asking them the same question back. Truly, I didn't care what they thought of their lunches but figured I needed to have proper etiquette.

"We both chose the fish. It was divine, really straight out of the ocean," Dorothy responded, then added, "I'm looking forward to the speakers this afternoon, aren't you? Particularly the therapists talking on mental health. Such a crucial topic for any newsroom. In fact, I can't think of a more important one."

I grunted a response and looked around for Stephanie again. She had lingered back in the courtyard while the rest of us were headed into the ballroom. Maybe she had to check in with her assistant or something. But still no sign of her, and now the emcee was climbing the stairs to the stage again and welcoming us to the second part of day one.

Seventy-five minutes into one excruciatingly long session about how to better cover crime, and not one sign of Stephanie. What the hell? I had spent most of this session ignoring the speaker and trying to imagine what could have happened to Steph. Did she ask to be moved to another table? That would piss me off. More than once, I swiveled my head around the room to see if that had been the case, but there was no sign of her.

Did she get sick? We both had chicken and I felt fine, so I didn't think it was food poisoning; plus, it doesn't hit that quickly, does it? Did she call her assistant and find out there was an emergency back in Madison? Or . . . and this was the thought that both annoyed and titillated me . . . did she bail on this conference just because she was as bored as I was?

If she pulled that, I was irked that I hadn't done it first, annoyed that I was forced to sit here and endure the blah-blah-blah of nonsensical talking heads while she was out tanning by the pool or whatever she was doing. But it also impressed the heck out of me. It took some balls. I loved a woman with balls, and it made me feel a surge of further attraction. Maybe we were kindred spirits. We could ditch the rest of the entire conference and find a hot tub somewhere. Hmm . . .

"OK, folks, quick bathroom and beverage break. Back in ten," the emcee said, and people began standing up and milling about, the din of voices creating a hum in the room as the house lights went up a touch and light classical music came across the PA system.

This was my chance. I sure as shit wasn't going to sit here for another ninety minutes next to Dorothy and Alan and listen to someone lecture me on mental health. The best thing for *my* mental health was to get away from this talk on mental health. If Steph bailed, why not me? I could just rejoin the group at the evening cocktail party. There was only that one session left anyway. No one would miss me.

Dorothy and Alan had turned to speak to some people at the table next to us and were ignoring me. Bitch. Geek. Fuck them. I grabbed my messenger bag from the back of the chair and strode out the exit and straight to the elevators. The thought of hitting the pool for a bit and then turning on the TV—maybe there was golf—and flopping across my king-size bed with a twelve-dollar beer from the room minibar was pretty appealing. I would charge it to the company.

The elevator dinged at the sixth floor, and I stepped out and turned toward my room. A guy with a light blue worker's shirt and dark blue pants with a ring of keys on his side was knocking on a door two down from mine.

"Maintenance," he called. "Is there a broken refrigerator in your room?"

Glancing at the worker, I saw the guest open the door a crack. Ignoring it, I was about to swipe open my door when I heard a familiar voice.

"No, I'm OK. False alarm."

It was Stephanie. My hand stopped an inch from the card reader, and I cocked my head to hear more.

"It seems to be working now," she added.

"Do you want me to come in, ma'am, and take a look?" the worker pressed. "The kitchen staff told me you had to get ice to keep medicine cold."

"No, thank you. I'm fine. I think—I think—it just wasn't plugged in all the way. It works now. I must have bumped it when I was unpacking. I'm sorry for the hassle."

"OK, ma'am, if you're sure. We want you to have everything you need during your stay."

"I'm good, thank you. I will call if there are problems."

"OK, very good, ma'am." The worker turned, saw me looking, and gave me a small nod. I nodded back to reassure him that he was doing a fine job taking care of his guests.

So that was why she left, I thought. She asked for ice to keep medicine cold in her room. Huh. A little odd but OK. Since we were both playing hooky, though, this felt like a perfect time to see if she wanted to hang out.

I waited for the maintenance guy to get on the elevator. Putting my key card in my back pocket and running my hand through my gelled hair to make it smooth on top the way I liked it, I tested out my breath into my hand to be sure I didn't have any lingering effects from lunch and walked the few feet to her room.

For a second I stood silently and put my ear to the door, waiting to see if I could hear anything coming from her side.

It was all quiet. No TV noise, no talking on the phone, no hair dryer or anything else. Hotel walls were so thin you could often hear your neighbors rustling about or even tell when they were flushing the toilet. But in her room you would have no idea anyone was there.

Lifting my hand, I rapped my knuckles lightly on the door. Silence. Waiting for a beat, I rapped harder.

Now I heard someone stir and her voice.

"The fridge is fine, thank you."

"Stephanie? It's Trent. From the conference. How ya doing? You OK? You never came back after lunch."

Silence again. I raised my voice, this time almost to a yell.

"Steph from Mad-town? Did you hear me? It's Trent, from Atlanta."

There was a further rustling, the door unlocked, and her eyes peeked out. She looked tired, eyeliner starting to smear. The room was dark behind her, and I guessed that the curtains were closed.

"Well, hey there," I said cheerily and leaned my arm against the door frame in a casual but flirty stance to try and perk up her mood. "How ya doing? We missed you at table four."

"Oh, hi, Trent." She sighed. "I'm sorry I didn't come back. I have a migraine."

"A migraine? I thought you were having refrigerator problems."

"No, that's fixed now . . . and . . . how did you know that?"

"I just saw the maintenance guy talking to you. I'm two doors down. Listen, if you need any help with anything in your room, no need to call maintenance. I'm a super handy kind of guy. I fix everything. Just give ol' Trent a ring and I'll come down to help you."

Truth was, I wasn't handy at all. I called repair people for everything, but she didn't need to know that. Women always seemed attracted to handymen. Maybe the idea of that would help. I flashed her my million-dollar smile, the one I had paid the dentist practically that much to create. From braces as a kid—twice—to the veneers I had on the front teeth now to the professional whitening every six months.

"Thank you, I'm fine," she responded and started to close the door, but I stuck my hand out and stopped it from shutting.

"Whoa, whoa, slow down. I'm sorry you have a headache, but maybe a drink will help. I decided to bug out early from the conference too. Maybe you and I should just play hooky."

"Really, Trent, I have a terrible headache. I get migraines and this one is bad. But if I rest tonight, I'll be back tomorrow fresh, I'm sure."

We both paused, looking at each other. My hand was on the door, still keeping it from closing. I could smell her floral perfume. How I would love to get more time with her. The thought of that ass walking away from me at the conference in the little black dress. I tried one more tack.

"Listen," I said, fishing with my free hand into my back pocket. "Here's my key card. I have another one. I'm going down to the pool for a bit. If you want to hang out, just let yourself in." I winked at her.

She didn't say anything for at least ten seconds, and I wasn't sure which way this was going to go, but then, to my delight, she took the key card.

"Thank you, Trent. If I feel better, I'll come down, but if not, I'll catch up with you tomorrow. I'll be sure to look for you. I promise."

"Right on," I said with another million-dollar smile. "Mi

casa es su casa—come on by. You don't even have to knock, just come in. The minibar is stocked."

She smiled.

"Goodbye *for now*," she said with a flirty lilt to her voice that I hadn't heard from her yet. She pushed the door closed, and I heard the latch turn. Silence followed.

Well, well, I thought to myself. *The Trent-master strikes again.* Now we were making some progress. She had opened the door a tiny bit, both literally and figuratively.

I whistled loudly as I walked back to my room, hoping she could hear me. I was sure she'd swing by. Even if she didn't come down this afternoon, I felt we were on the right path and something might happen before my flight home.

CHAPTER 28

Trent

At the Conference

When I got back from the pool, I waited a long time for Stephanie, finally dozing off sprawled across my king-size bed with the hushed whispers of golf announcers in the background. I woke up and it was time for cocktail hour. Still no Stephanie. I had been eager for some flirting, hoping for some needed sex at this conference. Now I felt all backed up. Stepping into the bathroom, I decided to give myself a release. I just had time for a quick jack-off before cocktail hour. Shutting my eyes, I put together a fake body—the glistening hair of a woman I had passed in the airport, the face of a model I had seen on a billboard, the boobs of a favorite teacher from high school, Stephanie's ass.

Doing my business quickly, I wiped everything off on a hotel towel and dumped it on the floor along with other towels I had used. The staff could clean up after me. That was their job.

Putting on a collared shirt monogrammed with my initials on the cuff, tucking a personalized handkerchief into the pocket, putting on my best $300 jeans and some Allen Edmonds shoes, I headed down, still hoping to see her.

Dozens of people were milling around the outdoor fireplace, eating hors d'oeuvres and drinking from bottles of beer or glasses of wine, but no Stephanie. I was disappointed but tried to hide it, walking up to a new group of people and giving them the ol' Trent charm. It worked, as it always did, and soon that group went out to dinner in the Little Italy part of San Diego and then hit a dance club. The five of us cool people (which did not include Dorothy or Alan, of course) stayed out way too late and had too much to drink. I nicknamed our group "the Power Players" and told everyone how much better we were than anyone else at the conference.

Now it was Friday, day two of the conference, and I was hurting as I pushed the curtains back and squinted at the bright California sun, turning my head away and rubbing my temples. No treadmill today. It would take every bit of effort I had just to get downstairs.

Part of me wanted to skip, but I had done that yesterday. Plus, Stephanie had better be back from her migraine. She missed a lot last night. The best bonding at a conference happens with dinner and drinks, and man, we had some fun. There was even one woman in our group from Jacksonville who I had flirted with, and she had flirted right back. I would put her a couple of notches below Stephanie in the looks department, but she would do if I just wanted a conference fling. We would see. I first wanted to edge up to Stephanie again and see if that went anywhere today.

Into the hot shower I went, lingering an extra long time as I tried to shake my headache and sore throat; then it was on to shaving, getting outfit number two on, gelling up my hair, and heading downstairs. I didn't have time for a full breakfast today, opting instead to grab a pastry and a coffee from the continental breakfast. *There goes my diet*, I thought, but my body was craving sugar and caffeine. I knew it would be a long stretch before lunch, and I braced myself.

Today our table assignments were shuffled, name cards out to show us where to go. My original foursome was scattered, and I found myself with three people I hadn't met yet. Dorothy, Alan, and Stephanie were at different spots around the room.

Or I should say Dorothy and Alan were.

Stephanie's name tag sat in front of an empty chair all day. I kept looking over to see if she was slipping in late, trying to look inconspicuous, but she never showed.

A tinge of anger welled up in me. She ghosted me yesterday after showing some promise, and here I was, hungover but making it to day two, and she couldn't even pop down after she told me a day of rest would cure her migraine.

By the afternoon break, I was done with her. Bitch. Cop-out. Cold fish. I turned my attention to the woman who had flirted with me the night before. And I never thought about Stephanie again. Until the next week.

CHAPTER 29

Trent

After the Conference

I got home later than I wanted Saturday after another long flight. In fact, I almost cashed it in entirely, but the neighborhood bar called my name, and I walked over for a few nightcaps. The place was billed as one of Atlanta's oldest bars and had apparently been in that spot since the early 1900s, surviving as condos and apartments went up around it. I liked it for its dark ambience.

I was weary, so I sat alone at the end of the bar near the door, nursing a gin and tonic. A woman I didn't recognize walked in and surveyed the place. She was wearing a top that really showed her tits.

I perked up and gave her the Trent slow look-you-up-and-down as a flirtatious opening, and she took it, immediately coming over to me and saying, "Hey, is this seat open?" We started talking. She was cool and pretty sexy. Said her name was Jasmine. She was new in town and super flirtatious, touching my arm and leg as she talked. I started thinking this might be a nice end to my trip, and I went to the bathroom to pop a

Viagra, just in case. Given my tired state, I figured I could use the boost.

When I got back to my chair, we talked for a while longer, and I was just about to invite her back up to my place when she said she had to go home for the night.

"Aww, no, don't leave yet," I implored.

"I'm sorry, I really do," she said. "But give me your number and I'll call you. This has been fun. You're a super guy."

"You give me your number first," I answered, noticing that forming actual words was getting harder to do.

"No, I will call you. I promise, Trent," she said. "In fact, I'll text you a sexy picture when I get home. You've never seen anything like this." She winked.

Well, that sounded enticing. What could I do but give her my number and hope like hell she followed through? I could text her back something equally fun. Maybe we'd meet up here tomorrow night.

Stumbling the two blocks home, I face-planted into bed and slept with my clothes on for most of the night. Waking up around six a.m. to use the bathroom, I checked my phone and was irked to see there was no text with a sexy picture. Still tired, I stripped down to my boxer shorts and went right back to bed.

Sunday was the NFL playoffs, and I wouldn't miss that for anything. My plan had been to hit the gym for a workout to keep that old BP down for the doctor, then meet up with some buddies at our favorite sports bar, the one with ten TVs, bottomless wings, a pool table, darts, and good Bloody Marys.

But when I woke up again at ten a.m., I had the worst stomachache I had ever had.

"Ugh," I moaned, rolling over in bed and clutching my gut.

I rushed to the bathroom and threw up. What the hell? I never got sick.

It was all I could do just to crawl back in bed.

I'll sleep it off and then go meet the guys, I told myself, burying my face into a pillow and moaning again. Within seconds I was out.

When I woke up again, it was three p.m., and I had missed the first game entirely. I also had five texts from my buddies at the bar wondering what was going on—and zero sexy pictures from Jasmine.

"Well, fuu-uuck me," I said aloud and texted my friends that somehow I got the "Rona" or some other virus at the conference.

My stomach was still feeling tight and painful, but at least I wasn't wildly nauseated anymore. Moving from bed to couch, I turned on game number two bitterly. Who gets sick and sits around like a loser on an NFL Sunday? I thought of my buds at the bar, laughing and whooping it up, maybe playing the retro video games the place also had. It was a good spot to meet chicks too. Fuck, fuck, fuck. I barely ate the rest of the day and hit the bathroom a few too many times. I found myself dozing on the couch.

By 8:30 p.m., I even contemplated texting my secretary to say I needed a sick day Monday, but I never took sick days, priding myself on how steely I was. All those wimps who used every sick day they had and then complained about not having more. Nope, not me. I would go in come hell or high water.

But Monday morning, I had a pounding headache in addition to the stomach symptoms not being fully gone. I still had diarrhea, my throat was dry, and my bloodshot eyes burned.

"Motherfucker," I said to my reflection in the mirror. I

looked like hell. Would this actually be my first sick day in years? People at the station had heard me make fun of others who were constantly out sick. Was it my turn to be the butt of a joke? That thought made me ill in a different way.

If there were two things I couldn't stand, it was getting laughed at and appearing weak. Weakness was not the trait of a leader; my team needed to see me strong as an ox at all times. If their leader was down, how would they go on?

But I felt like crap. Reaching for my phone, I made that call to my secretary that I never wanted to make, clearing my throat as it rang on her end.

"Trent, good morning," she said. "How was your trip?"

"Yeah, hi, Mary, it was good, but I seem to have caught . . . some kind of bug." It was embarrassing for me to even say the words.

"Oh no!" she responded. "You don't sound that great. Do you need to take a day off?"

"I don't know," I answered, shifting uncomfortably from one foot to the other at the thought. "Maybe I'll just take the morning and come in later."

If I could just buy myself a half day, maybe I'd be better.

"Trent, your voice sounds pretty rough. Why don't you take a day to rest so you'll be back tomorrow? You have that sales meeting with clients. Remember? They want to meet some of the news people. Might as well be fresh for that. I know it's a big deal to Bill and the sales department."

Oh, man, I had forgotten all about that. But she was right. This could potentially bring in tons of advertising dollars, which paid our bills and my salary. Katrina's monetary demands of me were getting bigger and bigger—the kids needed new clothes, new shoes, more lessons, yada yada, and I was feeling stretched very thin. Had even been holding off on some monogrammed shirts I'd been wanting to get. If this client came on board with all of their dollars, maybe I'd receive a bonus in my next check.

"Listen, Mary, if I take the day off, tell the newsroom I just extended my trip."

"You don't want them to know that you're sick?" She sounded puzzled.

"Nah—people get weird about germs. Better just to say I stayed a bit longer."

"OK, you're the boss, but really, people don't mind if someone takes a sick day."

No weakness, Mary, no weakness. You give an inch, they take a mile. They smell blood in the water, they circle like sharks. One crack in the facade is sometimes all it takes.

"I haven't taken a sick day in five years, and this isn't going to be my first," I said. "Tell the newsroom I'm on a plane today and I'll be in tomorrow."

Fatigue was calling me back to bed, and I wound up sleeping most of the day again. When I woke up in the afternoon, I checked emails—I had almost two thousand new ones since I had departed for San Diego. Life of a news manager. Sighing, I decided they could all wait for tomorrow, when I was officially on the clock.

An hour later, I felt like I could finally shower, shave, and put on clean clothes. I started to feel more myself, and my stomach growled. There were only three things in the fridge, though, so I used DoorDash to order a basic chicken-and-noodle dish from a place down the street and ate on the couch flipping between two NBA games. I fell asleep early and, thank God, woke up bright-eyed Tuesday, ready for work.

Driving to the station and parking my Range Rover in my favorite spot away from the rest of the cars—I couldn't risk a scratch being with the proletariat—I bounded into the newsroom feeling strong and healthy.

"Good morning, Leslie, Zac, Warren, Terrell, Alice," I bellowed as I went. When the news director walks into a room, everyone should know. People straightened up when they heard me; they stopped chatting and turned to their desks. It pleased me to see what kind of effect I could have just with a few words.

My office was a glass-walled space on the side of the newsroom that actually drove me a little batty. Sometimes a person needed privacy, and I was a fish in a bowl in there, couldn't even scratch my balls without the newsroom seeing.

I flopped down into my extra wide ergonomic chair. It was a gift from our GM, Bill, for Christmas the year before and was the most comfortable goddamn thing ever. I was just firing up the computer when my assistant news director, Jorge, came in.

"Hey, how was San Diego?" he asked.

Jorge was a nice guy. Not news director material, in my opinion, but decent for an assistant. To be honest, he had been a diversity hire my GM had rammed down my throat. When the position was open, I had preferred a white guy from a smaller market, but was overruled in favor of getting more people of color into management.

"Great, man, stayed an extra day. How was everything here?"

"Good, really good. Got some stuff to catch you up on later."

I nodded. By 8:45 a.m., I had picked the stories I wanted. I knew some stations did manager meetings before the regular newsroom meeting, but I always thought of that as a waste of time. One person would be making the decision in the end anyway—that would be me, the head honcho, the chief enchilada—so why prolong it by pretending to hear everyone's ideas and opinions? Reporters just wanted to know what they were assigned to and get out the door. Those long, lingering meetings of my past, when I wasn't in charge, were painful to even think about. I ran things my way now, and it was the best way. People always told me I was very efficient, and I considered that a high compliment. Who didn't love efficiency, especially in a newsroom?

At nine, we gathered in our conference room, me at the head of the table at the whiteboard. A quick look at the weather with our meteorologist, a run-through of overnight crime and court cases from our assignment desk, and I could start putting reporters into those stories. Lickety-split, done and done.

Anything else happening that day in the city would be what we called "pace"—short stories, like thirty seconds, shot by a photojournalist but not with a reporter. The producer would write it up and put it into their shows to make the pace of the show go faster.

My philosophy was so simple I couldn't believe it wasn't patented: Reporters go to crime and breaking news and court cases. We load the show with these and put the fluff at the end.

Another station in town was doing a whole bunch of issue crap, like politics and "meet the candidates" and "this referendum means blah-blah-blah" shit. *Who cares?* People wanted three things: crime, breaking news, and weather. Maybe a dog-rescue story thrown in every few months, but that's it. I had everyone out the door on their stories before 9:15, and I could see how much my staff appreciated my decisiveness.

The meetings made my morning go fast. There was the web team meeting and the sports meeting, upcoming election planning, and a meeting about how many stories we could fairly do for Black History Month without shorting all of the other specialty months. So many goddamn ethnic and other months. But I just shut up and approved a robust plan.

I also had my weekly check-in with Bill. He was the only person in the building who could tell me what to do. As I sat down, he jumped right in:

"Welcome back, Trent. How was the conference? Did you learn anything worth sharing?"

"Not really," I said, struggling to remember anything that was actually talked about. "Went to all of the sessions, but we do things pretty darn well around here. People should look to *us* for ideas."

"That's good to know. What would you say was the most enlightening session you attended?" Bill pressed.

I tried to flash back to the program book, to remember the actual titles of the sessions. The only one that came to mind was mental health, the one I hadn't attended. Could I BS my way through this? Of course I could. I was Trent McCarthy.

"Mental health, Bill. Such an important topic for any newsroom."

"I agree, a critical topic, especially for our younger employees who seem to be more in touch with their feelings. And what did you learn?" Bill said, leaning forward in his ergonomic chair.

"Well, uh . . . they talked about why it's so important, you know, stress and other triggers, and ways you can stay calm, like breathing or exercising." That sounded plausible. I looked to Bill to see if he bought it. Amazingly, he seemed to.

"Terrific. Please write up other tips you learned about mental health and send them to me by the end of the day tomorrow. Our newsroom will be better for the knowledge you gained at the conference. I'm glad I sent you."

Aww, shit. Now I would have to BS this assignment. Thank God for the University of Google.

"Tell me about the news directors you met there," Bill said. "People in from all over the country?"

"Oh, yes, Boston to Kalamazoo and everywhere in between," I replied, thinking of Dorothy, the stoic bitch, and Alan, that little geek.

"Anyone have anything interesting to share about the way they are producing news in different markets? I'm always fascinated by learning from others."

"Um . . . not really, Bill. I mean everyone has their own style, but as I said, I don't think anyone holds a candle to us."

"OK," said Bill. "Well, let's adjourn for now. I will see you at the sales meeting after lunch."

"You got it," I said, popping quickly out of my chair, happy to be free. Plus, I had to start googling "mental health" to see what I could cobble together as my pretend session from the conference.

I made it through some other boring planning stuff; then it was lunch and time to prep for the sales meeting.

Swinging by the men's room to make sure I looked sharp, I smoothed my hair and straightened my collar. The receptionist always kept mints in a little glass bowl, so I popped by there to grab one. Nothing worse than meeting someone you wanted to win over with lunch breath.

The clients were from a mattress chain that had just opened more than four dozen new franchises in our area. They wanted to advertise but needed to see which station would be the best fit for them for the max amount of dollars, and they were ready to open their wallets and flood the airwaves. They were standing in our news conference room with Bill, admiring the view of downtown as I walked in.

"And here comes our news director," Bill said.

I turned the wattage on the Trent smile as high as it would go and walked over with my hand extended, saying loudly, "Trent McCarthy, the pleasure is all mine!"

We sat down around an oval glass-topped conference table. Bill hit a button so a drop-down screen descended at the front of the room and a video began to play. It featured a local band singing a jingle with images of Atlanta mixed in and video of our on-air talent out and about with station-logoed microphones. The music came to a crescendo and the words "Home is where the heart is: NBC6, Atlanta" flashed across the screen. I saw one of our saleswomen dab at the corner of her eye.

"It gets me every time," she sniffed. Another salesperson handed her a tissue.

"Welcome to our wonderful city and to NBC6," Bill said, spreading his arms wide. "We're simply thrilled to have you opening up Mega Mattresses all over the metro. How can we help you get the word out?"

They began talking about the many mattresses they offered. The company was looking to advertise across all stations but would put most of their money into the place that felt like it best aligned with their values. Bill turned to me.

"Trent runs our entire news operation, so he can talk about our values. In fact, he just attended a conference in San Diego and will be writing up a report for me on how we can better serve the mental health needs of our staff."

I had to go into full-on bullshit mode. It reminded me of college when a professor would ask for a two-thousand-word paper and I'd stretch it by saying the same things in several different ways. We all had tried the font trick too, making the font bigger to get to more pages, but professors always caught that one. No, it was better if you just had the gift of gab.

"Mega Mattress aligns with our brand perfectly," I began, and saw Bill nodding. "We are all about comfort and safety. The stories we do matter because our community needs to feel safe. We report on the bad guys getting locked up so that you can feel better when you tuck little Johnny into a Mega Mattress at night. We follow through on cases every step of the way through the court system, so that you at home don't miss a thing. Our investigators are out there working for you. If there's wrongdoing, we will uncover it. If something is hiding in your medicine cabinet that could kill you, we will expose it. There is not another station in this town that works as hard to keep you and your family safe for a good night's sleep. Channel 2? They hardly even cover crime. Channel 8? Try watching them, they're all about politics. And I think they're very partisan, by the way. You look around at the others, and I guarantee you'll make your way back to Channel 6. We are mega-right for Mega Mattress."

I flashed my smile, proud of myself for sticking the landing like an Olympic gymnast.

"That's wonderful, Trent. What a nice description. And how do you help your own employees with mental health?" asked one of the women.

I had to scramble on this one. The only things that came to mind were days when I wasn't helping at all. I had mocked a producer just last week for telling me her kid was having a mental health crisis and she had to take the day off. "Isn't he in college?" I had asked. "Does he really need *his mommy*?" I had also turned down an offer from a local therapy organization to host a mental health awareness day with our staff because I thought it sounded like BS. But now I had to answer. The only things about mental health that leaped to mind were some of the talking points Alan and Dorothy had told me during our table session.

"We value the opinions of everyone in the newsroom. It's a democracy, not a dictatorship, and I think that sets an important tone. Everyone knows they can come to me. My door is wide open, literally and figuratively. Mental health is almost as important as physical health. It all starts up here . . ."

I tapped my head. I was on a roll now.

"If you get that right, everything else will follow right to here." I tapped my heart.

"Lovely, just lovely," sighed the Mega Mattress woman, and I could feel my tail feathers rising.

"Diversity is also very important to us," said a man seated next to her. "Can someone speak about the diversity here?"

The salespeople spoke of how over 50 percent of their staff were women or people of color. Bill then talked of our Equity, Diversity, and Inclusion training, which was mandatory every year. I hated every minute of the videos we were forced to watch; had cheated, in fact, on the most recent test we had at the end of the video and asked Jorge to help me out, saying I was "so busy."

Bill turned to me now.

"Tell them about diversity in our newsroom, Trent."

"Diversity, yes, so important," I began and pulled yet another Trent rabbit out of the hat, talking of Jorge and other people of color in the newsroom. "And just look at us on air," I went on. "We're like the United Nations!"

I laughed loudly, but others only gave a slightly nervous giggle. Maybe that wasn't PC? What the hell could you say these days if you couldn't compare yourself to the United Nations?

"Trent will now take you on a tour of the newsroom," Bill said. "It's fun to see what's behind the magic, right? I'll be back in my office, and I'll catch up with you at the end."

They started following me down the hall. Having given hundreds of tours over the years, I knew what people liked to see. I would save our glistening studio for last. First we would swing by and meet some of the anchors they admired on TV every day. Viewers always got excited by that.

We walked up to the desk of Leigh, our female five, six, and eleven p.m. anchor, and I began introductions. She was a pro and started charming them with a story about how her sister had found the best mattress she ever had at a Mega Mattress. I wasn't sure if it was true or not, but it seemed to be working.

A noise came from my phone in my pocket. It wasn't a ringtone; it was more like an alert you get from one of those apps you don't use often. Slyly pulling it out, I snuck a peek. It was my doorbell-cam app from home. Living in a condo in a nice neighborhood, I rarely had seen this thing go off. No one bothered me, and I wasn't one of those people who ordered from Amazon all of the time.

The app was giving me an urgent warning that someone was at my place. Stepping a few paces from Leigh's desk, I couldn't believe what I was seeing.

Two police officers were banging on my door.

Leigh glanced over at me. I pointed to my phone so that she would see I needed her to keep up the pace while I took care of an important matter. Leigh was used to subtle cues like that as an anchor, and she just revved up another story and kept the group engaged while I went to my office.

The officers were banging hard. And calling my name.

"Police, open up!"

What the hell was going on? My mind was so confused by the sight that I didn't know how to react. I had to play it cool, but I also had to get home. *Now.* Before they literally broke down my door.

Mega Mattress folks were being introduced to others by Leigh. I felt a surge of gratitude to her. I would repay her with a beer. She and I were good friends. Yes, we had one drunken slipup and made out after a holiday party many years prior, but that was old news. She trusted me and I trusted her. We helped each other out.

Leigh had her phone as she did the tour, so I hurriedly texted her.

Emergency. Do me this solid and finish the tour. Tell them a news matter arose for me and apologize. We need this client.

Her eyes shifted to my office, and she gave an ever-so-slight nod. I nodded back, grabbed my coat from the hook, and bolted for the parking lot.

My condo was just five minutes away. I had chosen it for that very reason. Keeping my eyes on the doorbell-cam app as I went, I saw the officers bang a few times more and then begin peeking in windows. There had to be some massive misunderstanding. I would clear this up and maybe even make it back before Bill noticed I was gone.

The cops were just starting to walk back to their squad car as I came up and threw the Range Rover into park. Jumping out, I yelled, "Hey, what's going on? I live here."

"Are you Trent McCarthy?" one officer asked. He was bald as a cue ball but had a thick goatee, so his face looked strangely out of proportion.

"Yes, and why are you here?" I asked. "What the hell is going on?"

"Sir, I need you to step over here," the second officer said. He was a smaller Asian guy with a very loud voice. "Take your hands out of your pockets and raise them up."

"What the . . ."

"Sir, keep your hands up."

I glanced around anxiously to see if any of the neighbors were watching. How would this go over at the next HOA meeting?

Officer Goatee came over and started patting me down. Finding nothing but my keys and wallet, he was satisfied and nodded to Officer Deep Throat, who then stepped forward.

"Sir, we received a 9-1-1 call from a concerned citizen that a woman might be in danger here."

"*Whaattt?* Who called 9-1-1? Who said they were in danger??" My mind didn't know where to turn. Was this Katrina's doing? "I have absolutely no idea what you're talking about. I was at work when I got a notification from my doorbell cam."

"Sir, we are responding to a 9-1-1 call. Is anyone in the residence at this time?"

"No, I live alone. No one is here."

Officer Goatee pointed toward the front door.

"Mind if we have a look around?"

"Sure, you can look around," I said. "There is no one here. I have no idea how this could happen. Are you sure you have the right address?"

"This is the address that was phoned in."

I walked confidently up the front walk and unlocked it.

"Come right in, look in every damn corner," I said. "There is not a soul here. If my ex-wife did this . . ." I let the sentence trail off.

"Are you divorced?"

I glared at him. What did he think I meant when I referenced an ex-wife? But it probably wasn't wise to get too mouthy, so I said:

"Yes."

The officers started poking around, opening closet doors and peeking behind the couch. I took them to the bedrooms, the office, the bathrooms, and the dining room. We ended back where we started.

"See?" I said with satisfaction. "Not a soul. Can I go back to work now? Somehow you fellas got the wrong address."

"Wait here," said Officer Deep Throat, and he went outside to the squad car. Officer Goatee stayed in the living room with me. I could see Deep Throat talking into the radio to someone. Goatee tried to strike up a conversation.

"What do you do for a living, sir?"

"I'm the news director at Channel 6. I run a newsroom of over a hundred fifty people," I said. "I know your chief very well. We interviewed him for a story just last week."

"Oh, that was you guys? The one on the police-community basketball game? That was a good one."

"Yup," I said. "So, can I go now? I was in the middle of an important meeting when this happened."

"You should be clear in a minute, sir," said Goatee as Deep Throat got out of the car and gave a thumbs-up that we saw through the front window.

"You're good to go. Sorry for the inconvenience, but if someone calls 9-1-1, we're obligated to check it out."

"Make sure that never happens again. Get your facts straight or I'll have my investigative journalism team look into fake calls to police."

"I'm sure it was a misunderstanding," said Goatee tersely and left my living room. I followed behind him and locked the front door.

They got into their squad car and drove off, and I sighed deeply.

What the hell was that? I looked around one more time for

the prying eyes of neighbors, but it appeared all was quiet, and relief flowed through me. Now I had to hustle back, though. I had never even told Bill I was leaving.

Jumping into the Range Rover and flying toward the station, I formulated an excuse in case I needed it. Something that would make me a hero.

Back in the parking lot, I sprinted through the back door and into the newsroom. Leigh was at her desk, but the Mega Mattress people were nowhere to be found. Walking over quickly, I leaned down and whispered, "Where are they?" We were so close I could smell her hair spray and some kind of berry lip gloss.

"In Bill's office wrapping up," she whispered back.

"Thank you, you are amazing." I gave her a little pat on her shoulder.

"That's what they all say," she shot back with a smile.

I needed to say goodbye properly to try and seal this deal, so I strode back to Bill's office. Thankfully, they were all still there, and Bill was showing them a framed Wayne Gretzky hockey jersey on his wall.

"I'm so sorry about that," I said to the group. "A reporter in the field texted me. She was having a mental health crisis right at that moment, so I ran out to assist her. That's the kind of newsroom we run, the kind of care we give."

"That is sooo inspiring," said one of the women, and her coworkers nodded as she added, "Everyone needs a boss like that."

We all shook hands and wished the Mega Mattress people well, and Bill's assistant showed them to the front door.

"Well?" I asked. "Do you think we got 'em?"

"I think we have a good shot," Bill said. "By the way, which reporter was in crisis?"

Now I had to lie to my boss. It was not a good feeling, but I had no choice. I picked the youngest, most fragile female, the one who always seemed on the verge of tears.

"Hannah. But we're all good now, she's in a much better place."

"Excellent, Trent, just excellent leadership," Bill responded, and I walked back to the newsroom knowing I was coming out on top, as I always did. I was a winner.

CHAPTER 30

Trent

Tuesday Overnight

I was sleeping that night when I heard pounding. It took me almost a full minute to come out of unconsciousness, look at the clock, and process that someone was banging on my front door.

Again.

"What the hell is going on?" I said aloud, sitting up, rubbing my eyes, and beginning to register that there were flashing police lights outside of my window. A dog was barking at a neighbor's house.

Hurriedly, I threw a robe over my boxers and scurried to the front door. When I opened it, there were two new officers there, a white woman with her hair in a tight bun and a Black guy. Before I could say anything, the Black guy yelled, "Hands up and come out the door."

Too stunned to argue in any way, I complied. My mind was still trying to wake up. The officer frisked me, put my hands behind my back, and put handcuffs on. I finally found my voice.

"Officer, I haven't done anything," The tone didn't even sound like mine. It was squeaky and reminded me of Alan's. I shuddered.

"Stop talking," said the officer, who then turned to his partner. "Take him to the squad car. We'll look around."

Two more cop cars came squealing to a stop, and four officers jumped out and started heading for my door.

"There's nothing here, I didn't do anything," I protested, but no one seemed to be hearing me. There was the sound of feet pounding on concrete and the wood floor as they stomped their way in. My beautiful heated wood floor.

The female officer took my arm and steered me toward the car. She said nothing, opening the back door and pushing my head down so I wouldn't bump it. I guess that was polite.

I sat there, shivering in my robe and underwear, looking back at my house and trying to put pieces together that made absolutely no sense. I was in a state of shock, I knew that, but also not in a state of worry because I knew that this was another misunderstanding. A big, fucking huge one that the chief was going to hear about. These officers would lose their jobs. That thought made me smile. I could sic my I-Team on the story and have them find out why innocent people were getting swatted with fake calls. This was ridiculous, ludicrous actually. The biggest miscarriage of justice I had ever seen.

Neighbors were popping on lights and starting to peer out of windows and around curtains. How awkward. I'd have to tell them about this horrid mistake and reassure them that I was 100 percent innocent and that our police department was a total joke. I yawned and wished I could scratch my eye, but my hands were bound behind me.

Minutes ticked by and more cop cars pulled up; one guy had a notebook, and another had a camera with him. What in the fuck were they looking for? They sure as hell weren't going to find it.

Seriously, me, a news director, sitting in a cop car with

handcuffs on. I should sue the pants off them. Yes, that's what I'd do. Sue them so hard I could retire early. Maybe this would be a blessing in disguise. I could pay off Katrina so she'd be out of my hair and move to the Bahamas, all on the dime of the Atlanta PD.

The male officer finally walked back with a determined look on his face. I was sure he was about to apologize and I could start my rant against him and the entire department. He opened the door and roughly yanked me to stand up next to the squad car. It lacked the gentle touch the female officer had used when she had protected my head.

"What the hell?" I protested. "Watch it, and undo these cuffs right now."

"That won't be happening," he said sternly, looking me straight in the eye. "Do you want to explain why a woman's phone, wallet, and jewelry were buried in your backyard?"

"Woman? What woman?" My mind was a blur. Did someone who lived here before me do something nefarious?

The officer took a small notebook out of his breast pocket and opened it.

"Name is Stephanie Monroe. Does that ring a bell for you?"

"Whhaaaaa?" I choked out, and I'm sure my face looked as shocked and confused as I felt.

CHAPTER 31

Bill

After the Conference

I hadn't slept since Chief Newman called me in the middle of the night to tell me about Trent. I had known the chief for years, been at Rotary Club meetings and National Night Out events with him. We had a good relationship. In fact, I was the one who had pushed Trent to send a reporter to cover the police-community basketball game the previous week. That was not the kind of story my news director would have taken to naturally. Trent didn't enjoy putting reporters on light stories, but I knew we needed a little balance from the sea of crime we offered up on the air. There were times I wondered if Trent was truly the person to lead us into the future, but then he would surprise me, like when he went to take care of Hannah in the field, or how he wowed the Mega Mattress people, and I'd be right back in his corner.

Being a heavy sleeper, I didn't even realize my cell phone was ringing until at least the fifth ring. Fumbling for it groggily, trying not to disturb Maxine, I knew before I even answered that anything at that hour had to be bad news. My throat felt froggy as I croaked out, "Hello?"

"Bill, Chief Reggie Newman here. Sorry to disturb you in the middle of the night, but I have some news you will want to hear . . ."

My first thought was, how did he get my cell number? I guessed the police had their ways. My second thought was that the news must be even larger than a massive shooting or building collapse for the chief to be calling me, the general manager, in the overnight hours. This sort of thing should go to the news director. Why not bother Trent?

"Chief Newman, that's OK, what time is it?" I asked, fumbling for my glasses.

"3:53. I wouldn't bother you if it weren't urgent . . ."

And that's when he told me. It's nearly impossible to describe the emotions one has when hearing that the man running your newsroom is sitting in the police station accused of murder.

And that they have evidence.

I saw a karate chop cleanly dividing two parts of my world: the before this happened and the after. It would never be the same. This was clearly going to be one of the defining moments of my career, if not my life.

The hours after that were a blur of calling my boss and his boss and his boss until I reached the CEO of our entire company, trying to implore him and everyone else that people are still innocent until proven guilty; trying to soothe our newsroom when the news came out; having fellow GMs from around the country reach out with shock and sympathy; *not* having certain people reach out who I thought would (I guess you do find out who your friends are); having anchors like Leigh in my office sobbing and having to comfort them; still having a newsroom that needed to be run and pulling Jorge aside to tell him he needed to take charge; having HR up my ass nearly every hour trying to get more information; having our PR people up my ass asking if we needed to put a statement out to the media; finally releasing that statement saying we were aware of the situation and would cooperate fully in any investigation; and spending every second not putting out an immediate fire in the aftermath trying to wrap my own head around how this could be possible.

And then one of the Mega Mattress people left me a voicemail.

"Bill, we have to tell you that we're all shocked and horrified by this turn of events. As you know, we are a company that prides itself on our values. Before today, you were our number one choice. Although everyone in this country is entitled to a fair trial, we don't believe NBC6 is the place for us to put our advertising dollars. We'll be buying ad time with the other three stations in town, particularly Channel 2. Their belief system aligns much more closely with ours. Thank you."

I tried to reach them three times to get them to change their minds, but they wouldn't answer my calls.

Wednesday night, the police held their second press conference, where they named the two potential victims, women named Stephanie Monroe and Jasmine Littleton I had never heard of. Stephanie was said to have been at the conference with Trent. I didn't sleep at all that night, pacing my home office. Maxine tried every trick in the book to assist me—cocktails, a sleeping pill, a shoulder massage—but nothing helped. She finally retired and I stayed up, stopping my pacing only long enough to look up any morsels of information people were reporting.

TMZ ran a promo teasing that they had interviewed people who worked at the conference hotel; a competitive outlet in Atlanta dug into Trent's past and found speeding tickets, his divorce record, and a DUI; CNN had police sources telling them the evidence was damning, even without bodies. An industry gossip website called GTV cited a "station insider" as saying many felt Trent had a wicked mean streak and a history of bullying subordinates and sexually harassing female employees. A friend of Trent's ex-wife went on the air and said Katrina had almost filed a restraining order once after he got physical with her. This was all new information to me.

Despite my fatigue, I had to go into work Thursday and put on a brave face. Midmorning, I was walking to the vending machine area to get a Coke—my second of the day—when I saw one of our reporters, Hannah. She looked exhausted. I'm sure I did too. I stopped her for a moment in the hallway.

"Hannah, how are you? I saw your reports outside of Trent's place. You're doing good work in a very tough situation." I always thought it was nice if the GM could say a few encouraging words to young reporters. It made them feel seen.

"Thank you," she said softly, looking down. "This has been the hardest assignment of my career."

"I'm sure it has," I responded in my best soothing and calming voice. "Remember that everyone is innocent until proven guilty in a court of law. But yes, this has to be especially difficult for you given what Trent did for you Tuesday."

She looked back up and cocked her head.

"I'm sorry, what?"

"When Trent went out and met you in the field. You know, mental health is incredibly important to all of us at the company. We will do everything we can to help our team. We're all in this together and my door is open anytime you need it."

"Tuesday?" I could see wheels turning in her head. "Umm . . . could you have me confused with another reporter? I never saw Trent in the field."

"Are you sure?" I asked. "He told me that he ran out to help you . . ."

"I've never seen Trent out in the field with us, ever," she said, a look of confusion on her face. "And I don't think mental health is very important to him. I heard him say once that it should be renamed 'woman-tel health' because men don't get bogged down in it."

"Oh, uh . . . I must have misunderstood what he told me then. I'm sorry."

Quickly I turned away, my head now pounding with the possibility that Trent had lied to me. Why would he do that? Why would he make that story up about helping Hannah? Where did he go? Was this part of the timeline of the murders? Jesus God, what was happening?

Returning to my office, I saw I had a new voicemail. Hoping it was from Mega Mattress and I could make a last-minute effort to keep them, I picked up my desk phone and hit play. An unfamiliar deep female voice rang out.

"Hello, my name is Dorothy Robinson and I'm the news director at ABC7 in Boston. I'm sure you're going through a lot right now. I just wanted to reach out on behalf of my colleague Alan Kozinski and myself. We were at the News Coverage Summit in San Diego last week with Trent. Sat at the same table with him. We've already shared our observations with police, but I thought you might want to know that Trent skipped out on part of the conference. He just got up and left during a break and never returned that day. Missed the entire mental health discussion, arguably the most important piece of the entire conference. If I could be so bold, sir, to also explain some of the other things we observed, please call me back. I just think his boss needs to have as many pieces to the puzzle as possible."

I couldn't dial her number fast enough.

Hearing how he glommed on to Stephanie from the get-go turned my stomach. Dorothy said Trent never took notes at the conference, left before the mental health session without so much as a word, returned for cocktail hour and got increasingly drunk and loud, telling off-color jokes that made people uncomfortable, and then looked hungover the next day. I was filled with rage by the end of the conversation.

Trent had lied to me about attending the mental health session. How was he going to prepare that report for me? Would he just google "mental health"? And he had also lied about seeing Hannah in the field. That made two times he said he was somewhere and it turned out he wasn't. Plus, Trent's assistant, Mary, had contacted me to say that Trent asked her to lie Monday and say he was on a flight even though he was sick.

Lying was an absolute no-no in my book. If someone made a mistake, they should be honest about it. I drew the line at lying. And where was he during these times he was lying about? Was this when he was doing criminal activities? And even if he wasn't guilty of murder, he'd still contributed to the loss of the Mega Mattress account.

I picked up my desk phone again and called HR.

"Fire Trent McCarthy. I'm not waiting for a trial. Fire him now."

Letting someone go had never felt so good.

CHAPTER 32

Trent

The Wednesday After the Conference

I was still in my bathrobe and underwear when we got to the station, but the police at least did me the dignity of offering some jail-issued clothes and moving my arms around so they weren't cuffed in back anymore, just in the front, slightly more comfortable. Then they sat me in an interrogation room.

My head couldn't compute what was happening. I was numb. Going along with their orders like a robot, I figured Bill would show up soon and rescue me and this whole giant mess would be cleared up. I couldn't wait to get out of here, to get a lawyer and hold a triumphant press conference where I made them look like absolute shit. I'd be the hero. I just had to survive this craziness first.

Plopped in a hard-backed chair, I was across a small table from two detectives. I decided to speak first and not wait for them.

"This is a terrible misunderstanding. I haven't done a thing. Not one thing. It's unbelievable. I'm an innocent man and you're making me out to be a criminal."

"Be quiet and answer our questions," said the first detective.

He had a portly belly and thinning brown hair flecked with gray. His partner, who had a full head of dark hair and an accent that sounded as if he was from some Latin American country, started in.

"Is your name Trent Jonathan McCarthy?"

"Yes."

"Do you live at 4240 Horizon Lane in the Peachtree Village neighborhood of Atlanta?"

"Yes."

"Do you know a woman named Stephanie Monroe?"

"No. I mean I met someone with that name at a conference last week, but *I never saw her again*! We barely crossed paths."

"So you have no idea how her wallet and cell phone might have been buried in your backyard?" Officer Spanish sounded combative now.

"*No! Good God, no!* I told you that already. This is a giant setup or a hoax or something. Is she trying to frame me? Is it my ex-wife, Katrina? Have you asked her, for fuck's sake? She's after my money."

"Trent, why don't you start by just telling us what happened when you left the conference?" Officer Portly Belly said in a gentler tone. That calmed me for a minute, and I took a long, ragged breath.

"OK, nothing happened. I got on a plane, came home, went to a bar that night for a couple of nightcaps, came home, fell asleep, felt sick actually on Sunday and stayed in. I even had to call in to work Monday I was so sick, and I never do that. Then I went to work Tuesday, and all this shit started happening. Police showing up at my door and dragging me out of bed and accusing me of something I didn't do. It's fucking bullshit, and you all will pay through the nose! *I'm going to sue your asses off!*"

My blood pressure was rising again, and I thought of my doctor and his warnings.

They ignored my comment about suing and just kept going.

"So you never saw this Stephanie again?"

"No!!"

"She didn't return to Atlanta with you?"

"Hell no! I got on a plane and came home by myself. I told you, I knew that chick for only a few hours. She even bailed on the conference early. You can ask anybody who was there. In fact, do. Ask Dorothy from Boston and Alan from Kalamazoo. They both met her too and then saw her take off. I'm not crazy. She disappeared and *I never fucking saw her again*."

"Trent, did you see anyone else on Sunday or Monday when you were home? Go anywhere? See any friends, family, coworkers?"

"No, I told you I was sick. I stayed in."

"So you have no alibi other than the fact that you were home sick?"

"It's not an alibi. *I was home sick.*"

From there, they just kept asking me questions and questions and questions until I almost lost my mind. I had to describe my job, my relationships, my childhood, and reenact every second of the conference and my return back home.

I decided not to tell them that I had skipped the mental health session, though. One, it would place me and Stephanie out of the conference at the same time, and two, it would tip off Bill, my boss, that I had lied to him. His cardinal sin was lying and people had been fired for doing so. I figured if Dorothy or Alan opened their big mouths and said I wasn't at the session, I would explain that I had needed some air and got up for a moment, then watched it from the back of the room.

Dorothy and Alan wouldn't know if it was true or not—their backs would have been to me the entire time.

As the questioning droned on and on, I just kept trying to make sense of anything, literally anything, that was happening. Stephanie Monroe? That bitch had to be framing me. There was no other possible explanation.

About two hours into questioning, Portly Belly decided to drop the biggest bomb, though.

"Trent, can you explain why blood and hair were found in your apartment?"

"Whaaaat? What are you talking about?" I was in a panic now. What the fuck was happening?

"We found blood, hair, and this . . ." Portly opened a manila folder, took something out, and pushed two photos across the table at me. "Can you explain why these were in the breast pocket of your sport coat?"

They were pictures of women's underwear. I had never seen them before.

I began to stammer. "I . . . I . . . I swear on my children's lives. I have no . . . no . . . no idea."

"Trent," said Officer Spanish. "Semen was found on the underpants. And there's something else: Investigators found a second woman's ID buried in your backyard and DNA from that woman, Jasmine Littleton, in your suitcase. Can you explain that?"

Jasmine? Wasn't that the name of the chick I met in the corner bar the night I returned from the conference? The one who stiffed me on the sexy picture?

I opened my mouth, but words would not come out.

"It's not looking very good for you, Trent. Why don't you just tell us what really happened?"

CHAPTER 33

Trent

The Thursday After the Conference

They set bail at $1 million. I was confident our company would pay for it. The parent company of NBC6 owned dozens of stations across the US and raked in money every year, especially political years, when candidates threw attack ads at each other. NBC6 definitely could afford it, and we'd get it all back and then some when we sued the pants off the Atlanta Police Department.

There was no way I was going to jail for this ridiculous story the police had concocted. DNA found in my apartment? Absurd. Personal belongings buried in my backyard? Insane.

As I lay awake at night in my jail cell staring at the ceiling, thoughts kept running through my head. It was either some woman trying to frame me—Stephanie? Katrina?—or the police themselves. For what reason the police would do it, I didn't know, but they could have planted evidence when they barged into my house in the middle of the night.

The one thing I was sure of, as sure as I was of anything ever in my life, was that I had not seen Stephanie Monroe since she had peeked out of her door at the hotel. Was she truly dead? I mean, if so, that sucked for her, but I had nothing to do with it. My conscience was completely clear.

They allowed me three phone calls. Since I was still sitting in jail waiting for the magic words "Bail has been posted," I started with Bill. When he answered, we both had to sit through a "This call is coming from the Fulton County Jail and may be recorded" message and then a beep. I heard him take a deep sigh. I jumped right in.

"Bill, this is the most asinine, ridiculous, insane, warped, twisted, fucked-up—pardon my French—thing ever. You know I'm 100 percent innocent. I did *nothing*. I never saw Stephanie after the first day. I don't know who this Jasmine person is. I'm going to sue them for character defamation too. I trust NBC6 will pay my bail?"

There was silence. It went on for so long that I thought our connection was lost.

"Bill? Are you there?"

"I'm here, Trent."

"Did you hear what I said?"

"Yes, I heard."

"So when can I expect to get out of here?"

"Trent, NBC6 and our company are not going to post bail. You need to stay put until the trial."

"*What?* What are you talking about? You're going to leave me here to rot? Who's going to run the newsroom?"

"Jorge has assumed command. Trent, your employment at NBC6 has been terminated."

"Wait a minute, wait just a goddamn minute." Little bits of spittle began to fly out of my mouth as I talked. "You can't fire me. I did nothing wrong. Tell me what I did wrong. I'm innocent!"

"You lied to me, and that alone is a fireable offense. I informed HR yesterday. They will clean out your personal belongings and put everything in boxes for you."

"I didn't lie to you," I implored. "I'm telling you the God's honest truth. I did nothing. This is all a huge hoax or a setup. That will be proven in court!"

"Trent," Bill said, and I noticed suddenly how tired his voice sounded. "Where did you go when you told me you were comforting Hannah in a mental health moment?"

Uh-oh. Had he talked to her? Was the jig up? I had to scramble.

"I was on my way there, Bill, when I got diverted. She did have a mental health crisis, and I was on my way to talk to her. I do that for my employees. If she's not telling you the details, maybe she's embarrassed. We learned that in our session at the conference. People sometimes get timid."

I held my breath waiting for his reaction.

"So, you were at the mental health session at the conference?"

"Of course I was."

"The time for lying is over, Trent," Bill said. "Tell the truth."

"What do you mean? I was there."

"I've been told by people who were there that you left and never came back."

People who were there? He must mean Dorothy and Alan. Once again, I had to scramble.

"I ducked out for a minute to check my messages and came back in and stood at the back of the room. I saw the whole thing."

"If that is the case, then tell me who the speakers were. I pulled up a recording that the National Press Foundation had so I can compare. Go on, tell me, who was speaking that day? How many speakers? What did they talk about?"

"I—I—don't remember their names. They were all mental health advocates, giving us tips and stuff."

I could feel my footing in this conversation slipping. I was grasping, and he was about to sink my battleship, just like the game I had played as a child when my brother would revel in beating me. I was scrambling to protect that last little corner before the final peg went into my boat.

"Trent, I don't believe you. Describe for me even one of the speakers. What did they look like?"

Battleship hit and sunk, my entire career slinking with it under the murky water.

"I'm sorry, Bill," I whispered. "It's true, I didn't get to that session. But that's the only thing I haven't been truthful on. I didn't want you to be upset with me. I had a migraine, and I went to my room for a few hours. It was the only session I missed."

"There is absolutely nothing else I can do for you. I am sickened by these allegations, just sickened. And disgusted by your continual lying. It's taking all of my willpower just to speak on the phone with you. If you did these things . . . God help you . . ." He let his voice trail off. "No matter what, your employment is terminated."

And he hung up. I held the phone receiver out from my ear and just stared at it. I wanted to take it and smash it on the counter in front of me, pulverize it into smithereens, but there was a guard eyeing me, so instead I just yelled out, "*Goddamn it.*"

"Watch your mouth," he sneered. "Two more calls."

Who the hell to call now? Who would help me in this situation? Not my brother—we had been estranged for a long time.

My mom was gone, and Dad had Alzheimer's. I hadn't been to see him in at least six months. A few aunts and uncles came to mind, but they had no money.

Then I thought of my Sunday football drinking buddies. They were all well-off and high up in their respective fields. They would help a bro out, wouldn't they? I would do it for them if they were in a pinch. Well, maybe I would. But they should do it for me. I called my friend Scott. He was CEO of a boat-dealership company and had two houses, plus a yacht.

"Trent?"

"Yeah, Scott, hey, I'm in a jam here. I don't know what's going on. I need you to know I am completely innocent and have done nothing wrong. To prove it, though, I gotta get out of this place. Have you seen the bail? Can you float me some and I'll get you back? I'm planning to sue the entire police department."

The guard shot me a look but didn't say anything.

"Aww, Trent, man, I feel for you, but I don't have that kind of money."

"Come on, Scott, I know you have it. You gotta get me out of here. I can't stay in jail as an innocent man."

Scott was quiet, and I heard his breathing. I thought he was about to say yes, and I felt a surge of hope in my chest.

"Trent, man, I'm sorry. I need to stay away. I can't have my name tied up in this. We're just looking to buy out Southern Sails. I can't get embroiled in some scandal."

"Scandal? What scandal?" I asked. "This is all bullshit, 100 percent bullshit. They'll be making a movie about how I was wronged one day. I think the police might have planted evidence."

"Trent, you're in jail for murder. Two women. Your name is all over the news, not just here but nationally. You're trending on every platform. You were the first story in my national news feed. I don't know if you did it or didn't do it, that's for the courts to decide, but I can't bail you out. And that's final."

This time I was the one to hang up. I put my head into my hands and began to rock back and forth. I was fired. My friends wouldn't bail me out or even want to be a part of this.

There was only one person left to call.

"Katrina . . . you have to listen to me. You know I would never hurt anyone. I really need your help."

"I don't want to talk to you. The kids don't want to talk to you. You're a fucking monster!"

"The kids want to see me. I want to see them. I need to get out of here. I need bail money."

"Oh, you want to see them, do you? Is that why you blew off the last visit you had a few weeks ago?" she spat. "And yes, you have hurt people. You hurt me, physically, you know it. You hurt me psychologically too. No, Trent, you made this bed and you will lie in it. Fuck you."

And she hung up on me. Apparently, no one was going to say a proper goodbye ever again.

"Time's up," the guard said, and I replaced the receiver with an extra loud thud. "Watch it," he added as he jerked me up out of my chair and took a firm hold of my arm through the prison jumpsuit, steering me back to the jail cell. As we walked past some of the other prisoners' cells, one called out:

"Took out two women, huh, pretty boy? Did you do it just for fun? I'll show you some fun in here."

I shivered. It was like every jail movie or TV show I had ever seen, from *Shawshank Redemption* to *Orange Is the New Black*.

When we got back to my cell, I lay down on the hard

mattress, turned toward the wall, curled into a ball, and, for the first time since third grade, began to cry. Quietly, though, so no one would hear. What could have happened? How did I get entangled in this mess? My mind struggled to put pieces together that made no sense at all.

CHAPTER 34

Lucy

The Wednesday After the Conference

Robert was shell-shocked and wild-eyed as I escorted him back to Madison from Atlanta. He fell into a state of mumbling answers for basic questions, and I took the lead on every aspect of getting us home and getting him to his side of the townhouse before returning to my apartment. Of course I was distraught too, but somehow I had shifted into an autopilot of determination. I was sure grief would come later.

Police still had not found any bodies, but they had some DNA from Jasmine Littleton from hair and blood samples, and both women's personal belongings were buried in Trent's backyard.

Things were starting to leak out—Steph had withdrawn large sums of money both in San Diego and Atlanta. Police surmised that she and Trent started a hot romance at the conference and he convinced her that he needed money for his growing child support payments. The pair traveled together to Atlanta, but then something went wrong. Maybe Steph refused to take out more money, or maybe it was just that he had a temper. Regardless, she wanted to get away from him—we knew this from her texts to Robert—but then he killed her.

How this Jasmine woman fit in, we didn't know yet. She was labeled as a drifter from Madison. How did she wind up dead in Atlanta too? When did Trent meet her?

His picture was all over the news now. Even his own station had to report on it. I called up NBC6's story to see how they were handling it. A grim-faced young reporter named Hannah did a stand-up outside of Trent's condo, police tape behind her. When she threw back to the anchors, they looked stunned and spoke in hushed tones. The female one named Leigh said they would stay on the story and update people with further details as they came in. I wanted to use the skills I'd learned in a women's self-defense class and kick Trent right in his baby face, but I couldn't shake the strong sense that something was just not adding up—that Reiki gut feeling again. If Steph had really met the man of her dreams and wanted more time off, why wouldn't she have told us? Why would she lie about having a brother?

Opening a new tab on the computer, I went to LinkedIn and called up Trent's profile. There he was, all frat-boy smiles with wickedly white teeth, grinning away with the NBC6 logo behind his head. He didn't look like the type I thought she would fall head over heels in love with. His LinkedIn made it clear he was a market-hopper, someone who never truly put down roots, always thinking there was something better, more money, more prestige. I had seen plenty of them in TV.

I looked to see what sorts of things Trent had posted on LinkedIn. It was all egocentric, photos of him holding awards with braggy captions that said things like "So honored to be honored again! Huge night for NBC6 at the Atlanta Broadcasters Association Awards!"

I checked Twitter/X and Threads. Trent's second-to-last tweet came the day he had flown to San Diego for the conference. He took a selfie of himself grinning at the Atlanta airport with the caption "Wheels up—ATL to SAN!" It had three likes.

But it was his last tweet that truly intrigued me. I peered at a group picture of about ten men and women in what seemed to be an outdoor courtyard at the conference hotel.

"The Lunch Bunch, best News Directors in the country!" it said.

The woman next to him was clearly Stephanie, but her head was turned to the side so that all I really saw was her hair. I did recognize her pink blazer. She was not tagged in the post like the other news directors were. There were twenty likes on this one. Clicking to see who, I noticed that all eight of the other tagged people who seemed to be at the table with Trent and Stephanie had liked it and retweeted it, but she had not done either.

It was as if Stephanie herself were trying to tell me something.

Lying down on my yoga mat in the savasana pose, I was exhausted but not ready to sleep. My mind whirred, but I forced it to slow down as I began to meditate. After twenty minutes, I felt much better and shifted my mind gently back to a place of contemplation.

Think, Lucy, think. Steph's texts about Mark Ruffalo were so weird, but clearly she had been in Atlanta. She was sending Bruce and Robert voice memos and photos and texts. Her cell phone was found there, and Jasmine's was now traced to the nearest tower to Trent's place too.

An idea hit me.

TMZ had identified Steph's tablemates from the first day of the conference as Dorothy Robinson from Boston and Alan Kozinski from Kalamazoo. They were among the last known people—other than Trent, a maintenance guy, and strangers on the flight to Atlanta—to see and talk to her.

Dashing to my laptop, I returned to LinkedIn and sent direct messages to Dorothy and Alan, explaining who I was and that I had some strange texts from Steph during the conference and wondered if something wasn't adding up. I put my phone number, asking if they could talk.

I didn't expect an answer right away, maybe ever. I figured I might get a curt "thanks but no thanks" response, if anything, but just thirty minutes later, as I was unpacking my travel bag in my bedroom, my cell phone rang. The area code was unfamiliar.

"Hello?"

"Is this Lucy from WISC in Madison?" a deep woman's voice asked.

"Yes."

"This is Dorothy Robinson. You wrote to me on LinkedIn. I'm absolutely sick about your coworker, and I'm so very sorry. Anything I can do to help. What would you like to ask me, and what's this about weird texts to you?"

So we began to compare notes. Dorothy made little clucking noises or said "hmm" as I detailed for her what we had seen back in the newsroom and how we began to wonder if someone had her phone. Then she told me how Trent had been awful from the get-go, flirting with Stephanie.

"But Stephanie seemed rather uninterested," Dorothy summed up. "Which is part of the reason I'm so confused by this."

"Me too," I agreed. "So then came lunch?"

"Yes, and we sat at opposite ends of the outdoor portico. Then she was gone. I never saw her again."

"Anything else?" I asked, starting to feel desperate. "I just feel like it wasn't her sending those messages to us."

"No, that was it," said Dorothy. "I'm sorry I don't have more for you."

"Did you see what she was wearing or eating?" I was flailing for anything now, trying to visualize her on this patio having lunch.

"A pink blazer and a black dress. As for food, no, I didn't. Wait . . . actually, now that you mention it, I just remembered. Trent told me and Alan afterward that he and Stephanie both had chicken."

A ripple of adrenaline shot through me.

"Chicken? But she's a vegetarian! Steph wouldn't have chicken. Did they offer a vegetarian option?"

"Why yes, they did," said Dorothy. "Do you think this means something?"

"Dorothy, can I ask you a favor? Can I send you a recent photo of Stephanie, and can you confirm that it was her you saw at the conference?"

"Certainly, I'll do what I can. It was such a brief time sitting next to her and we were focused on the speakers, but I'll try."

I fumbled for my photos and pulled one up from just a few weeks prior: a going-away party for a coworker where Steph had her arm around the woman's shoulder, both grinning for the camera. Texting it to Dorothy, I held my breath.

"OK, hold on, I'm putting my glasses on," she said. "Hmmm . . . if memory serves, that's her. Same hair, for sure. I'm sorry I don't have a really clear mental image of her face that differs from this picture. There is one other thing we could try, though. We all had to sign in when we got there. Do you know what Stephanie's signature looks like? I could call the National Press Foundation and ask for a copy of the sign-in sheet. We could compare."

"Yes!" I cried out. "That's a good idea. Steph is a lefty. Is there anyone who can help us confirm that a lefty signed in?"

"Lucy, I have just the person. I'm a former investigative

journalist, and you're getting my juices flowing. I'll get the signatures from the NPF and call my contact."

The next morning, just as I was doing my Pilates and trying to stay calm about all things Steph-related, my cell rang again. Dashing for it, I saw that it was Dorothy. I answered breathlessly.

"Lucy, I got the NPF sign-in sheet and sent it to my handwriting expert. It's definitely written by someone who is right-handed. We've got something here. And that's not all. I went to your website and found a video of Stephanie giving a mission statement about your station. I wanted to compare her voice to the one I remembered from San Diego since the face wasn't a clear mental image for me. Lucy, I don't believe that's the same voice I heard at the conference. We need to call the police."

PART FOUR

CHAPTER 35

Jasmine

The Day of the Flight

17A was my seat, and I walked down the aisle thinking of the new me, the happy me, the energized me, so different from the beaten-down me I had become with Glenn.

A woman was already in my row, sitting in the aisle seat. She had brown hair and a kind-looking face. I decided to try out the refurbished me.

"Hey, I'm in the window seat," I said, hoisting my carry-on to the overhead compartment. She nodded and stood up to let me in. I set my fringed purse in the seat between us and added, "I hope we have an empty middle seat, don't you?"

"That would be nice," she replied.

Glancing down the aisle to see who else might be boarding, I noted a little old lady with curly gray hair, glasses, her coat over her arm, and a slight limp. She was moving gingerly, checking her boarding pass at each row. She stopped at ours.

"I think I'm here with you two," she said. "I'm sorry to make you stand up."

"No problem," said the brown-haired woman. She stood

again, offering to put the old lady's coat and purse in the overhead. I reluctantly moved my purse to the floor by my feet, and the older woman lowered herself into the middle spot, buckling up and looking back and forth at the two of us.

"Well, isn't this nice?" she said. "I get to be with two lovely young women. Are you sisters? Your hair is different, but you look similar. I bet you want to spend the trip talking!"

The stranger at the aisle and I glanced at each other, puzzled, and chuckled.

"No, we're not sisters," I said.

"Silly me," said the older woman. "Would either of you like a stick of gum?"

She pulled a pack from her pocket. The brown-haired woman politely declined, but I decided maybe it would help calm my adrenaline and I took one.

"It's funny you say that about sisters," said the brown-haired woman. "My coworker told me about this website, Find My Doppelganger, where you can easily find someone who looks like she could be your sister, even your twin."

"I don't know much about doppelgangers . . . or websites," said the old woman and we all laughed. She was wearing a white sweater and what you would call "sensible" slacks and shoes. Slightly pudgy in the way you don't mind a grandma being so you can fold into her lap, she reminded me of my own grandma, and I felt it was another sign from above. I only wished this stranger smelled of patchouli instead of something that seemed to be an odd cross between mothballs and baby powder.

"Where are you both going today?" the older woman asked, looking to the woman on the aisle first for an answer.

"I'm headed to San Diego. Denver is just a layover. I'm going to a work conference," said the woman.

A conference, look at you, I thought. I certainly couldn't keep up with her on a professional level, so I decided not to go for the conference–in–New York idea in case she started talking hotel points and things I didn't know about. Keep it simple.

"Denver for me. Visiting a friend," I replied. That was vague enough.

"Oh, how nice," the old lady replied. "I'm going to see my son and grandson in Fort Collins. They'll be picking me up at the airport. I do wish they lived closer. My grandson is getting an award this weekend."

"What kind of award?" asked the woman on the aisle.

The older woman started telling us all about the community service her grandson did and how the local Rotary Club was honoring him.

"Well, I hope you have a wonderful time," said the woman on the aisle, and I nodded.

We all settled in, the plane took off, and I looked out the window at Madison receding behind me, my heart pounding with adrenaline about this escape and relief starting to pulse down into my cells.

As we reached cruising altitude, the older woman got up to use the restroom, and when she came back, she said, "Ladies, I noticed there's an empty window seat just two rows back. I think I might move there and take a little nap. It's been a busy day already. You two have a nice flight now."

I brought my purse off the floor and back onto the middle seat. The stranger did the same. I could see her more clearly now that no one was between us. They say you can size someone up in seven seconds, and my read was: wealthy. She had on a nice sweater and low leather boots, and I could smell a hint of a floral perfume now that mothballs and baby powder were not between us. I was surmising that this person going to San Diego was one of those businesswomen I had always wanted to be, someone like my sister. Her watch was the kind where she could answer emails or check her heart rate. The pearls in her ears seemed real. I imagined someone gifting them to her in a velvet box after a meal with champagne, maybe for a birthday or holiday.

I thought of the unfairness of life. Why did she get to jet around the country in lovely clothes when it took me over a year to save up enough for just this one flight? I wanted to feel her life for a few moments, so I decided to initiate further conversation.

"My name is Jasmine. Are you from Madison?"

"I'm Stephanie," she responded. "And no, I mean, not from Madison originally. Indiana. I've been there about ten years, though. You?"

From there, we got into a long conversation. She told me she was a news director at the CBS TV station in Madison. I didn't know what a news director actually did until she explained it. It was crazy to imagine that she was in charge of all of those anchors and reporters and everyone else. And it was extra fascinating as I had just been watching that channel for weather to plan this trip. I told her I thought the weather guy was cute. She laughed and said he was just voted Madison's favorite in a local magazine.

I turned to what she did outside of work: Did she have kids? What would she do in San Diego? I just wanted to chat with someone, to distract myself, and I was fascinated by her world. The conversation kept going, and she cracked open like an egg. I learned she had an adult son. She was divorced. She talked about owning a cat and said her neighbor was cat-sitting. She told me how she always got her neighbor a little trinket in the city where she was—a mug or a magnet, that kind of thing.

Listening to her, I felt jealousy rising up. What a life. A

high-paying job but no man around to tell her what to do or drag her down. A woman in charge of a TV station and seemingly in control of her own destiny too.

When she asked me what I did, I blurted out the first thing that came to mind. I was surprised that it involved my mom: "I'm a nurse's assistant at a retirement home." I hoped Stephanie had no knowledge of the nursing industry that she would press me on, but she didn't seem to.

She asked me if I had a husband or boyfriend. The question startled me, although I had just asked her the same thing, so it was only fair. Still, it took me a second to respond. I didn't feel I could properly voice it without emotion showing through, so I just shook my head and averted my eyes.

Meanwhile, my story about the weekend away grew. It was an old high school friend, I fibbed, named Allison. "And what are you going to do in Denver?" Stephanie asked, and I responded with the only thing I was pretty certain every Coloradoan did: "Hiking."

"I've never been to San Diego," I sighed, taking a bite of a pretzel from the little bag the flight attendant had handed out. "Are you staying by the ocean?"

"No," she said. "That would have been nice. It's a Hilton five miles from the beach, and I probably won't even have time to see the water."

As we talked, something began to occur to me. It started as a tiny germ of an idea, but the more she divulged about herself, the more it blossomed. I studied her face. We did have similar features. Not exactly the same, of course, but if I had her hair and fancy clothes and took off my John Lennon glasses, I could reasonably pass for her. The little old lady had been right.

My eyes flashed to our two purses sitting in the middle seat, and I thought of her wallet in there with her ID and credit cards. Could I steal those when she wasn't looking? Could I take on the identity of this stranger sitting next to me on a plane? It was ridiculous, ludicrous, right?

But was it? Maybe the universe was trying to give me the break I had been craving, that I had been deserving for so long, that I had literally prayed to my grandma about before I got on this plane. I mean, I had to have been placed near this particular person for a reason, right?

I had thought of my escape for so long, nibbling my fingers to the nubs and trying to figure out what I would do with my freedom from Glenn once I gained it and how I could live. This woman had to have tons of money in her bank account. If I had her ID and her cards, maybe I could drain her account and be off to Mexico or somewhere else south of the border that felt even safer than Denver. I started to imagine cutting my hair and dyeing it. I could easily pass for her at a bank or in a store if I did so. I kept asking her questions, and I tried to memorize her mannerisms, the way she paused at times and slightly tilted her head, the way she smiled, just in case there were security cameras where I went.

If I could get my hands on her money, I could dash off immediately and it would be enough time for me to be home free. If she noticed anything missing, she would be racking her brain for how it disappeared, but she would never suspect the person on the plane with her, would she? Or *would* she? If she started yapping to the police, my whole story might blow up.

I needed to use the bathroom and get to a space where I could think for just a moment.

"Do you mind if I slide by you and go to the restroom?" I asked. "I'll just leave my purse here."

"Of course," she said and stood up to let me pass.

In the bathroom, locking the door, I was panting with nervous energy. If she got up to use the restroom as well and also left her purse, I would have full access to it. I already knew a ton about her from our airplane conversation. Her job, her background, her family and friends. I even knew where she was staying. If I wanted to follow her, I could easily do so. Imagine if I showed up at her hotel out of the blue? The thought gave me jitters. What could I do if I found her there? What would she do if she saw me?

Another thought moved in, like an approaching thunderstorm, dark and full of lightning bolts. What if I took this one step further and actually *became* her? How would that look? What would that mean? If she disappeared and I became Stephanie, the high-powered, rich TV executive, even for a few days, I could truly disappear. Because then I could have her entire wallet, her laptop, her clothes, whatever else I wanted, and I could hide in plain sight until I hid out of sight. A beach in Mexico, a tiny out-of-the-way town no one bothered to look at.

I imagined the little beach cottage I could buy: just enough for one person, decorated in shabby chic, the way I had done my apartment in Madison before I moved into Glenn's place and was forced into his style, which was what I would call a true bachelor trailer. He had zero interest in decorating and didn't like the knickknacks, hooked rugs, plants, and brightly colored furniture I wanted to bring along.

"Let's sell it all, babe, and go on a trip together with the money," he had said when we first started living together. "I've got stuff, we don't need more." And in the cloudiness of early love, I had agreed, thinking about a romantic getaway somewhere, but he pocketed the money and kept putting off the trip until he told me that "household expenses" were getting to be too much, blaming the president for rising inflation.

Now I stood in the tiny airplane bathroom, fantasizing about how I might decorate this fictional beach house in a fictional Mexican beach town with the fictional money I was going to steal from the real woman seated back in row 17. Squeezing my eyes shut, I slowly counted backward from ten until my breathing steadied. *Just be natural, Jasmine*, I said to myself. *Maybe Stephanie won't even need to use the restroom and this whole little fantasy will disappear.*

Walking back to our row, I felt lightheaded, almost sick to my stomach waiting to see what would happen. I knew it was now or never as the first tiny dip of the plane descending a notch had started. The FASTEN YOUR SEAT BELT sign was soon to go on, I was sure.

When I got to the edge of our row, Stephanie stood up to let me in, but then said, "I'm going to use the restroom too."

My adrenaline shot up. *Keep it cool. Jasmine, keep it cool. Don't look happy or surprised or anything.*

"Sure," I said in as natural a voice as I could. She turned and went down the aisle. My hands started to sweat. Her purse was just inches from me, a Kate Spade in a robin's-egg blue. It looked wildly different from my purse with the tassels and fringe, worn down from so many years of use.

Wait, I told myself, *be patient, not yet.* I snuck a peek behind me toward the restrooms. She was just going in.

My body felt like it was not even itself. Glancing across the aisle, I saw a middle-aged couple with their eyes shut, their shoulders leaning against each other, his hand covering hers. There was no one else who could possibly see a thing; the flight attendants were busy in the galley.

Quickly, almost in a robotic trance, my hand slid toward Stephanie's purse and pulled it to me. I glanced back one more time. The bathroom door remained shut. Gently gliding the zipper of the purse open, I felt inside for her wallet. It was right there, cool to the touch and firm, made of good leather, I could tell.

Keeping an eye on the couple across from me, I slid the wallet out and opened it, glancing down. Her driver's license was right there: Stephanie Monroe. I also saw three major credit cards, a handful of specific store credit cards, a debit card, some sort of work ID, several insurance cards, and a photo of a handsome young man in a graduation cap and gown.

The driver's license slipped out of its plastic holder easily, and I gently eased it into an inside pocket of my purse. I was just about to take a credit card too when the woman across from me stirred, opened her eyes, and said to her husband, "I think we're landing soon, honey." My heart leapt into my throat. Here was Stephanie's purse open next to me. Although I doubted they'd notice across the aisle, I couldn't be 100 percent positive. The man mumbled something I couldn't make out, and I thought I heard the bathroom door click at the rear of the plane. I wasn't sure if it was Stephanie coming out or whoever might have been in the other tiny restroom, but I couldn't take the chance. I had just seconds now.

The woman turned her gaze to look out the window, and I zipped Stephanie's wallet shut, shoved it back into her purse, zipped that too, and put the purse in the exact spot it had been.

To make it look like I was busy, I reached for my phone and earbuds just as Stephanie walked up. I thought I might have a stroke, her contraband with me now like a tiny beating heart.

Sure that my facial expressions would give it away or that I was visibly sweating, I needed a mental break. I wasn't confident I could keep up conversation with her either, so as soon as she sat down, I said, "It's been so great to chat with you, Stephanie. I'm just going to rest for a bit before we get there."

Then I threw in one more lie to double down on it. "My friend wants to go out tonight."

"OK, sounds great," she answered. "I'll do the same. I could use a rest too."

You know how when you're a child and play Marco Polo at the lake or at someone's pool and you're supposed to keep your eyes shut but you really don't? You keep them open just a slit, just enough so that no one notices? That's what I did for the rest of the flight.

Faking that I was sleeping, I leaned my head on the window shade but tilted my body in such a way that I could still see her. I needed to know if she went into her purse—and if she did? Well, I truly didn't know what I would do. My entire escape plan could be blown by that if she demanded that the flight attendants empty my purse and the police came.

God, I was stupid. Maybe I was as dumb as Glenn said I was, but as soon as that thought entered my mind, I stomped on it again and again, like a person in a barrel turning grapes into wine. I was smart. Screw Glenn.

Think, Jasmine, think.

Stephanie had tilted her seat back as far as it would go and had her eyes shut. Should I return her ID now so that no one would know? That was absolutely too dangerous. Not only was she right here, but I would never get the chance to get it again. But if she noticed her ID was gone and accused me, what would I do?

Watching her through the slits of my eyes and keeping an eye on the middle-aged couple, now fully awake and fussing to find a missing boarding pass for a connecting flight, I put my hand carefully into my purse and found the side pocket. Stephanie's ID pulsed in my palm. Wrapping my fingers around it and making sure Stephanie remained zoned out with her earbuds in,

I slipped it from my purse and up toward my chest, keeping my hand cupped protectively over it.

Pretending I had an itch in case the couple across the way looked over, I pushed the ID into my bra, the plastic edge poking me uncomfortably and reminding me of what I had done. But it was safer there. If the flight attendants made me empty my purse, they would find nothing, and I could act as horrified as Stephanie.

Did you leave your ID on the ticket counter in Madison? I imagined myself saying, feigned sympathy in my eyes.

But Stephanie paid no mind to her purse. She rested, and I pretend-rested, my adrenaline so high I would have needed two of Glenn's Ambiens to get me to feel even a tiny bit sleepy.

As we descended through the clouds and into the range of Denver, I looked down and saw snow-capped mountains and sprawling suburban areas, and I began to feel scared. Where would I go? What would I do? I knew no one, and I had no place to sleep that night.

The hazy plan I had dreamed of for a year was all in front of me: get to Colorado, figure it out. But the plan that had just twinkled at the edges of my psyche during my conversation with Stephanie began to dance again. It was like one of those giant blow-up, vinyl creatures you see at car dealership openings, where the arms and legs move around wildly and the body dips and lifts in all sorts of awkward movements, bolstered by a fan of some sort. That's how I felt. A little out of control but buoyed by air.

It was the same feeling I had at the Halloween party in high school.

I tried not to think of it, tried to push it back deep into the depths of my memory. It was so long ago—why think about it now? It had been an accident, right? I hadn't meant to hurt Allison that badly.

Or had I? I knew in my heart how angry I was at her, how jealous I was of her life.

Allison always had the best clothes and prettiest hair of anyone in school. She treated me horribly when a small bit of kindness was all that I wanted, the least that I deserved.

Still, the incident itself was an accident. At least that's what I had been telling myself for decades just so I could sleep at night.

Flashes of the party at Drake's massive house in Maple Hills came to mind as the plane moved closer to Denver and I looked out the window. Drake's rich parents out of town. Music thumping: "Monster Mash" someone had put on a loop. People drinking from orange plastic cups. The Kool-Aid, spiked with who knows what, ladled out of a punch bowl. Fake spider-webs and skeletons on the walls. A group passing joints around.

Allison throwing her head back and laughing, her perfectly straight teeth glowing, her lips with the brightest red lipstick I had ever seen. All of the boys flocking around her.

My costume was homemade. My family lived in what was considered the low-rent part of our school district, while Allison and Drake both lived in Maple Hills, one of the wealthiest areas. It was even where the governor's mansion was located. We were all funneled to the same public schools, though, and it sometimes made for conflicts and difficult dynamics.

The Maple Hills kids clearly thought they were better than the rest of us, and some had started a group called "the Fun Bunch," huddling together and laughing about things we weren't supposed to be privy to.

Drake's parties when his parents were gone were well known around school, and our whole junior class was invited. I was so excited to go, thinking that maybe I could break through to some of the kids in the Fun Bunch. It was a group I constantly admired from afar.

I asked Raven to go with me. She and Anna were my only two friends, but Anna had to go to her grandma's birthday in Milwaukee that weekend and would miss the Halloween party.

Raven lived in the projects and had even less money than me. She was a scrappy girl, used to fending for herself. Raven's mom had been addicted to several types of drugs for many years and came and went from their tiny apartment at all hours. Raven was known as the go-to at our high school for any type of drug, including weed, ecstasy, you name it. She somehow had a pipeline to anything and everything.

Raven and Anna hated the Fun Bunch, but I thought if the three of us could break into their group, we could turn our entire high school experience around. Being in the popular group seemed like the only thing that mattered at the time.

For weeks, Raven refused to go to the party. As we were walking home after school on that Friday before Halloween, I tried one more time. Stopping at the corner where we turned our own ways, I practically begged her. Raven said no and accused me of being a sellout by sucking up to the Fun Bunch. I told her she was an asshole for not even trying. She told me to go fuck myself and stomped off. I tried to think of a strong retort, but the only thing that came out was "Well, you go fuck yourself too!" She flashed me a middle finger over her shoulder. I was hurt and angry but hardened my heart. I would go alone.

I worked really hard the next night to look like a cute kitten, hopeful of catching the eye of one of the Fun Bunch guys. Mom and my siblings weren't around to help, and unlike so many of my peers, I didn't have my driver's license yet. Mom had been putting it off, citing the cost. I biked to the store and got supplies. Cheap black eyeliner from Walgreens went across my cheeks in long, thin lines to create cat whiskers, and I fashioned perky ears on a headband with pipe cleaners and cloth. I had on a white sweatshirt and a pair of white gloves that used to be my grandma's. They were the one thing I was given when she passed.

I had to take the bus and walk the rest of the way to the party. The first person I saw upon arrival was Allison, also in a cat outfit but completely different from mine. Hers was jet-black, full-body, tight, and glittering with rhinestones. It came with a long, thick tail that Allison held in one hand and constantly swung around. Her hair was extra shiny, and she somehow had what looked like real whiskers glued to her face. A perfect black headband studded with more rhinestones sat on her head, pink cat ears rising in immaculate triangles. I overheard someone whisper that Allison's parents had spent a fortune on the costume at the most expensive Halloween store in town.

After Kool-Aid-drinking and pot-smoking, someone suggested we all play Ghosts in the Graveyard, a game we knew from elementary school. For old times' sake, they said, and the whole group of high and drunk teenagers spilled out onto Drake's wide back lawn. It had wooded areas off to each side and sat nestled up against a lake.

We all laughed and chased one another around. It was fun, and I was actually enjoying myself and making a little headway with one of Drake's friends, I thought, until Allison ran past.

"What a pathetic cat outfit, Jasmine." She sneered with a cackle of laughter.

I felt a white-hot flash of anger, pure rage, mixed with humiliation.

Allison and I had never been friends. Not even close. She had looked down on me ever since about second grade for no reason I could tell other than our addresses.

She immediately turned her attention back to her friends.

"I'm an Allie-cat," she called out, and people started yelling, "Hey, Allie-cat, meow!"

Embarrassed by my outfit, I ran to hide behind a tree that was off to the side, keeping an eye on her. Watching that long, thick tail run this way and that, hearing her annoying laughter, watching the boys trip over themselves to find her in the darkness.

And then, suddenly, she was running to hide in a spot behind a different tree near me, and Drake was following. They didn't see me.

He tickled her; she giggled wildly. He pushed her against the tree and they started kissing—sloppy, disgusting kissing with heavy breathing. I crouched down, watching his hands running all over her.

"Drake, I'm a virgin . . ."

"Come on, Allie, tonight's the night . . ."

Before I knew it, he was peeling off the catsuit, and to my surprise, she wasn't protesting. He tossed the suit to the side, and it landed with a crunch on the dried leaves near me. I crouched farther back.

He was taking off his vampire cape and pulling his pants down. They resumed kissing, the perfect whiskers on her face starting to fall off, the headband tilting crazily to one side. He pushed her to the ground and forced her knees apart, and she said, "Drake, please be gentle."

He didn't reply. Allison made weird little noises like she was in pain. It didn't seem all that gentle to me, but I was still a virgin too, and this was the first time I had seen actual sex take place.

Other kids were still running around all over the open backyard, laughing, and no one noticed what was happening in the dark by the trees. Drake gave a final grunt just as the buddy I had been flirting with yelled from the gigantic, wraparound back deck.

"Drake? Where are you, man? We're going inside to do Jell-O shots!"

Drake jumped off Allison, pulled on his underwear and pants, grabbed his cape, and ran off without a word. She lay there naked and panting in the dark, her catsuit still away from her, crumpled on the leaves.

The backyard emptied as kids ran inside for the shots. Allison stayed still for a minute, catching her ragged breath, and then she turned her head to look for the suit. That's when she saw me a few trees over. I think my white sweatshirt and gloves might have been illuminated by the moonlight.

"Jasmine? Is that you? Were you *watching* us?" She sat up and scrambled to cover herself with her hands while frantically reaching in the general direction of her costume, feeling in the dark.

I shook my head.

"You were, you crazy bitch." Her right hand was covering her breasts as her left fumbled for the suit. "I'm going to tell everyone that you just sat there and watched us." She paused and added, "We do it all the time, you know."

I couldn't help myself from firing back, "You said you were a virgin."

"I didn't say that. You're a liar!"

And that's when I snapped. I did. I can admit it. I think the fact that I already felt like I had lost Raven as a friend that night, that no one had helped me get ready when her parents spent a mountain of money on her, that I had to take the bus when she probably drove up in a Porsche, combined with Allison's continued vitriol, pushed me over the edge. I grabbed for her catsuit before she did. I didn't know what I would do with it. I think I planned just to run away so that she would have to be naked in the woods and somehow make her way back to the party, as ashamed as she had made me feel.

But she lunged toward me and growled like a dog.

"You are so fucked up, Jasmine. Your cat outfit is a piece of shit, just like you."

And the next thing I knew, that long, thick tail on her outfit was being wrapped around her neck. I intended just to scare her, to make her lose her breath for a minute. I wanted to see her begging me, her eyes terrified, her hands on the tail as it roped around her neck, clawing at it. Me in the position of power for a change. It was like a grade school game where you make someone pass out. That was my intention. I didn't think about what would happen after she woke up. How much trouble I'd be in. It just felt good to watch her writhe in agony for a moment.

The tail kept getting tighter and tighter and she was gagging.

By now, the party had moved entirely inside, and someone changed the soundtrack to thumping rap music. No one could see us; no one could hear us.

My arms felt like they didn't belong to me. I was superhuman and powerful, out of control of my own limbs.

I noticed her face turning slightly bluish and her eyes bugging out, but it still didn't register how close she was to dying. We had just learned about asphyxiation in health class, but none of the lessons came back to me in the moment. She was desperately clawing at the tail and trying to kick me. I pulled it even tighter.

And then, suddenly, before I anticipated it, she stopped gagging and went limp, her eyes wide and vacant, only two whiskers still stuck on her left cheek, the headband on the ground. She slumped over, her face falling into the dirt and leaves with a hard thump.

I stood, horrified, the tail and the suit still in my hand, her lifeless body in front of me. An incredible mixture of emotions passed through my body in that moment, a mix I had never felt all at one time, before or after: power, fear, horror, and, I had to admit, a tiny flash of joy.

Instinct took over, and I threw the rhinestone catsuit as far as I could toward the woods and ran to the other side of the backyard, where I had to stop to puke by a log, the thought of her face-first on the forest floor, her limbs splayed at weird angles, seared into my brain. I kept heaving until I had nothing left, wiping spittle from the corners of my mouth and trying to swallow away the horrible mix of Kool-Aid, alcohol, and stomach acid that was still on my tongue.

But as I sat down on the log panting, I realized exactly what I had to do.

I needed to pull myself together, go back into the party, act natural, and blend in. And I knew with complete clarity all of a sudden that Drake would take the fall for this. His sperm inside her. A clear rape and assault. It was him or me, and it wasn't going to be me. I didn't owe him anything. He had never been kind to me either.

Walking quickly back to the deck and slipping through the glass doors, rap music pulsating in my ears, I beelined for the snack table, downed a full glass of Kool-Aid, and gobbled cookies with frosted ghost faces until my mouth finally tasted better. Another glass of Kool-Aid and my senses started to dull. Soon I was on the dance floor, moving with more fervor than I ever had, waving my arms around wildly.

People began to ask where Allison was, but someone said they thought she had a curfew and was picked up by her mom and no one panicked. I stumbled back to the bus stop, throwing

Grandma's gloves away in the garbage can by the bus shelter. I got home after midnight and puked one more time before bed.

Allison's body was found in the late morning, and Drake did take the fall, his future ruined. Her friends mourned like I had never seen. Over a thousand people came to her funeral in a megachurch that had to provide overflow rooms. I faked grief while I watched the real tears from my classmates flow and flow and never stop. Jealousy overtook me again. If I had died, I would have been lucky if ten people from high school had come.

I was never the same, of course. Nightmares, headaches, my grades dropped even further than they had been. I fell into a deep funk. I abandoned any idea of being near the Fun Bunch. I couldn't even look at them anymore.

Raven and I never talked about our fight that Friday night, but we did move on, becoming friends again, cautiously at first and then more firmly as time passed. Raven, Anna, and I continued running around with the hardened crowd and got in trouble for shoplifting, underage drinking, and driving without a license.

For more than a year, I never told anyone what happened.

One spring afternoon our senior year, Raven and I were out back smoking cigarettes after school by the baseball field.

"I never thought I'd pass frickin' chem," Raven said, handing me the cigarette. "Asshole gave me a D-minus, but it's enough. What a messed-up high school this is. So much shit has happened. I still can't believe that bitch Allison was killed by her boyfriend. Stuck-up little snot walked around with her nose in the air like her shit didn't stink, though. She deserved it."

I looked at the concrete and said nothing, taking a small drag.

"You were there that night. You didn't see anything?" Raven asked. We were just two months from graduation. I wanted to go to cosmetology school and move somewhere far from Madison, to start a new life away from these memories.

I said nothing, jiggling my foot nervously. Raven stopped smoking and cocked her head, looking at me quizzically.

"Jazzy?"

The boys' baseball team was practicing in the distance, the sound of a bat hitting a ball and a coach yelling. I still said nothing.

"Jazz?" She looked worried.

Suddenly, I felt like telling someone, an explosion of a year and a half of secrets bursting from behind my ribs and making their way to my mouth.

It came out in a rush as Raven stood slack-jawed, staring at me. To be honest, I don't know if she fully believed me. Maybe she thought it was a tale I was telling just to sound important. After all, there was no evidence for anything other than the fact that several eyewitnesses had seen Drake run off with Allison to the trees and not return for twenty-five minutes. DNA convicted him.

"You can't tell *anyone*, not one soul," I begged, suddenly not sure if I would regret divulging this.

"I won't, I promise," Raven said and continued to stare at me, eyes wide. "Holy shit, Jasmine. You're my hero!"

We never spoke of it again. But I saw her giving me side glances in second-hour Spanish. She was trying to figure out whether to believe me, I could tell.

Two weeks later Señora Goldberg handed us a quiz on the geography of Mexico. She had put the major spots on there—Mexico City, Cancún, Puerto Vallarta, Tijuana—but there were smaller ones too: Guadalajara, Oaxaca, and a little fishing village called Puerto Escondido.

Raven leaned across the aisle from her desk to mine and

whispered, "If we ever get enough money, let's run away to Puerto Escondido, OK? Just you and me. Doesn't it sound like paradise? *Puer-to Es-con-deed-oh.* I'll meet you there someday." She grinned.

"Puerto Escondido, yes," I whispered back, looking at the map and how the town nestled up against the ocean, picturing a white sand beach and endless sun. It couldn't be further from Madison, Wisconsin, in my mind or from the nightmares that still kept me up at night.

Raven, Anna, and I continued to hang for the rest of the semester, but then Raven met an older guy at her waitressing job and suddenly she was busy with him, and that summer was when I started having unprotected sex regularly and found out I was pregnant from one of the going-nowhere guys in our high school group. Mom was forced to pay for the abortion. After that, Mom told me I would have to do cosmetology school on my own. I only lasted a semester.

Raven moved with the guy from the restaurant to Atlanta but spent time back in Madison too. Her life was as transient as mine, and she worked her way through a series of hustles, drug deals, and low-level work. She never mentioned Allison again, and neither did I.

Now, as I sat on the plane by this Stephanie woman, I was thinking that Stephanie was probably in the Allison crowd of her high school. The popular group with the moms who bought them rhinestone catsuits and had their daughters' hair and makeup done at a salon just for a party. I bet Stephanie had mountains of friends in high school and tons of friends even now to go with her piles of money.

I looked at Stephanie's fingernails as she rested: a perfect manicure, each nail a pale pink. I had never had a proper manicure in my life, couldn't afford it. Had to paint my own nails, and they were always messy. I bet Stephanie had spa days all the time, getting full manis and pedis, sitting in saunas and steam rooms and lying on tables for massages with hot stones. I'm sure she enjoyed facials where experts worked to minimize any wrinkles.

Her ID in my bra poked at me again, reminding me that I had her driver's license but not her money. I needed those credit cards, needed the chance to disappear into her life if I wanted to.

When we got to the gate, I said, "Well, listen, Stephanie, wish me luck in Denver! Have a great time at your conference!"

"Thanks—have fun visiting your friend. Nice to meet you."

She pulled down the old lady's purse and coat and handed them back to her.

"Thank you, dear," the woman said. "You both have wonderful trips now."

"You too," I said with a smile.

We walked off the plane, and I waved to Stephanie, turning left, following the signs toward ground transportation, as she turned toward her gate.

But instead of going any farther, I ducked into a different nearby gate and pulled out my phone, pretending I was checking messages. I needed to give it a few minutes for her to get farther away and then see what time Stephanie's flight left. I had to either get on that exact plane or another one soon after to follow her to San Diego. I would have to pay cash again.

Standing up and slowly making my way to where I could see the row of gates, I made sure she wasn't unexpectedly coming my way. Seeing nothing, I dashed to the closest bathroom and into the handicap stall, where I'd have more room.

Unzipping my carry-on, I quickly pulled off my jeans and

top and changed into an entirely different outfit, including Glenn's red flannel shirt. Then I stowed my John Lennon glasses in my purse, twisted my hair up as high as it would go, and put my Dodgers cap back on, tucking in all of the wisps of hair under it.

When I emerged from the stall and looked at myself in the mirror, I was pleased. It was as close to a total change as one could get without hair dye. For good measure, I grabbed my makeup bag from my purse and started applying dark eyeshadow and heavy strokes of blush.

Before I had dropped out of cosmetology school, one of my favorite classes had been Transformative Makeup, really making someone look different. We used contour sticks, foundations, and color to change the look of someone's features. Although I couldn't afford the expensive contour sticks now, I did a poor man's version with what I did have, all Walgreens makeup I had purchased over the course of many years, some past their expiration point or cracked, but oh well, they wouldn't kill me.

There was a tube of lipstick at the bottom of my purse too—an orangey color that really didn't look very good on me. Someone had left it on the sink in the women's bathroom at the bar weeks ago and never came back, so I kept it. Now it became an integral part of my disguise.

Swiping it on, I was further satisfied that anyone walking past me in an airport would not recognize me as the same person I had been just minutes before. Different clothes, different hair, hat on, glasses off, major makeup on my face now. The only thing the same was my fringed purse.

Going back into the handicap stall, I reopened my suitcase and pushed the purse into it, sitting on the top to squish it down until I could get the zipper to close. The suitcase strained against the bulk but held up. There, now the purse was hidden too.

Slipping from the bathroom, I imagined myself as a stealth ninja, occupying the quiet corners of the airport where people wouldn't be looking. I walked close to walls, kept my head down, and maneuvered behind crowds or in and out of spaces with no one taking a second glance. Moving quickly, I found the monitors where all of the departing flights were listed and located what had to be Stephanie's San Diego flight, the only one leaving anytime soon. It was about a dozen gates down in that same concourse.

My next stop was the counter where a gate agent had just finished welcoming passengers onto a plane to Phoenix. She was tidying up the desk area as I approached.

"Hi," I said. "I just had a change of plans. Can I buy a ticket to San Diego here? Whatever your next available flight is, please."

"Sure, honey." She began typing. After a few moments she said, "All I have left is the back row."

"No problem." I felt relieved. I could hide back there more successfully.

"Can I pay cash?"

"You sure can."

She handed me the boarding pass with a smile. "Have a good flight!"

I steadied my breath as I walked away. This was happening. This was actually happening. Now I needed to avoid detection before the flight and during boarding. Once I was in my seat, I would feel more confident. I would be one of the last to deplane, so I didn't think Stephanie would see me. If she got up to walk to the rear of the plane to use the restroom, I could literally pull my baseball cap over my face the way I had seen others do when they wanted a nap.

Cautiously I approached the general area of the San Diego gate, still staying one gate down as I surveyed the scene. It was crowded, people starting to fill every seat, but no Stephanie. I backed myself into a wall and glanced around.

There were three gift shops, four restaurants, a first-class lounge, and multiple bathrooms. She could be anywhere. I would have to wait. Moving to a vantage point that was more of a diagonal from her gate, I pushed myself into a dark corner and stood there, alert as a cat, quiet as a Buddha.

After about fifteen minutes, I saw her. She was walking down the concourse.

I shrank further into the wall, willing myself to take up less space.

She scanned the now overflowing waiting area and sighed before heading to an empty seat and wedging herself in.

I would wait until she boarded and then board myself. I didn't want to be last—people sometimes looked up at those who were last to board, everyone who was already seated eager to get moving and annoyed that these people might be delaying them. I planned to slip into the line at just the right time to move with the masses and be undetected by her. I only had to get past her row to the back of the plane and I'd be home free.

With my head down and my change of clothes and overall disguise, I was maybe 80 percent confident I could do this. But that 20 percent was starting to tear up my stomach. What would I do if she recognized me? I would simply have to lie, to pretend I was someone else. With the change of clothes and makeup, if I admitted I was the person who was on her last flight and said I had a sudden change of heart to go to San Diego, she would be incredibly suspicious.

No, lying was the only way. I bit my nails as I thought about the whole horrid scenario that could unfold. I'm walking down the aisle, and she looks up and says, *Jasmine? Is that you from my last flight? What are you doing here?*

My mind shot back to cosmetology school. There had been a woman in my class with a thick Southern accent. I always enjoyed listening to her speak, and now, as I stood there, minimizing myself against the wall, I conjured up that accent again and silently rehearsed saying *Sorry, ya got the wrong gal* in a strong Texas twang. Hopefully that would be enough to throw her off the trail.

My only other concern was that Stephanie might be in the same row as me, but I dismissed that. Anyone traveling for business was not going to be in the last row, the one where you couldn't push your seat back and were right next to the bathrooms. No way.

I watched her do various things on her phone. As they began to call rows for boarding, I held my breath, praying I was right when it came to where she'd be sitting. She boarded with the second group—not first class, but still a way better seat than mine. I slipped into line ahead of about a dozen other people and handed the gate agent my boarding pass.

Stephanie's ID poked again at my left breast, and I gently rearranged it to a more comfortable position. As the line moved through the jetway to the plane, I took a deep breath and pushed the brim of my cap lower to cover more of my face. I wanted to look for her, to see exactly where she might be sitting, but the risk was too high. If I looked up, full face, and she happened to be looking to the front of the plane at that exact time, I could be screwed. Better to keep the head down. Walking that way all the way to the back of the plane, I felt like I might faint the entire way.

The last rows were already packed except for my empty seat. I would have to be in the middle. As I reached my row, the flight attendant stopped me.

"Hey, we're getting real full up top back here. I might need you to gate-check that roller."

My knees went weak. Gate-check? I hadn't considered that possibility. There was no way I could part with this bag. It had everything I owned in it, literally everything, including my purse. Without it I wouldn't have a cent.

"Uh . . ." I stammered, unsure how to handle this unexpected curveball. I couldn't make too big of a scene, but there was no way I would allow this bag out of my sight. "Is there anything we can do?" My voice came out weak and thin, and I could see how pathetic I looked in her eyes.

"I think there's room next to my bag," a guy with a wide smile in the row up from me said. He winked. "I don't like waiting for bags when I land either."

Clicking open an overhead bin, he lifted my suitcase so easily it could have contained feathers. With a small push, he got it in next to others.

"Well then, problem solved," the flight attendant said, and relief coursed through me.

I took one quick peek up toward the front of the plane, trying to see if I could recognize Stephanie. I thought I saw her, also in a middle seat.

Wedging into my spot, I stayed there for the duration of the flight, my cap tipped partially down and my mind racing for my next plans. By the time we landed, Glenn would be blowing up my phone. My stomach tightened at the thought, memories of him dragging me by my hair into his truck, screaming at me for trying to leave him. His anger would be unstoppable on this one. He would be ballistic that there was no steak dinner waiting for him too.

I planned to never answer his calls again. In fact, I would block his number so that he couldn't keep bothering me. I couldn't keep lying to him about my whereabouts—that time had passed. It was now time for the disappearing act.

And I had this plan, this crazy plan, that had come into my mind. Get Stephanie's credit cards. Maybe more. Maybe. I might bail on the big part, the really big part, and just take the credit cards, but I would get a few things lined up just in case.

I wished I could be writing down the order of things for my next moves—it would be easier to remember and keep track of—but I couldn't risk my seatmates seeing anything. This would all have to be in my head. I bit my fingers as I rehearsed the order again and again: land; get off the plane; get a rental van—it dawned on me that I would need one with a wheelchair lift, just in case; figure out which Hilton was five miles from the beach in La Jolla; look up cheap motels within a few miles of there; find a Walmart; buy scissors, hair dye, plastic gloves, and the largest suitcase I could find. Maybe get something slightly nicer than what I was wearing to complete the look that I was a high-powered executive.

Next would be getting to Stephanie's hotel in the middle of the night. The rest was almost too much for me to think about. I knew what I planned to do, knew what I needed to do in order for this to truly work, but the thought of it was making my stomach turn. What if it didn't work? What if it did? Each thought was almost equally horrifying, and yet I was on autopilot now. A woman on a mission.

Any missteps might ruin me, I needed to stay focused. One task at a time. I could always back out of the plan if I got too scared. But I could never go back in. This was my only chance, my only true way of escaping Glenn, my mother, my siblings, everyone. There was literally no one in my world that I couldn't do without. Sure, I would miss Anna and the bar waitresses, but friends came and went. I would find someone new to hang with in Mexico.

Money. I was hemorrhaging my own money, and it was only the first day of my departure. The ticket to San Diego, a rental van, a motel room, a suitcase, hair dye, all expenses I hadn't counted on when the day had started. That was why I needed to do what I needed to do. I needed Stephanie's money first and foremost; the rest would unfold for me in some way. Nothing could be accomplished without money. If I had just been able to grab Stephanie's credit card in addition to her ID, would I be planning what I was now planning? I wasn't sure. If I had, perhaps I could have stolen some of her money before she realized it, but I also wouldn't have access to her full accounts; I wouldn't have her laptop and phone and clothes and everything else I coveted about her.

She seemed nice enough, I reasoned as I bit my nails, but she had been able to live the wealthy American lifestyle for a long time. Long enough. She was a grown-up version of Allison, expensive shampoo and doting parents and money dripping off her.

It was my turn to have a dream. I was so sick of other people getting all of the breaks, and she seemed to be one of those people. Probably a fancy high school followed by a fancy college fully paid for by her rich parents. A handsome husband who was captain of some team while she was a cheerleader. A perfect pregnancy and amazing child. A family who still held Thanksgiving around a cozy table with a log crackling in the fireplace, playing board games after dinner, laughing and sharing inside jokes as they ate homemade pumpkin pie with dollops of real whipped cream on top, not the kind that came in a can like I always had.

I bet she had a walk-in closet draped with clothes and jewelry too. I could see her house and her life in my mind. Banquets and art openings and who knew what else on weekends. As I thought about it, I got angrier and angrier. It was time for me to have a life of luxury and ease. I would be outthinking and outsmarting everyone, from Glenn to Stephanie. I just needed to take this one gentle step at a time.

It was dark outside when the plane landed. I couldn't believe I was in San Diego instead of Denver, how different a day could be from how you envisioned it. Looking toward the front, I saw Stephanie and the rest of the passengers standing up and collecting their bags. Her robin's-egg blue purse flashed at me as she put it over her shoulder.

"I'll get your bag," the man with the big smile said and pulled it down, plopping it on its wheels and even spinning it the right way and lifting the handle for me. "There you go."

He seemed so fatherly it gave me a sharp pang for the man I never knew.

Pulling my phone out of my pocket, I turned it off airplane mode. It took a few seconds to catch up, but then the text button lit up with eight new messages and the phone icon showed six voicemails. I knew what they would say before I even opened or listened to them. All from Glenn, of course, in an escalating staircase of anger. Yet I couldn't help myself from hitting play on the first voicemail.

"Jasmine, baby, where are you? I love you so much. Don't do this. What are you thinking? Come home, sweetie. I'll change, I promise . . ."

In the sixth and final voicemail, his tone had completely changed.

"Are you fucking serious with this shit? You're going to tell me you're making me a steak and then take off? I will find you, Jasmine. You can't hide. I will hunt you down. And I do mean hunt. You won't ever get away with this, bitch."

A shiver hit me and I felt a renewed purpose. I had to hide from this psycho permanently. The thought of the hunting rifle he kept hanging on the living room wall made my whole body go numb.

This was the new me, though. Deleting all of the voicemails, I went to my contact list and scrolled to his name, hitting block. I was never going to hear from him again. Glenn's anger sharpened my focus. I glanced ahead to where Stephanie was and thought, *Sorry, but this has to be done. There is simply no other way. Time for a woman to help a woman out of a jam.*

We all shuffled off the plane. I saw Stephanie walking far down from me, headed toward baggage claim. I followed the signs to rental cars. It took several agencies to find a wheelchair-lift van. After getting the keys, I sat in the parking lot calling up Hiltons in the area and mapping the distance to the beach until I found hers. Next came motels. One was just a mile from the Hilton. There was a Walmart down the block from it. Perfect. Steering the car that way, I kept repeating to myself, "I'm in California, I'm in California, I'm half a country away from Glenn and going to be further soon."

The San Diego landscape already looked so different from Madison, even in the dark. The air was warmer, a sea breeze in it, palm trees dotting every street. People were out running in shorts and T-shirts; a bright red light-rail train went whizzing by; the houses had Spanish-tile roofs and were built lower to the ground, many a sort of a creamy peach color I wasn't used to. This was a different world, that was for sure, and I couldn't wait to take a big bite out of it once I had money and nice clothes.

At Walmart, I studied the rows of hair dyes, carefully slipping Stephanie's ID out of my bra and looking at her hair color. A medium brown, I would call it, and I found a shade labeled just that. Adding hair-cutting scissors, plastic gloves, the largest suitcase I could find, a decent-looking professional top on a sale rack, a new purse in a bland shade of beige, a Diet Coke to keep me up, and some beef jerky for protein, I took my haul to the motel and got to work.

Standing in front of the mirror, I said a little goodbye to my long blond hair and started chopping. Once I got it to the proper length and it looked reasonably even across the bottom, I turned to the dye. The color went on easily, but I had to wait thirty minutes for it to set, so I flipped channels and nervously drank my soda and nibbled at the beef jerky. My appetite was not very strong, and my stomach was tight and tense. Abandoning the jerky on the nightstand, I chewed my fingernails instead and thought about the next move in my chess game.

It was getting close to eleven p.m., and I needed to wait until I was sure Stephanie would be asleep. Any sort of conference was bound to kick off by nine a.m. at the latest, so I was sure Stephanie would try to be asleep by two. I also guessed she had checked in with the evening team at the Hilton. I wanted to arrive when the overnight team was there so that no one would possibly remember her checking in earlier, just in case. After working in hotels myself, I knew there would be a shift change when the 2:30-to-10:30 p.m. crew left.

Sliding Stephanie's ID out of my bra again, I studied her picture for a long time, then looked at myself in the mirror. It was uncanny how much I now looked like her if you had never met me or her. If you had, you might notice that I was a little thinner with a slightly longer chin and eyes set farther apart, but our noses were close enough, and the rest could definitely be missed by anyone who didn't know either of us. And she had told me in our conversation that she had never met any of these news directors.

Stepping into the shower to rinse off the hair dye, I turned the hot water up almost as high as it would go, washing off Glenn and my past. Taking the soap and scrubbing every inch of my body, I got all of the blush, dark eyeshadow, and orange lipstick off with a washcloth, then watched as the brown hair dye circled the drain and slithered away.

I thought of Stephanie, totally oblivious to my plan, in her hotel room a mile away, thinking she was getting ready for a conference. I was sorry for what I might do, I truly was, but I couldn't see another path. And I had asked my grandma to guide me, then been seated by this woman. Wasn't that a sign from the universe? Clearly, I was supposed to meet Stephanie and use her for whatever I needed.

Blow-drying my hair with the tiny hair dryer that was stuck to the wall of the motel bathroom, I changed back into the nicest clothes I had with me, including the shirt I had just purchased at Walmart. It was made of thin material but had a floral print and a simple neckline. It looked better than the mostly dirty and crumpled clothes in my own suitcase. I was passable as a conference attendee arriving late at night. I wasn't planning to use my fringed purse at the front desk. Not only did it not look like it belonged to a professional woman, but I was cognizant that there would likely be security cameras in the hotel lobby, and if anything were to go awry, I didn't want to be recognized by Stephanie in any way, shape, or form.

I swapped out my own driver's license for Stephanie's,

slipping her ID into the plastic holder of my wallet and putting my own license into my bra; then I tucked the wallet into the new beige purse and returned to the bathroom to apply makeup. This time I tried to emulate what Stephanie had on in her ID photo and what I had seen on the plane. Neutrals and pinks. Nothing gaudy, nothing that screamed, *Look at me.* Just boring, professional makeup. When I was done, I stepped back and admired my work, turning my head from side to side. It really was uncanny. Grinning at my image, I clicked off the bathroom light and returned to bed.

It was still not yet midnight, so I lay down carefully on my back, so as not to mess up the makeup, and shut my eyes, willing myself into a meditative state. Visions of my recent life began to dance: the bar on rocking nights when everyone and everything seemed fun, the early days with Glenn when he would make me pancakes in the morning and deliver them to me in bed. How he insisted on opening that passenger door. *Stay with the good thoughts, Jasmine,* I told myself. *Don't think about the bad.*

I drifted off.

But suddenly, Allison's face came to mind, red lips, head thrown back, laughing at the party, tail in her hand; that was followed by the thought of Glenn's face laughing after he smothered me with that pillow. I shuddered, jerking out of the half-sleep.

I sat up and slugged the rest of the Diet Coke, pulled the tags off the big suitcase, put a few more items of my own clothing in there, plus my baseball cap and makeup in case I needed them, and went to the minivan outside.

CHAPTER 36

Jasmine

Going to the Hotel

It was only a few minutes to the Hilton, and I pulled into a spot where I could see through large picture windows into the lobby. The clerk at the desk was a heavyset older woman who sat looking at her phone.

There was almost no one coming and going. To be sure, though, I waited. Fifteen minutes later, a few partiers got out of an Uber and staggered into one another, laughing loudly as they walked through the sliding glass doors. The clerk looked up and nodded at them. A guy came down and asked for something. I saw the clerk reach into a drawer. Her hand emerged with a toothbrush, and she passed it across the counter. I studied the direction the guests walked in so that I would look like I knew where the elevators were and wouldn't have to ask. I needed to look as if I had been there before.

By one a.m., there had been no guests in the lobby for at least thirty minutes. It was time. My heart started pounding, but I reminded myself again why I was here and how this would help me. *One step at a time, Jasmine. Just do this one step. If someone gets suspicious, you run, get back to Walmart, buy black dye, cut your hair to a pixie cut, and get the heck out of Dodge.*

Slowly I slid from the driver's seat and walked to the rear of the minivan to retrieve the suitcase. It was huge, meant for a family going to Disneyland or something. I hoped I didn't look too comical, but I couldn't think of another way. Drawing in one more breath of the San Diego air that just felt different, I threw my shoulders back and kept my chin up in a confident, professional stature, then strode as calmly as I could toward the lobby.

The glass doors slid open and the woman at the desk looked up. Smiling, I glided over. Someone at a previous job had once told me that if you keep smiling and look confident, people will believe just about anything you say.

This was it.

"Hello, I checked in earlier, but I seem to have misplaced my room key."

"OK, no problem," the woman replied. "What's your room number?"

"Oh, I'm such a dummy. I go to so many conferences for work," I faked. "I'm sorry, but I don't remember."

"We can look it up. What's your name, and may I see your ID, please?"

"Sure, Stephanie Monroe, I'm here for the news conference." Opening up my Walmart purse, I pulled out my wallet and pushed the ID forward. My heart was a jackhammer. She glanced at the ID, then up to my smiling face and back down again.

"Very good, Stephanie. Room 630—here you go. I'll give you two just in case you lose one again."

My mouth went dry, but I kept on smiling. She slid me two key cards, and I thanked her and turned toward the elevators, trying to walk at a normal pace.

Stepping onto the elevator, I had a feeling of being outside of my body, of this being a movie and not really happening. I was lightheaded.

The sixth-floor hallway was quiet, not a noise to be heard. I really couldn't believe I had made it this far, had followed Stephanie and done everything I needed to do to impersonate her and get a card to her room.

But a new thought came into my mind. What if Stephanie had more than just the main door lock on in her hotel room? What if she had one of those security locks that acts like a chain and doesn't allow an outside visitor to come in? My confidence faltered as I walked toward room 630. What would I do then? All of the money I had just spent would be blown, a total bust. I would have to slink back to my motel in shame and figure out what to do. Maybe I could try again the next night, or the next, if I had to. It wouldn't be ideal, me as "Stephanie" coming into the hotel in the middle of the night all the time, and I only had a few nights to do this. She had told me she was flying home this weekend, and today was Wednesday, but maybe the real Stephanie would forget the latch or be too drunk one night to use it.

Rolling the suitcase down to 630, I stood outside her room for a moment, summoning up the final bit of courage I needed to go through with this. *Now or never, Jasmine, now or never.* Putting my ear to the door, I thought I could hear the low hum of a TV but wasn't sure. There was no movement, though. She must be asleep. And if she wasn't? If she heard me and called out *Who's there?* when I opened the door, I sketched a plan to lower my voice an octave and say, *Housekeeping, sorry, mistake*, then dash away before she saw me.

Pulling a rubber glove from my pocket, I put it on before touching anything. Couldn't risk DNA being discovered.

My hand went to the metal of the door handle, and I let it sit there for several seconds before gently touching the key card to the black square reader above the handle. It made a soft click, and the light turned green. Pushing the handle slowly down, I braced myself in case the safety lock prevented me from going farther.

But the door kept opening. There was no extra lock.

Holy shit, I was in.

Peering around, I saw it was dark except for an old episode of *The Golden Girls* playing on TV. Stephanie was sleeping on her side, a bottle of some sort of prescription on the nightstand next to her. I recognized her hair in the semidarkness. She must have crashed with the TV on.

Letting the door close very quietly behind me, I moved like a ninja again, resting the giant suitcase against a wall so it was out of the way and setting my purse on top of it. Surveying the scene, I saw clothes hung neatly in the closet and expensive shoes—oh, those shoes—lined up on the floor. Black pumps, cream flats, funky tennis shoes, running sneakers. They sparkled like jewels to me. Her robin's-egg blue purse sat on top of the long, flat dresser. A quick glance into the bathroom showed me expensive cosmetics, a curling iron, and a flat iron.

I could hear her deep breathing. She was sound asleep. Moving with a little more confidence now, I got to her side to see the prescription medicine bottle next to her. Picking it up, I read the drug name: zolpidem. That was the official name of Ambien, the same drug Glenn used. Wow, what a coincidence. I knew this drug, knew how it knocked him out. The fact that this fancy lady had to use it too made me silently laugh. It must be another sign from Grandma. This was almost too perfect.

Grabbing the remote, I thought I might turn the TV off, the sound of canned laughter from *The Golden Girls* seeming too odd for the moment that was about to transpire, but then I realized that turning it up a few notches might be smarter, just in case someone were to hear anything. I hit the volume button twice, and the laughter got just a bit louder, the women arguing over an exercise class they all wanted to take. Female friendship. Would Stephanie have been my friend in the real world? I didn't think so. She was several economic tiers above me, and if I had run into her in high school, I bet she would have been living in Maple Hills. If I met her later in life, I would have been nothing more than an anonymous service worker to her. Yes, she chatted with me on a plane, but I was sure she'd forgotten all about me by now, moving on to her gorgeous friends and clothes.

My guess was that she had probably spent her whole life tipping people like me but never going beyond. Did she volunteer for battered women's groups? I doubted it. Did she donate money to causes that would truly help anyone? Debatable. She was a richy-rich, what we called a "Maple Hills Molly" when I was growing up. Polite, not disparaging, but not truly in my corner either. The kind of person who had probably never been in a car not advertised as "luxury." The kind of person who thought organizing a glittering banquet fundraiser with silent auction items that included trips to Paris, box seats at sporting events, and full spa days was truly helping the homeless. I had been a cocktail waitress at some of those events, eavesdropping as the moms gave one another tips on the top cruise lines, the new boutique in town, and the tutors they used to help their kids get into the best colleges.

It was comeuppance time. In some ways, it felt like the

entire underbelly of America might be cheering with me. The workers who really made conferences like this possible. Those cleaning the toilets, making the beds, mixing the drinks, and cooking the food; those driving the airport shuttle vans and working late nights at a bar just to make ends meet; those like me who had been living in a trailer home.

What I was about to do felt oddly like a lifetime of vindication against the elite, the ones who had it so good they didn't even recognize it. Their gripes were about how they couldn't get a reservation at a popular new hotspot or how the contractors had screwed up the bathroom remodel *again* by using the wrong tile *again*. They didn't have a clue what real life was like.

The bed was littered with so many fluffy white pillows that one had fallen to the floor. I picked it up, keeping an eye on Stephanie. She was out.

Positioning myself next to her, I planted my legs wide to create a base of support. Her eyelids fluttered, and she let out a soft snore. My heart jerked for a moment. I had been a lot of things in my life. Up until this point, premeditated murderer had not been one of them. Murderer, yes, I guess, but not premeditated. There was a difference. Everyone thought it was Drake—except Raven, who knew the truth. But my reputation was clean in most people's minds.

Here I was again standing on a cliff in my world. I could go back right now, put her ID in her wallet, leave her room, never bother her again, never see her again, and figure out my next move without her, or I could go through with a moderate version of my plan, stealing a credit card or two and then leaving. If I enacted the full plan, though, I would have access to everything she owned and plenty of time to make a run for it.

I pondered the three options for a moment as I stood above her. If I left now, I would have wasted time and money getting to San Diego for no reason. If I stole her credit cards, she would surely notice at some point tomorrow, so my window of opportunity would be very, very small. The choice seemed simple. I rolled her onto her back, took a deep breath, and closed my eyes.

CHAPTER 37

Jasmine

In the Hotel Room

Glenn's face is what came to mind first. I imagined that the person under the pillow was him, a weak, pitiful version of him, and I was the physically strong one.

Then I pictured Allison. Her words from the party flew through the air at me in Stephanie's hotel room like tiny swords:

What a pathetic cat outfit, Jasmine.

You crazy bitch.

You are so fucked up, Jasmine.

My mother floated to my brain next. Her telling a friend she never should have had a third child. Her calling me "Little Piggy" and making me wear pigtails. That final card with the words "Have a very Merry Christmas."

This trio of people taunted me as slowly, slowly I brought the pillow down and covered Stephanie's face, pressing as hard as I could.

Within a few seconds, I heard her coughing and fussing about. I pressed harder. She began to flail. She was stronger than I thought, and I had a sudden fear that she might overpower me. The angle I was at was not going to work, so I kept pressing and climbed onto the bed, straddling her waist for a firmer position.

I thought of only Glenn again, and renewed strength came into my limbs as I pressed down.

Stephanie's arms and legs thrashed wildly, but I was winning. I heard her gasping for air, *The Golden Girls'* laugh track offering a sickly ambient noise.

My breathing was ragged, but my limbs felt electric with adrenaline. Sweat popped out on my forehead.

Slowly, her movements got lighter and less frequent and then stilled. I kept the pillow on her face for an extra sixty seconds, counting carefully to myself.

Lifting the pillow a few inches, I took a peek around the edge, ready to restore it if she moved at all.

Her face was frozen in a state of shock, mouth and eyes open, a single tear falling from one eye toward her temple. Seeing her dead made my stomach curdle, and I raced to the bathroom and threw up the beef jerky and Diet Coke.

I had just killed someone. For a second time. What. The. Fuck. Like murder, real premeditated murder this time. A woman I barely knew, a woman who had woken up in her home in Madison that morning without a clue that she would be gone within twenty-four hours in a hotel room in San Diego.

But it needed to be done, I reminded myself. There was no other way. She'd had a way better life than mine for however old she was. It was my turn to have a way better second half of life.

OK, now I had to focus.

Her face was disturbing me, so I got the pillow and placed it back over her head. Picking up my phone, I used it to google "rigor mortis." It would set in about three to four hours after death. OK, I had to get her scrunched into the giant suitcase before then, but I had a tiny bit of time. Grabbing her laptop, I flipped it open.

There was a yellow Post-it note stuck to the screen. It said "Phone and laptop passwords: EvanFred0503."

What? How could anyone be *so* stupid as to advertise their passwords? I felt like I had just hit a bull's-eye in darts, cranked a home run out of the park, or earned a gold medal in figure skating. I mean, WTF?! This had to be yet another sign from my grandma that I had just done the right thing. There was simply no other explanation.

"Thank you, Gram," I muttered, bringing my hands into a prayer motion and looking up at Stephanie's hotel ceiling.

I had no time to waste in celebration, though. Logging in, I started opening all of her pages and scrolling through to see what I could learn. She had tabs across the top for work email, personal email, something called LinkedIn (which I had heard Anna talk about but had never tried myself), Facebook, Twitter (or whatever it was called now), Google Docs, and TikTok. First, I took a quick peek at her personal email. There was a back-and-forth with some female friends about tickets to Florida for a girls' trip.

"Bring on the vacay—I need it! Strawberry margs are definitely calling my name! I booked us a super cool Airbnb on the beach!" Stephanie had written in the last one. Another richy-rich privilege the rest of us didn't get to have. Weekend getaways, Airbnbs on the beach. *Not going to happen now, spoiled bitch,* I thought as I glanced back at the bed.

Next I went to the files under the desktop icon. Scrolling through ones with boring titles like "Taxes," "San Antonio trip photos," and "New friend, Diana," I finally spotted the one I was looking for: "Passwords." This was it, the holy grail.

Clicking it open, she had everything neatly laid out by category, and I spotted the one I was hoping to see: banking. It listed all of her passwords for her online bank accounts. They were variations of "Evan" and "Fred" and numbers, sometimes with an exclamation point or some other sort of punctuation at the end.

I had done it. I had hacked into exactly what I would need to drain her money.

Next I looked at LinkedIn. It was some sort of professional work site, and I checked her profile, hoping to learn more, to memorize details so that I could spit them out in the morning when I attended the conference.

I had to make an appearance as her, I knew that, to make my story believable. She couldn't just not show up at the conference at all. Someone would question her absence, maybe call back to her station. No, her name tag had to be picked up, her presence visible at least for a bit. A day was my plan. She had told me on the plane that she had never met any of these people, that there were thousands of news directors across the country and this group was all new to her. I felt confident I could pull off being her for a day, but to be sure, I needed more info.

Her background on LinkedIn was laid out to me clearly in a résumé-style list: went to DePaul, was from Indiana originally, had worked in Chicago before Madison. That was easy enough. Just in case, I looked up the mascot for DePaul (Blue Demons) and the names of the freshmen dorms so that I would sound authentic if anyone said they also went there. I scribbled these all down on my paper.

OK, Jasmine, what have you forgotten? I picked up her phone, and the password let me right in and I started looking through her texts. Who did she converse with? There was a chain with her son, Evan; a chain with what maybe was a sister named Renee who called her "Little"; a chain with someone named Robert; and a chain with someone named Bruce. Those were all at the top, the most recent. Based on the conversations, I surmised that Bruce was a coworker and Robert a friend, maybe a neighbor. My plan was to try and buy time with all of them until I could get the money that I needed. Make sure they weren't suspicious.

It was only Wednesday night now, so I knew I had some wiggle room. If I faked being her at the conference tomorrow and then spent Friday dealing with bank stuff, it seemed that it would all work out perfectly. I would find some excuse to extend her trip via text with friends and family and then just stop texting at some point and ditch the phone. They would never know. They would think she just disappeared into the night and would never find her.

As for the body . . . my eyes flitted back to the bed . . . I had to get moving. I needed to fold her limbs into the giant suitcase before rigor mortis overtook her, and then I had to wait. I couldn't take her out of here now—the same desk clerk would be on duty, and it would be weird for me to leave with the giant suitcase so soon after checking in.

No, I would have to do that in a different shift, and I had a plan. This close to the ocean, there had to be out-of-the-way spots to dump a body in the water. I would need weights, of course, so that she didn't float to the top. I bit my fingernails and thought. I should have gotten those at Walmart too. Damn it, my first misstep.

Then a thought thumped its way across my temples. I was in a hotel! There had to be a gym, the kind with lots of hand weights all lined up and ready for use. My eyes darted to Stephanie's rolling suitcase. I could take that bag to the weight room at an off time, fill it with some weights, and wheel it back here, where I could put the weights in the big suitcase with her. My only concern was that the body not smell in the meantime. I could wheel it out during the day even, or the evening, after the conference tomorrow, but I couldn't do it right now. I might need some ice to keep her cold. First, though, getting her into the suitcase.

Going to the bed, I started to pull her toward me. She was damn heavy. Not an overly large woman but heavy nonetheless. I grunted and groaned as I twisted her this way and that. Positioning the suitcase next to the bed, I let her drop into it with a thud, hoping it didn't wake other hotel guests; then I folded her up into the smallest size I could make her, pushing her limbs. She just barely fit. Testing out closing the suitcase, I was thrilled that it worked. No one would have a clue if I rolled her out right through the lobby. But the smell? I went back to my phone and googled: It can happen within twenty-four hours. There must be an ice machine down the hall. Just to be safe, I could pile some ice around her, but not just on its own—that would melt and make the suitcase wet and gross. I needed some bags.

Looking around, I didn't see an ice bucket, but in the closet there was one plastic bag clipped to a clothes hanger and labeled LAUNDRY. In the bathroom I saw a couple of hair ties. Those could help to keep the bag tight.

Taking the bag and slipping out of the room and down the hall, I peered around for the ice machine. But it was not on one end of the hallway, not by the elevator, and not on the other end of the hallway. What the heck? Every motel I had ever worked in had an ice machine and soda vending area. As I walked back to my room, it hit me. The few really fancy hotels I had been employed by never had them. You had to call housekeeping for ice. Damn. A miscalculation. What to do now? I guess I had twenty-four hours to figure it out before she really smelled.

When I returned to the room, it was almost 2:30 a.m., and I surmised the conference was starting in six or so hours. In order to be Stephanie, I would need to wear her clothes and act like a news director. I couldn't start transferring any money or making any rash moves in the middle of the night. That would be suspicious. No, it had to look as if Stephanie herself had just decided to skip out on life after this conference. That would have to happen during the day.

Going to her closet, I surveyed her clothing, feeling the fabrics with my fingers. Most of my clothes came from Goodwill, but hers were clearly many notches up. A green shirt was so buttery to the touch that it felt almost magical; a pink blazer had a thickness to it that showed it was made well; a navy sweater looked and felt cozy. We were close enough in size that I wasn't too worried about the fit but decided to try everything on anyway. I didn't want to show up at the conference looking odd.

Stripping down to my underwear and bra, I started trying on each piece, turning this way and that and looking at myself in the mirror. The green shirt was just a bit too baggy for my liking. Her pants were roomy in the waist. Either I would be hiking them up all the time or I needed a belt, which I didn't see. She had a cute little black dress, though, and that looked good on me. I loved the way the soft material felt on my skin and admired the flowiness of the skirt. Twirling in satisfaction, I grabbed the pink blazer and put it over the dress. Pretty. The blazer fit me well.

Now for shoes. I picked up a pair and looked at the size.

Damn, she was one size larger than me. The tan-and-cream flats she had in the closet wouldn't work then—they'd be falling off. My best bet was a sort of a high-heeled tennis shoe thing. I could wear two pairs of her socks inside those if need be. I went to the drawers of the dresser to hunt for socks, and that's when I saw her pretty bras and underwear. Even her practical-looking underwear was nicer than anything I owned. She also had a bunch of Spanx in there and a multitude of sock options. I couldn't help but try on a black lacy bra and a pair of bikini underwear. It felt so good to have nice clothes on. I decided to wear those the next day too, not my old ratty pair.

Next I moved to the bathroom and inspected her makeup and smelled her perfume. So nice, so well-made. The names on the sides of the makeup were brands I knew you couldn't find at a drugstore. The perfume had an Italian-sounding name. Spritzing some on my wrist, I took a satisfying whiff. It was like a bouquet of flowers, very different from the patchouli I usually wore, but this was the new me now. I was going to be keeping this perfume, that was for sure.

Out of things to do and with several hours yet to go, I changed into her workout clothes, since her pajamas were still on her, then got into the king-size bed where Stephanie had just been but moved to the side away from where her body had lain. That was too creepy. I had a big role to play the next day, so I needed some sleep. Looking at her iPhone to see when she had her alarm set, I kept it that way and put her phone next to me on the nightstand. Finally, I clicked the TV off, *The Golden Girls* flickering to darkness, and I shut my eyes.

CHAPTER 38

Jasmine

One Day After the Flight

I wasn't sure if I would sleep, but the next thing I knew the alarm was going off and sunlight was poking around the edges of the heavy curtains. Startled, I sat up and rubbed my eyes.

Where was I?

It all came flooding back.

Glancing over at the suitcase, I saw Stephanie's body, still and curled into a fetal position. My stomach roiled. Somehow by the light of day things always seemed worse than in the middle of the night, the black magic of darkness gone.

Shit. I had killed this woman. Now I had to *be* her. Quickly I got up and made coffee with the room coffee maker. There was a minibar stocked with alcohol and snacks, and a small placard listed the outrageous prices. Still, I was very hungry, and I didn't want to risk room service, so I broke open some of the fancy cheese and ate that along with a chocolate bar, downing it all with coffee.

I took a shower and got dressed in her underwear and bra, the black dress with the pink blazer, and the funky shoes with two pairs of socks. Spraying the Italian perfume all over me, I put on her makeup and jewelry, took her robin's-egg blue purse and returned her ID to her wallet, then added her phone and mine to the purse, plus the sheet of hotel stationery where I had put my notes about Stephanie's life. I was ready.

Zipping the suitcase all the way, I put it into the corner of the room and plopped Stephanie's suitcase on top of it, just in case, so that someone who entered wouldn't see anything to suspect.

I knew from my days working at motels and hotels that housekeepers would be happy when there was a room they could skip, so I hung the DO NOT DISTURB sign on the exterior of the door handle.

Even though I had done everything I could think of, the elevator ride down had me filled with anxiety. I was heading into a strange place to pretend to be a woman I wasn't, at a conference that had topics I knew nothing about. But I had to do this little charade for at least a day. It was part of my master plan. I would just be as quiet as I could and not draw attention to myself.

When I stepped off the elevator, there was a big sign that said WELCOME TO THE NEWS COVERAGE SUMMIT. An idea hit me. Pulling Stephanie's phone out, I snapped a picture, went to her Facebook page, and posted it with the caption "I'm in San Diego for a conference. Can't wait to learn new things!" Within thirty seconds, the first like came in, and I smiled.

When I entered the ballroom, a young woman with short hair, a nose ring, and a name tag that said WILLOW was the first to speak to me.

"Good morning, can I help you find your name?"

"Yes . . . uh . . . Stephanie, Stephanie Monroe." The words sounded so unfamiliar on my lips.

"Monroe . . . here you are. Your table assignment is on the corner of the tag. Looks like you're table four. Can you sign in, please?" She handed me a pen.

The guy whose name was above mine, Trent Something-or-other, had signed so largely that it spilled into my box, but I wanted mine to be small and almost illegible anyway so that no one would know that it wasn't really Stephanie. Scribbling her name, I turned to find my table.

The ballroom was crowded, and most people were at their spots already. As I approached table four, I tried to walk in a steady, confident way but felt like I might faint. Three others were already there. A tall woman in a dark blue pantsuit and gold earrings, a short guy with curly hair and glasses in a gray suit that looked like it was made of cheaper material, and a taller guy with broad shoulders and slicked-back hair with a suit coat over a T-shirt. *Steady, Jasmine*, I told myself, *steady and calm.*

"Are you the fourth person at table four?" the tall guy asked and flashed me a smile with teeth so white I knew they had to be fake or at least mega-bleached.

"Yes," I said, controlling my voice and trying to project confidence. "My name is Stephanie Monroe."

"Trent McCarthy, NBC6, Atlanta, and it certainly is nice to meet *you*, Stephanie." He gave me a full up-and-down look. I realized that this was likely the guy who signed his name in such a sprawling way, and based on that, his white teeth, and his leering eyes, I did not like him.

The woman and the other guy introduced themselves and asked what station I was from. My mind raced back to the piece of paper where I had scribbled notes, the one that now sat in Stephanie's purse on my shoulder. I couldn't remember the call letters of the station she worked at, but I knew it was CBS in Madison, so I said that and they seemed to accept it without any further questioning. We sat down, and the emcee went up onto the stage.

"Welcome, one and all. We are so excited to have you at the News Coverage Summit. I hope you all had a good trip to beautiful San Diego. We have a jam-packed few days for you, so let's get going!"

What the hell am I doing here, I thought as the speakers started up. Most of what they were talking about didn't make sense to me. I mean, I got it in a broad sense, but they were throwing around terms like "FOIA" and "VOSOT" and "package" and "stand-up" and "nat sound" and "track" and "MMJ" that were like Greek to me. I tried to stay still and stoic, though, just sitting quietly as if I were absorbing all of the information. I couldn't help sneaking a peek at Stephanie's phone once or twice to make sure no one had called or texted her (they hadn't) and at mine to make sure Glenn hadn't somehow been able to get ahold of me (he hadn't). There were two texts to me from Anna asking me if I was OK and telling me that Glenn was pissed, but I ignored them for now. The good news, though, was that there were now a dozen likes and a few comments on the fake Stephanie Facebook post I had put up. Perfect.

As we were getting close to lunch, I began to feel nervous again. Listening quietly to speakers was one thing. Conversing with strangers and pretending to be Stephanie was another.

"OK, folks, before we break for a wonderful lunch, I want to invite you all to turn to your tablemates and share things that are working in your newsrooms. Go ahead—don't be shy. Be sure everybody gets a chance to share!"

The room began humming with conversation. My anxiety spiked. What was I going to say? At table four, Trent took command, as I could have predicted.

"Dorothy . . . Alan . . . Stephanie." He pointed at each of us and looked piercingly into our eyes. I tried hard not to avert mine. "In Atlanta, I run a tight ship. I've learned over the years that if you give an inch, most will take a mile. It's also important for the boss to be decisive, so I choose what we're covering each day and stick to it. Crime is rampant, and we're known as the breaking news station. People turn to us for that, and we have to live up to it. It bleeds, it leads. You know what I mean, right, Al? How about you, how do you run things up there in the Zoo?"

The wiry guy spoke. "Well, we actually take the opposite approach from your style," he said. "We try to hear all viewpoints in the newsroom about what we should cover. I think that makes for the best newsroom atmosphere. It should be a democracy, not a dictatorship."

Immediately, I liked him more than Trent. Then the woman took her turn in a warm voice.

"We're trying community journalism in Boston. We have assigned reporters to specific neighborhoods and they are embedded there. Some even live in those neighborhoods. We do what we call 'hometown stories' and profile restaurants and people in addition to breaking news, politics, and, yes, crime. But crime is not our focus. I think people want solutions-based journalism, not just an amplification of problems. We're actually trying *not* to run out breathlessly to every breaking news scene. Just because crime happens and is the low-hanging fruit doesn't mean it automatically gets anointed to the top spot."

I knew I was next, and my mind was scrambling for something, anything to say.

"So what about you, Steph? How do you do it in Madtown?" Trent asked and grinned with those ridiculous teeth again. My distaste for him was growing.

"Umm," I answered and spit out the first thing I could think of. "We kind of do a little bit of everything you all said. You know, we just do our best to cover the news every single day."

"Uh-huh," Trent replied. "But like, what is your style?"

"My style?" I gulped. What did that mean?

"Yeah, as a news director," he added, taking a sip of water and staring at me. Dorothy and Alan were also waiting for a reply. Trent went on: "Are you someone who likes to . . . punish others? Or do you prefer, you know, a softer touch?"

I saw him wink. His attempts at innuendo were so obvious. It reminded me of guys at the bar who just tried too hard. But I had to answer something.

"Oh, ummm." I shifted in my seat, uncomfortable. "Well, my style is to be nice to everyone—but tough when I need to. I can do it all."

They all just looked at me, and I wondered if I had said something wrong. I needed to get out of there.

"Excuse me, I have to run to the restroom."

Grabbing Stephanie's purse, I dashed for the bathrooms at the back. In the stall, my head was pounding. Being someone else was exhausting, and I was living off very little sleep and only cheese, chocolate, and coffee for breakfast. My stomach growled. I needed some real food. I would have to eat something at lunch, but my original plan to stay all day at this conference was seeming more and more difficult to achieve. It would mean I would have to put on the facade for a very long time, and what if they did more "sharing" things and I looked like a fool? Would I invite suspicion then? *One step at a time, girl,* I reminded myself. *Get through lunch and then decide.*

Emerging from the restroom, I saw the attendees making their way to an outdoor plaza area with a big fireplace. Tables were set up all around, and waiters and waitresses were starting to mill about. My plan was to get away from my current table-mates and just eat quietly with a new group. I drifted toward a table off to the side and near the back and was just about to sit down next to a woman about my age when Trent came up and pushed his way past her.

"Mind if I take this seat?" he said. "There's an empty one over there for you. Stephanie and I have some unfinished business to attend to." He winked at me. The woman huffed and walked away.

"Hiya, table-four friend. I thought we should get to know each other better," he said. As we sat down, he turned his body so that it engulfed me, making me feel trapped in my chair and unable to turn my head to talk to the person on my other side. Then he started asking me questions. My brain was tired, but I managed to have enough firepower to accurately answer where I went to school (DePaul), where I was from (Indiana), and if I had any kids (a son named Evan). Trying to deflect the conversation from me, I asked him about himself. University of Illinois (he even told me what frat he was in, as if I cared), divorced, two kids, wife wanted all of his money. It started to feel too personal for a business conference.

Trent looped his arm around the back of my chair in a much-too-familiar way as we spoke, and he leaned in closely. I could smell stale coffee breath and feel his sexual desire oozing off him, and it sickened me. I mean, we had only just met. Did this guy think I would just go back to the room and sleep with him? I had seen his type many times at the bar, too many. I found myself leaning away from him as much as I could. Thankfully, the waitress approached.

"Hi, I'm Miranda, and I'll be your server today. It's a pleasure to have you with us. Are you ready to order?"

Trent turned toward her. She was very pretty, with red lipstick that made her features pop. Red lips always reminded me of Allison, but I pushed that thought down. *Twenty-seven years ago, Jasmine, twenty-seven years ago.* Trent looked the waitress up and down.

"Hiya, sweetheart," he said. "I'll take the biggest piece of chicken you've got, all right?"

He put his hand on my wrist. Reflexively, I jerked it away. His touch reminded me of Glenn giving me the bruise that was hidden under the pink blazer. Who did Trent think he was? Touching me so soon? Putting his arm up over my chair, his legs splayed open in front of me? I could tell all of his clothing was super high-end; I could see the large silver watch on his wrist; could smell the eucalyptus bodywash that I had seen in the shower. But his gut protruded over his belt, and he had so much gel in his hair that it was practically shining.

"Stephanie, what would you like?" Trent asked, reaching for my wrist again. I put my hands in my lap.

"Chicken is fine," I told the waitress and tried for a slight smile. I needed the protein.

"Anything besides water?" she asked both of us.

"Coke," said Trent in that bellowing voice he had. I shook my head. I didn't want any more caffeine right now. The waitress walked away, and the person on the other side of Trent asked him a question about some sports team in Atlanta. Trent was forced to turn toward him, and I used that moment to angle my chair to the woman on my other side. I began asking her all kinds of questions just to keep the conversation going and keep Trent away from me. I could hear Trent and the guy he was talking to changing the subject and now comparing notes about how they had managed to scam various workers over the years to do things at their condos for less money than it should have been.

"And the guy barely spoke English, so I really got him good on that one! He never knew what hit him!" Trent guffawed, and I winced, anger rising as I thought of all of the workers I knew who scrambled for every penny.

We made it through lunch, me wolfing down some chicken and drinking a lot of water to try and clear up my headache. During dessert and coffee, Trent pulled out his phone.

"Let's get a selfie!" he said to the whole table. "The best lunch group at the conference deserves a picture!"

"No, really, that's OK," I protested, thinking that photo evidence was the last thing I needed. What if he posted it and someone who knew Stephanie recognized that I wasn't her? "We can do it later, OK, Trent?" If I could hold him off, I could disappear before this happened.

"Later? No, we have to do it now! Why put it off? Come on, gang." Trent was already hustling the entire group into a huddle, and most people were complying, the women fussing with their hair and sucking in their stomachs as they posed with one hand on their hips, trying to make themselves look thinner.

"Come on, Steph, you stand right next to me," Trent said, wedging his body tightly by mine. He put one arm around my waist and squeezed my side provocatively as he extended the other arm up with the camera in one hand. I was trapped again, trapped by a man and what he wanted. I started to feel angry. But the rest of the table was laughing and jostling in for the picture. They were acting like sixteen-year-olds rather than forty- and fifty- and sixty-something news directors.

"We have to get closer, I can't see you all," commanded Trent, and he moved in even more behind me as everyone scrunched together. He pushed his crotch against my behind.

"Whoopsie, pardon me," he whispered in my ear.

I fought back nausea.

To the group, he bellowed, "OK, picture coming in five . . . four . . . three . . . two . . . one . . ."

When he said "one," I turned my head, hoping he would see more of my hair than my face in the final shot or maybe it would be blurred.

"Going on social right now!" he called out. "Who wants to be tagged?"

"Me!" called several of the women, and the whole group began crowding around him.

Trent looked over at me.

"Steph, what's your handle?"

I didn't even know what that meant.

"I'll pass, thank you."

"Aww, come on. We're just having some fun. I'm going to caption it, 'The Lunch Bunch, best News Directors in the country.'"

Did no one ever grow up? People who ran newsrooms still did this kind of stuff?

I needed to get out of here. It was suddenly very clear that I couldn't possibly stay put any longer. If people kept taking pictures, if Trent kept coming on to me, if I kept having to talk at this conference and make shit up, I might lose it and make a mistake. My original plan to stay all day looked ridiculous. I needed to bail. And I was thinking about Stephanie in the suitcase. I had to see if housekeeping had obeyed my orders and not come in today. Plus, I desperately needed ice.

"I already posted on Facebook today, I'm good," I said.

"Suit yourself." He shrugged and called out, "Planet earth, here is your social media gift for the day!" He hit a button.

The group started dispersing back toward inside, and Trent pulled ten dollars from his wallet.

"Always tip waitresses, especially those who aren't hard on

the eyes," he said to me with a wink and slid the money under his plate. Disgusting creature. I tried to smile back.

"Come on, Steph, I'll walk you to table four." He put his arm out and crooked his elbow.

"Oh, thanks . . . I, uh. I have something I have to do. I'll catch up with you." I forced myself to smile again.

"Sure," he said, straightening up and running one hand through his gelled hair. "I'll keep your seat warm for you." He grinned like a Cheshire cat.

I went to the side of the portico and looked at both my phone and Steph's again, trying to act like some important news director checking messages. In reality, I just wanted to be sure there were still no texts for either of us. There weren't. I exhaled.

Our waitress was at our table, picking up Trent's ten-dollar tip. No one else was close by, so I walked over to her.

"Excuse me," I asked. "Do you know where I can find some ice?"

She looked puzzled. "Do you mean ice water?"

"No, actually like a bag of ice, or even two," I replied, hoping that the request was not too bizarre.

"Umm, I think we have some in the back," she answered. "Aren't you going back to the conference, though?"

"I'll go back in a little bit," I answered and thought fast. "I just have some medicine in my room that I'm trying to keep cold."

"Don't you have a refrigerator?"

I was starting to get annoyed by her questions but hid it and answered back quickly. "My refrigerator is broken. I have some medicine in my room that I'm trying to keep cold."

"What room are you in? I can send it up."

I hesitated. Should I lie? Should I tell the truth? Should I avoid the question? If I lied and they found out, they might get super suspicious.

"It's . . . uh, 630," I replied, then hastily added, "but I'll take them up."

"OK," she said. "Sure, I'll go get them."

I drifted back to the door closest to the elevators and waited for her, looking at my phone again. The waitress came back with two bags of ice neatly tied at the top with zip ties.

"Do you want help?" she asked. "I can send one of the guys in back to go with you."

"No, thank you," I said, and straightened my shoulders as she handed me the bags. "I appreciate it, though."

Turning toward the elevators, I tried to walk as upright and confidently as I could. It was only when I got into the elevator alone that I crumbled, putting the bags of ice down and hunching over, rubbing my throbbing temples.

Back at the door to my room, I was relieved to see the DO NOT DISTURB sign still in place, and even more relieved when I opened the door and confirmed that the bed was unmade and the towels in the bathroom not replaced. Clearly no housekeeper had been here in my absence. The suitcase sat across the room. I felt a bit sick looking at it. I needed to get Stephanie's body away from me as quickly as I could.

Disposing of a dead body was not an easy task. I had to think through a way that wouldn't arouse suspicion. I couldn't just roll through the lobby now in the middle of the day. Someone might ask me where I was going or comment that "Stephanie" was leaving the conference with a giant rolling bag.

The back of each name tag had a tiny schedule printed on it, and I flipped mine over to read what was happening. A cocktail hour that night caught my eye. Everyone in this group was sure to either opt in for the free drinks or crash out in their room.

There might be people in the hallway, sure, but likely people not from the conference—people attending a wedding or in town for some other sort of thing. I could walk down rolling my suitcase and maybe find a side door to get to my next destination, which was . . . where?

Kicking off the black tennis shoes that were too big for me and sitting at the desk, I googled "hidden places, coastline San Diego" and found one just a few miles from the hotel.

"Completely secluded and quiet," the description said. "A short bridge goes over the deepest part. Bring a flashlight, there are no lights."

That seemed spot-on to me.

Now I needed the weights. Again, the hotel gym came to mind, and I realized suddenly that the best time was right now. It was midday, and there were not likely to be many people working out. To be safe, I would try not to look like Stephanie as I went down there, in case anyone from the conference happened to be walking through the hallway and saw me.

Putting the ice in the suitcase next to her and changing out of Stephanie's expensive clothing and back into my crappy stuff, I pulled out my trusty baseball cap and tucked my hair under it, then stepped into the bathroom, did some transformative makeup tricks to make my face look a bit different, and got out my John Lennon glasses again, adjusting them on my nose. I had no idea if hotel gyms had security cameras, but I would look around the place first to make sure I didn't see anything obvious.

Wheeling Stephanie's smaller suitcase to the gym, I peeked in the windows. Not a soul. Just a row of treadmills facing some nondescript buildings and palm trees with steppers and bikes behind the treadmills. The free weights were off to the side, lined up neatly on a rack. Using the key card to click my way in, I scanned the walls and corners for cameras. Nothing I could see. It was as sterile and empty as could be.

The weights ranged from five pounds to fifty. I walked over and started picking up the various denominations to see what felt like it could weigh down a suitcase with a body in it. I figured I needed at least a hundred pounds.

Hoisting two fifty-pound weights off the rack and into the suitcase wasn't easy, and I braced myself for a story in case anyone unexpectedly walked in on me. I was a worker taking them for cleaning, I would say if the person arriving was a guest. I was a guest wanting to use them in my room for a bit, I would say if a worker came in. Just for good measure, I threw in two twenty-pounders. I had the suitcase zipped and was out of there without a soul bothering me. I couldn't wipe the smile off my face as I sailed back to my room. Every part of my plan was working.

Carefully, I manipulated the weights into the larger suitcase, wedged around Stephanie's body and the bags of ice. It was still early afternoon, and I knew the conference downstairs was ongoing. I needed to wait at least until cocktail hour and darkness to wheel Stephanie out, to use the wheelchair lift on the minivan to get the now incredibly heavy suitcase in, and to head to the secluded spot for the dump. In the meantime, I had to rest. I was going on very little sleep from the last two nights—the first being the night I left Glenn and the second the night I arrived here.

Drawing the curtains on the room and removing my baseball cap and Lennon glasses, I wiped off some of my transformative makeup, smearing my eyeliner and eyeshadow in the process. Oh, who cared? I just wanted to sleep. Lying down in the quiet, dark room, I was completely conked out within minutes. I was having a dream that my grandma was walking with me through a forest, down a path that was littered with purses all a robin's-egg blue. It was twilight, and Grandma told me we were going to the deep spot over a river. Just as I was about to ask her what river, I heard a knocking. It startled me out of sleep, and it took me a minute to realize this was not in my dream but here in the room.

"Maintenance," a man called. "Is there a broken refrigerator in your room?"

Oh, crap—my mind raced. Why was he here? How would he know this? The stupid waitress from lunch, that's how. I had to think fast. No one could enter this room. I jumped out of bed and went to the door, opening it just a crack and peeking out.

"No, I'm OK. False alarm," I said. "It seems to be working now."

"Do you want me to come in, ma'am, and take a look?" the worker pressed. "The kitchen staff told me you had to get ice to keep medicine cold."

Shit, shit, shit.

"No, thank you. I'm fine. I think—I think—" My mind scrambled. "It just wasn't plugged in all the way. It works now. I must have bumped it when I was unpacking. I'm sorry for the hassle."

"OK, ma'am, if you're sure. We want you to have everything you need during your stay."

"I'm good, thank you. I will call if there are problems."

"OK, very good, ma'am."

Relief flooded me, and I closed the door and put my ear to it to see if I could hear him moving away. Footsteps got softer, and there was the ding of the elevator. Exhaling, I turned to go back to bed when someone knocked on my door again. What the fuck? I froze and didn't respond. The knocking got harder. Without moving I called out:

"The fridge is fine, thank you."

"Stephanie? It's Trent. From the conference. How ya doing? You OK? You never came back after lunch."

You've got to be kidding me. That asshole had resurfaced again. I stayed stock-still and hoped he would go away. How did he even know I was in here? I had never told him my room number.

"Steph from Mad-town? Did you hear me? It's Trent, from Atlanta." He was practically yelling now. A sudden panic went through me that he might raise too much of a ruckus and others would notice. I had to respond in some way. Inching toward the door, I opened it just a slight crack again. I wasn't wearing the same clothes from earlier and I didn't want him to see me all the way.

"Well, hey there," he said and leaned against the door frame. "How ya doing? We missed you at table four."

"Oh, hi, Trent. I'm sorry I didn't come back. I have a migraine."

It wasn't too far from the truth.

"A migraine? I thought you were having refrigerator problems," he replied. My panic meter shot up again.

"No, that's fixed now . . . and . . . how did you know that?"

"I just saw the maintenance guy talking to you. I'm two doors down. Listen, if you need any help with anything in your room, no need to call maintenance. I'm a super handy kind of guy. I fix everything. Just give ol' Trent a ring and I'll come down to help you."

"Thank you, I'm fine," I responded and started to close the door, but he stuck his hand out and stopped it from shutting.

"Whoa, whoa, slow down. I'm sorry you have a headache, but maybe a drink will help. I decided to bug out early from the conference too. Maybe you and I should just play hooky." He grinned, his eyes radiating desire. I was repulsed.

This jerk wouldn't leave. I had to figure out how to shake him before he manhandled his way in. If he pushed the door hard enough, there would be no way I could stop him. Fear crept into the reaches of all of my limbs.

"Really, Trent, I have a terrible headache. I get migraines and this one is bad. But if I rest tonight, I'll be back tomorrow fresh, I'm sure." I threw in a smile in what I hoped was a slightly flirtatious way. It seemed the best way to get him away from me—the promise of more later.

"Listen," he said. "Here's my key card. I have another one. I'm going down to the pool for a bit. If you want to hang out, just let yourself in." He winked at me.

I stood there, frozen, trying to decide what to do. This jerk wanted me to come down to his room. Clearly I couldn't do that. The risk of spending more time with him, him asking me questions, plying me with drinks while he tried to get into my pants. It was all way too much of a gamble, and he made me sick anyway. He reminded me of Glenn, cocky and demanding. A flash of Drake came into my mind too. Forcing sex on Allison and then running off without so much as a word. Although I despised her, his actions had always made me feel angry too. Rage started to surge. Men. I was sick of them.

And then a thought came into my head.

Maybe it wasn't a bad thing to have his key card. In fact, the most sinister plan of all started to reveal itself. If I had his key card and he was gone at the cocktail party or elsewhere . . .

I held out my hand and took the card from him, giving him that shy, flirtatious, come-hither smile that always got guys.

"Thank you, Trent. If I feel better, I'll come down, but if not, I'll catch up with you tomorrow. I'll be sure to look for you. I promise." I gave him my most flirtatious smile.

"Right on," he said, and I sensed his triumph. "Mi casa es su casa—come on by. You don't even have to knock, just come in. The minibar is stocked."

Remembering Spanish from high school, I knew that "Mi casa es su casa" meant "My house is your house." I batted my eyes.

"Goodbye *for now*," I said in a purr and pushed the door closed. Turning the latch, I stood in silence, Trent's key card in my hand.

He had no idea what a huge mistake he had just made. I had a very strong feeling that Trent was another one of those rich people who had always gotten whatever he wanted. He probably didn't have to spend a cent himself for college and then likely paid some nerdy dude to write papers for him to get good grades and impress his wealthy parents. He probably had Daddy's money for anything he wanted and dated a hot sorority girl and then cheated on her with another hot sorority girl. I bet he had a crazy-expensive car and belonged to a country club and had his initials monogrammed on his shirts and had soft hands because he never truly worked a day in his life and left dirty towels all over his hotel room knowing some worker would pick them up and tipped cute waitresses and now believed he could get me to sleep with him just by flashing that stupid fake smile. He made me sick, so sick. The thought of his paws on me turned my stomach, but the thought of me turning the tables on him brought me a rush of joy. Oh, he wouldn't know what hit him, that piece of shit.

My newly forming plan would be payback for every woman out there who had to deal with guys like him everywhere. It might even be retribution on behalf of Allison, for the way Drake had treated her, and I couldn't believe I was thinking that.

I crawled back into bed and began to hash out my plan. I knew when the conference ended Saturday, thanks to the name tag. I would look up flights to Atlanta to get the general sense of when he'd be leaving; then I'd change my hair, pick up my money from Western Union, return my rental car early, and wait in the ticketing area until I saw him. When he was out of sight, I'd buy a ticket on the same plane and follow him there, getting an Uber behind him to his condo and texting one of Stephanie's friends that I had met a great guy.

Except after a short time, Trent wouldn't be so great anymore, and then I'd drop some sort of bomb on Steph's friend about him wanting to kill me. That would be the paper trail for police. The DNA would already be inside his condo without him even knowing it. And he lived in Atlanta—perfect. Raven came to mind. She would be happy to help—she had even told me so. She was always out to make a little cash and liked a good scam.

First, I needed to secure money. Getting out of bed and grabbing Stephanie's laptop and the hotel stationery and pen, I propped some pillows up behind me and set the laptop on my knees, then went back to "Passwords" and wrote down all of the ones for her banking accounts. I could go to an ATM with her debit card tomorrow. Right now, my plan was to draw $5,000 from each of her three credit cards and ask that it be wired to the closest Western Union. Five thousand seemed like a safe number. Not something so outlandish that it would raise giant flags, but the combined $15,000, plus whatever I could get from her debit card, would be enough that I could have a cushion to do what I needed to do in Atlanta, pay Raven, and get myself to Mexico.

The wire transfer was easy, and all three promised to be ready by eight a.m. Friday morning. Things were clicking into place. Picking up my phone, I scrolled through my contacts until I found Raven.

> Hey, girl, long time, no talk. Are you in Atlanta right now? Do you want to make $1,000?

She wrote back almost right away.

> Jasmine!!! I'm here. You know I want some of that $! What do I have to do?

> I need you to follow a guy and slip something into his drink for me. I'll text you the address. It's going down Saturday night. I'm coming to town. You free?

> For $1,000 I am. I got ya, sister. I'll be ready.

And with that, satisfied that I had done everything I needed to do, I shut off the light and finally fell fully asleep.

When I woke, it was dusk, and I could hear commotion in the hallway, people talking and laughing, doors closing.

Cocktail hour. It was here.

Shooting out of bed, I went to my window and pulled the curtain back a touch. My view was right over the courtyard where the big outdoor fireplace was, and I could see the first conference attendees starting to show up, mingling around the bar area holding beer bottles, glass tumblers, or wineglasses. Servers were milling about with appetizers on trays. The sixth floor was all for conference people, and based on the noise in the hallway, everyone seemed to be going. I watched as the courtyard filled up, hearing the ding of the elevator down the hall again and again until the hallway was quiet.

Continuing to peek out, I waited until I saw Trent. There he was, looking smarmy as always, walking up to the groups with the prettiest women and holding court. I couldn't hear him, of course, but I could see him gesturing, telling stories while chugging on the perennial bottle of beer in his hand. My eyes drifted across the courtyard and found Dorothy and Alan, my other tablemates, in an entirely different part of the cocktail party, standing around a high-top table with glasses of wine, seeming to have a deep conversation with a couple of other people. Trent headed back to the bar for another beer, and I knew the time was now. But I had to act fast, just in case.

CHAPTER 39

Jasmine

One Day After the Flight

Grabbing Trent's key card and some rubber gloves from the box I had gotten at Walmart, I slipped out my door and down two to his.

The latch opened easily and I was in. His curtains were open, his room also overlooking the courtyard. I knew I couldn't dare turn a lamp on or go near the window, just in case, but the light coming in from outside gave me just enough to see by. Going into his bathroom, I grabbed his razor and a small pair of scissors men used for sideburns off the sink counter and slipped them carefully into a pocket, then found his suitcase open in the main room. It was one of those fancy ones that had a bunch of little pockets for different things. Perfect.

Looking in his closet, I noticed a row of suit coats lined up and identified the one he wore that day. It had an inside breast pocket that was just what I was looking for.

Sitting on a shelf in his closet, there was a pile of monogrammed handkerchiefs, all crisp and white with little *TJM*s stamped on each. Although I worried he might notice one missing, I couldn't help it. I had to take one. I had a feeling it would come in handy for me, and he would likely either be pissed at his assistant for not packing enough or think a housekeeper stole one.

Peeking back in the bathroom, I was just about to leave when I noticed a towel on the floor. Picking it up to see if there were any hairs on it that might be useful to me, I saw it had a wet spot right in the middle, and suddenly, I knew. Hesitantly, I brought it to my nose. Semen. I was familiar with that smell. He must have jacked off before he went to the party and used the towel to wipe himself. I had seen Glenn do the same. Holy shit, the perfect item I hadn't even banked on. My plan just got more airtight.

Taking the towel, scissors, and razor back to Stephanie's room, I cut a little bit of Stephanie's hair and then pulled some of mine out from the root and set those aside.

I grabbed a pair of Stephanie's underwear and a pair of mine and smeared the crotch of each into the wet spot on the towel I had brought with me. That would plant his DNA there. Peeking out my window again, I saw that Trent was still telling what looked like an over-the-top story—laughing and clapping someone on the back.

Taking everything back to Trent's room, I returned the towel to exactly where I'd found it on the floor, and slipped my underwear and Stephanie's into the breast pocket of the coat he had worn that day. Knowing guys like him, he wouldn't wear the same thing twice and would never know it was there until the police did.

I took the hair I had pulled from my own head and the hair from Stephanie's and slipped the strands into a pocket in his suitcase that didn't look like it was used for anything.

Taking the tiny scissors, I braced myself for a bit of pain

and punctured my finger with the blade, wincing but adding a good amount of my blood to a different side pocket in the suitcase. I patted the scissors dry so that he wouldn't notice but a little DNA would hopefully remain, returned them to their spot, and glanced around for anything else.

On the desk was a stack of papers, and I drifted over, squinting in the growing darkness to make them out. On top was an itinerary, printed on NBC Atlanta letterhead and signed by some secretary.

"Details for your flight," it said. "Have a safe trip—Mary."

Listed below were his outbound and inbound flights from Atlanta. Quickly, I memorized his airline, flight number, and departure time for Saturday back to Atlanta. That would save me from having to try to track him at the airport. I could use Stephanie's credit card to buy the ticket. After all, I needed that paper trail so that it looked like she had gone back to Atlanta with him. Grinning with my finds and my good smarts, I departed Trent's room for good.

My next order of business was to get Stephanie out of here by cover of darkness. I waited and watched the cocktail party until it emptied completely out, people heading out to dinner. When I was sure everyone was gone and I saw only the waiters and waitresses cleaning up, I made my move, removing the bags of melting ice and dumping them out, zipping the suitcase with the weights in it shut, and bracing myself for the walk ahead.

There wasn't a soul on the elevator on the way down, and I only passed one couple in the hallway of the first floor as I went to the back exit. Moving into the perfect San Diego night air, I wheeled Stephanie to the minivan with the wheelchair lift. That had been my most brilliant calculation yet. I had known there was no way I was going to be able to lift her, and that was even without the weights, and I was proud of myself for thinking ahead and requesting it from the car rental agency.

With the push of a button, the side doors of the minivan opened and a lift lowered to the ground with the grind of mechanical gears. Rolling the suitcase onto it, I needed only to push another button, and up she went into the van. Climbing into the driver's seat, I punched in the address for the hidden lagoon spot on the coast and steered that way.

I was nervous I would see someone there, some nature lover out at night or a couple making out on the bridge, but it was pitch-black with no sound but the nearby ocean waves as I parked. Using my cell phone flashlight, I lowered Stephanie with the lift and rolled the suitcase toward the bridge.

It was so quiet and empty that I felt a prickle up my spine as I got closer. What if someone jumped me and I got hurt? I shuddered but kept putting one foot in front of the other.

The bridge had a railing, but the wooden slats didn't reach the ground—there was a big open space under it. I waved the flashlight at the water and tried to assess the depth. It was a lagoon off the main part of the coast and looked deep to me. It would have to do.

Thank God the suitcase, laid on its side, would slip under the handrail part of the bridge fairly easily. There was no way I could have hoisted it up and thrown it over.

As I manipulated the suitcase into place, I thought of one final coup de grâce. If Stephanie were ever found, it was not going to be me to take the fall. Trent's key card and his monogrammed handkerchief were still in my pocket. Taking them out, I found a crack in the wooden slats of the bridge and wedged them in there. Just enough that someone really looking would see, not enough that anyone would notice even in daylight.

Then I put my foot on the suitcase and got ready to push. For a moment, I felt remorse, guilt, even a touch of sadness. But then I remembered how *my* life was about to start. An eye for an eye. I needed to get rid of this woman to become the woman I was destined to be. And did I feel bad? Sure, a little, but she was a stranger on a plane, not a friend.

"Goodbye," I whispered to the darkness. It took multiple shoves and kicks to move the suitcase, which must have weighed close to three hundred pounds at that point, but finally it fell into the lagoon with a giant splash and sank to the bottom.

Hurrying back to the minivan, I got in, shivering not from cold but from adrenaline. For a moment, I put my head on the steering wheel and my body shook reflexively, but I had no time to linger. I had things to do.

Back to Walmart I went, and this time I bought the blackest hair dye I could. I would need that soon. Returning to my original motel room, I left the hair dye on the table, organized my remaining clothes, and put them in a pile on the bed. I looked at the red flannel shirt I had stolen from Glenn. No need for that anymore. I was going places where it was warm now, and I wanted every ounce of him out of my life, so I stuffed the shirt into my smaller rolling suitcase, put the suitcase in the minivan, and found an old dumpster a block down to pitch the suitcase and the shirt inside it.

Pulling into a convenience store parking lot with an ATM that was mostly in a dark shadowy spot, I took Stephanie's debit card out of her purse, checked the password on my list, and inserted the card. Her balance was $5,458.23. Jeez—who keeps that kind of money in a checking account? With my eyes gleaming, I withdrew the maximum it would let me in one sitting, $3,000, and stuffed it into her purse. By the next day I would have $18,000 of her money.

Checking Stephanie's Apple Watch, which was now on my wrist, I saw it was getting to be about the time some of the people who had gone to dinner would be returning. I needed to get back.

Driving to the hotel and slipping in the side door, I took the stairs this time to avoid the elevator and cautiously peeked out at the sixth floor, confirming it was empty before walking quickly to my room.

Thank goodness, the worst of it was over now. I had planted evidence in Trent's room and at the site where Stephanie's body was, and I had done the biggest thing of all: disposed of her. The room felt so much airier, lighter, without her presence, and I twirled around in a circle, admiring myself in the mirror. I wished I could have all of Stephanie's clothes from back in Wisconsin. I bet her closet was amazing. I pictured her living in a mansion with crystal chandeliers and a plush red couch, wineglasses in a glass cabinet, and a fridge full of fancy and expensive organic foods. But I could never go back to Madison, could never go anywhere near there. I needed to head south, to Mexico. I would have to live off the clothes she had brought for the conference for now.

Turning on the TV and flipping channels, I decided to treat myself to some more items from the hotel fridge and mixed up a rum and coke, then ate the popcorn and mixed nuts they had. Changing into Stephanie's workout clothes again for bed, I crawled under the sheets and decided to take one of her Ambien to make sure I slept. I had tried it just a few times at Glenn's place and knew that it was good when needed.

Before it fully kicked in, I got up and made sure the DO NOT

DISTURB sign remained and that the extra lock was in place. Not like her, I thought with a sardonic chuckle. Then I jotted down my plan for the next day: "Western Union, pack up and leave the hotel, check back into the motel, start dropping clues via text." With my next moves spinning in my head, I fell asleep soundly for the first time in months.

CHAPTER 40

Jasmine

Two Days After the Flight

When I woke, it was 6:30 a.m. and my mind was immediately filled with plans. I needed to start laying breadcrumbs that would lead the police to Trent.

I was just thinking about how to do that and I picked up Stephanie's phone to see if she had any messages. There was a text from that guy Robert. When I opened it, the first thing I saw was a picture of a cat in a chair licking its paw. The text read:

> Hi Mama, I miss you. I'll see you tomorrow! Love Freddie (and your favorite cat-sitter)

Aha, so Robert was the cat-sitter she had told me about. Now what was my chess move? As I was pondering this, a second text came in from him:

> Opened your package. It's bigger than I thought. Lots of options and settings. I think

you'll love it. It will make you feel great. Would you like me to put it next to your bed?

What the heck did that mean? Did Steph order a *vibrator* and ask her friend to bring it in? That was the only thing I could think of. How scandalous! A news director!

Nibbling my fingers, I lay in bed thinking. What would be a natural first thing to say to a friend to buy myself some extra time and to set up Trent, and what to say about the vibrator my cat-sitter had just opened? Sitting up, I started crafting a text, then read it over several times:

Thanks for the pic! So cute. Hey—I know this is super unexpected but I met an amazing guy at the conference and I'm actually going back to his place with him! Can you watch Fred for a little longer? I'll be back in touch to let you know when I'm returning. Thank you so much! And regarding the package, go ahead and put it in the bedroom. Maybe I won't need it anymore now that I met this guy, ha ha! Thanks.

That sounded good. I was acknowledging the picture of Fred *and* acknowledging the vibrator, plus setting up that I had met a guy and gaining some extra time. Taking a deep breath, I hit send.

The text back from him was almost instantaneous.

Girlfriend, you call me right now.
I want every detail.

Clearly I wasn't going to call him, but nibbling my nails more, I thought of the pluses and minuses of responding to him again via text. I didn't want to give away too many details just yet, didn't want to engage much. Ten minutes passed and he wrote again.

Don't you dare ignore me when
you have news like that!

I kept ignoring it and went to take a shower. When I got out, I had missed a call from him and there was another text.

You can't drop a bomb on me
and then ghost, uh-uh, ain't fair.
Who is this guy?? Is he cute?
Is he a news director? Does he
have a nice tush? At least tell
me his name and where he's
from.

Jesus, Robert, lighten up, I thought as I toweled off and rifled through the rest of Stephanie's clothing in her closet. Today I was going for the long flowery dress. I still needed to look like her for a few days so that I could get to Western Union today and get through security to Atlanta tomorrow.

Continuing to ignore Robert, I used Steph's makeup and perfume, put on her watch again and her jewelry, wore her clothes, carried her purse, packed everything else into her rolling carry-on carefully, stripped the bed as best I could to help the housekeeping staff, wiped down the bathroom for the same reason, and waited patiently until I knew the conference had started and everyone would be in the room hearing from speakers on topics that still confused me.

This was my time to slip out the side door again for a final time. I was never coming back here. I removed the DO NOT DISTURB sign from the outside handle and rehung it on the inside.

With all of Stephanie's items, plus the few I had brought, in her bag, I rolled it down the hall to the staircase and walked down this time, the bag not heavy, getting to the lobby. Slipping out the side door, I went to the minivan and drove to Western Union a few miles away. After a short wait in line, I had only to present Stephanie's photo ID and credit card and to know my password as an extra security measure, and I was handed $5,000 from each account, walking out with $15,000 in cash.

I wanted to be done with the minivan, so I took that back to the rental-car place and got an Uber back to my motel, asking the driver to stop for fast food so I could order some lunch. That way I didn't need to go out again.

Shedding each part of the tools that got me to this point and advancing my plan felt great. Car gone, money here, dead body gone, evidence planted. I was doing well. Back at the motel, I counted all of my money: $18,000 from Steph's accounts, plus some I still had from my job in Madison.

The bills looked great spread across the cheap, thin duvet of the motel bed. Eating tacos from Taco Bell, I thought about how I'd be enjoying real Mexican food soon. My eyes drifted to Steph's phone. I noticed she had two more missed calls from Robert and remembered I had not returned his morning texts asking me for more information. It was probably time. Still acting like happy, in-love Stephanie, I wrote:

> Hey! Sorry I didn't get back to you. Really busy day here at the conference. He's amazing. His name is Trent McCarthy and he's from Atlanta. We really hit it off and I just need to roll with this. Can you give me a week? I'm going to go back to Atlanta with him. I'll send you some pictures!

Pictures would be part of my paper trail for the police.

> Well, aren't you just the Queen of the Nile?! Of course I'll take care of Fred. Have an amazing time and call me when Trent is out of earshot. I want to talk to you! Every. Single. Damn. Detail.

I didn't respond. Instead, I picked up Steph's phone and called United Airlines, asking to be on the same exact flight Trent was on. I still had it memorized from the paper in his hotel room.

"You're lucky, just a couple of seats left," she said. "That route fills fast."

"I'll take anything," I responded. "My name is Stephanie Monroe, and I have my credit card right here."

In no time at all, we had it booked. I leaned back in the bed and kicked my feet around in joy, stifling the urge to scream along with it. I was kicking ass and taking names.

The rest of the day and night I stayed in at the motel, not wanting to draw attention to myself. I had my money and had formulated my plan, but to be sure I didn't make any missteps, I sketched it out on the motel paper using their pen. Both items felt cheaper in my hand than the versions at the hotel Stephanie had stayed at. There, the pen was heavy, the paper thick. It felt important when you were writing. Here, it was a Bic ballpoint that looked as if someone had chewed on the end of it, and it was missing its cap. The paper was of a thin, almost scratchy quality. Just another way the class system in America rewarded people like Stephanie, Trent, Allison, and Drake and cared little about people like me. The toilet paper was another example. It had been so soft and fluffy at the Hilton. Here I barely wanted to use it, it was so cheap.

Well, I would be jumping social classes soon, that was for sure. I tried to picture how people in Mexico would perceive me. I'd have nice clothes and jewelry and smell like Italian perfume. I smiled at the thought. It was my turn.

I made a list of Steph's cell phone contacts—who I thought they were and how I was going to respond to each. For Robert, it was falling in love and going to Atlanta. For people at work, it was a more ambiguous "something came up"–type thing, as I thought running off with a guy might seem odd to them at first. For her son, it was simply going to be that I was extending my trip. That one gave me a pang. I knew what it was like not to have a mom in your life, but if he had one good parent around, he still was doing better than me. He'd get over it.

Then there was Raven. I needed help with something else

from her, a new ID. I couldn't cross the border as Stephanie. That would ruin the whole thing. Texting Raven again, I offered her an extra $1,000 to help me get a fake passport for Mexico.

When do you need it?

ASAP. It's urgent.

Do you plan to come back to the US? Mexican authorities don't look nearly as hard as US authorities. If it's one way, I can do it. But it'll cost you $2,000, not $1,000.

I paused before texting her back. This was a pivotal moment in my life. Would I ever return to the only country I had ever been in? Ever? The answer was clearly no. I would be much safer there, and I would just have to build a new life.

Never coming back

I felt the finality of those words as I hit send.

OK, then text me a photo of you against a wall that looks like a passport photo. It doesn't matter what your hair looks like. I just need your face and I'll have my buddy do some digital work. What kind of hair do you want?

My eyes went to the box of hair dye.

Black pixie cut. I'll pay you in cash in person when I see you. Coming tomorrow.

I stood against a blank part of the wall of the motel, the paint on it a dullish gray, and snapped a selfie, then texted it to Raven, who gave a thumbs-up.

There was nothing much to do until the next day, so I spent a lot of time lying on the lumpy bed staring at the ceiling, which was painted a boring beige and covered in a texture that reminded me of mosquito bites. It occurred to me that I should be sure Glenn hadn't gone public about my disappearance, so I called up the website for Stephanie's TV station and scrolled around. No stories on me, thank goodness, but there were a lot of stupid videos about things like a baby giraffe at the zoo and the "World of Weddings" show at the expo center that weekend. Who created this kind of dumb stuff? Was it someone's actual job to do so? Scrolling further, I came to the national news section, and a headline caught my eye: "AI Voice Cloning Gaining Popularity."

This brought back a memory of something Anna had taught me.

"Check this out," she said one night after closing, leaning her elbows on the long bar, a tray of empty beer bottles and dirty glasses next to her. "I recorded my mom's voice and then put it into this software and it sounds *just like her*! It only cost me five bucks and was super easy."

She hit play first on the original audio of her mom and then on the replica. In the original, her mom was talking about a recipe for casserole, but in the fake she was telling Anna how much she loved her.

"How did you get the fake voice to do that?" I asked.

"You can write whatever you want, and the voice will read it. It just needs to learn the voice first, then it can say anything, and I do mean *anything*."

At the time, I had just laughed, thinking how weird it would be if I could get my own mother's voice to say whatever I wanted. Maybe she could finally tell me she loved me, that she was sorry for the awful ways she had treated me. But that seemed too bizarre and ultimately unsatisfying, so I hadn't thought much more about it until now.

Quickly I opened the article on the Channel 3 website and scanned it, taking in details. Another possible step in my plan began to formulate. Texting with Stephanie's friends and family was one thing, but I could *really* fake them out if I could get her voice to leave them a voice memo.

Sitting up and googling Stephanie's name, I hit "Videos," and watched with joy as several popped up: her speaking at a Rotary Club banquet, her being on some panel at a university, even a video posted by her own station where she was reading a mission statement about how committed they were to local news.

That one was the winner, winner, chicken dinner. It had the best, cleanest audio and was about a minute and a half long. Anna had told me the sample needed to be at least one minute. I couldn't remember the exact website Anna mentioned, but the article on Stephanie's station's page listed several, and I fished around until I found one that came with a free one-month trial.

Uploading Stephanie's voice took just a few minutes, and afterward the site asked me to type in whatever I wanted the fake voice to say. I was thinking ahead to the various texts I planned to send Robert from Atlanta, to draw out that Steph was in love at first and *later* in harm's way.

There would be one from Trent's house, one or two from sightseeing, and one from Trent's station. Voice cloning could be perfect for one of those. That would also be about the time I would be dropping the first hints that Trent wasn't the super guy I had made him out to be, so I composed this into the software program for her voice to read:

"Last stop: Trent's station! He's the boss here and he's very bossy with me—tells me exactly where we should go and what we should do and I just follow. Talk soon!"

Reading it over a few times, I was satisfied and hit "Create." Within minutes, my clip was ready. My heart pounded as I hit play.

Holy crap, it sounded like Stephanie. I couldn't believe it. I was giddy with possibilities now. Maybe she would even call 9-1-1 herself near the end of her time with Trent!

Speaking of Trent, it was time to plant the first seed with Anna too. I needed her to think that I had also met a wonderful new guy. Later that relationship would also take a dark turn, and I would be dead at his place too. For now, it was time to answer her original texts about whether I was OK. I picked up my phone.

Hey Anna—I'm more than OK. I met a great guy named Trent McCarthy. He makes me feel safe and beautiful. More details when I can!

OMG, Jasmine, that's awesome. I'm so excited for you!

Perfect! I was a genius. Filled with adrenaline at my tremendous smarts, I stood up in the middle of the motel room and felt like dancing. Stephanie's phone had Spotify, and I randomly picked a song.

The Temptations song "My Girl" started blasting out: . . . *my girl, talking 'bout my girl* . . . Yeeessss . . . What a good song. Flying around the motel room in ecstasy, I belted out the words. I wasn't sure if the girl in the song was me or Stephanie, but either way, I felt more alive than I had been in years.

CHAPTER 41

Jasmine

The Saturday After the Flight

I caught an Uber to the airport early, just to be sure Trent wasn't skipping out of the conference early and catching a different flight. On the way, I texted Robert:

Conference is over, heading
to the airport. Going to
Atlanta with Trent!

Another breadcrumb. He wrote back asking for more details, but I ignored it. At the airport, I had to be Stephanie to get through security and show my ID, but I could morph into anyone after that. I wore her nice clothes and carried her purse, lurking in the corners of the ticketing area so Trent wouldn't see me.

At last he came in. He wasn't paying attention to anyone, striding to the security line with his bag, the one that now contained women's hair and blood. He had a garment bag too, and I knew it was filled with suit coats, one of which had two pairs of women's underwear with his semen on them. I waited until he was through security before heading in myself. The guard looked at my boarding pass and ID and nodded me through with no issues at all. Another one fooled.

Once I passed the metal detectors, I hoofed it to the nearest restroom and did my switcheroo again in the handicap stall—gone was Stephanie's clothing, and on was mine, including the baseball cap and glasses. I doused my eyes in a crazy purple eyeshadow that made them look different, but this time I left my lower face alone. I had a different idea: a mask. *Thank you, COVID.* I had seen them for sale in the airport gift shop. That would help me disguise myself from Trent on the flight. I bought several for good measure and felt safer the moment I put one on. Only my eyes peeked out from under the baseball cap.

At the gate, I lingered back so Trent wouldn't see me and boarded near the end again, keeping my eyes down as I walked the jetway. I heard his voice as I was passing his first-class row, booming as he talked to the woman in the seat next to him. He was bragging about returning home from an "exclusive conference." Oh, I couldn't wait for what was about to hit him.

When we landed in Atlanta, I followed him through the airport from a safe distance to the Uber/taxi-pickup area. As he got into his Uber, I grabbed a cab and said, "Follow that car, but don't be obvious, please. I'll make it worth your while." The driver barely nodded and pulled behind Trent's Uber.

On the way, I texted Robert again:

Landed, heading to his place.

Then I texted Raven and told her I needed her to be ready to go.

Dress sexy and come with some sort of pill to knock a 6' 2" kind of burly guy out, make him so sick he needs to stay in for two days

I have just the thing

I asked the taxi driver to drop me a half block down from where Trent was getting out so that he wouldn't notice me; then I crept up to his building and pinged Raven the address. Taking out Steph's phone, I snapped a few pictures of the exterior that I would use to prove I was here.

There was a bench down the block, and I sat and waited for Raven, trying desperately not to chew my nails so I wouldn't look nervous. She came in an Uber thirty minutes later, a black leather coat over a tight white blouse showing her cleavage, with bright pink lipstick on. She had always been pretty, but she looked extra hot. I gave her a long hug.

"I can't tell you how much this means to me," I gushed. "Thank you."

"You got it, sister. Where's the creep?"

I pointed toward the condo.

"So you want me to follow him into a bar, pretend to hit on him, slip something into his drink that he'll feel tomorrow, and get out of there, right? I don't have to sleep with him, do I?"

"Oh, God, no, I wouldn't do that to you," I replied. "Yup, that's it, that's all you need to do."

"Piece of cake, Jazzy," she said. "Your passport is coming tomorrow."

"You're the best," I said. "Here's half the money. I'll get you the other half when I get the passport."

I reached into my purse, but she put her arm out and stopped me.

"Not here," she hissed, glancing around. A man all dressed in purple and with a poodle in his arms was walking across the street. He looked at us and raised his eyebrows but kept going.

"You can pay me all at once," she whispered.

Removing my hand from the bag, I tried to resume a casual pose. We waited longer. At least the time on the bench gave me a chance to catch up with my friend.

"So what are you doing now, Raven? Do you like Atlanta?"

"It's like any place, good and bad. I do what I have to do to make money . . . and to keep out of jail," she laughed. "Been there once. I will do anything not to go back, and I do mean anything. I'd turn in my own mother if I had to. It ain't easy to make a living, but I find ways. Just gotta stay one step ahead of the feds, you know?"

"Amen to that," I said, and we sat chatting on the bench for another few minutes. I told her about leaving Glenn and about stealing Stephanie's identity. I stopped short of the full murder, but I told her I wanted to frame Trent for some things. She nodded.

Finally, Trent walked out. He had changed since the flight but still had his greasy-looking hair slicked back.

"There he is," I hissed, grabbing her forearm. He turned right. "Let's go!"

We stood up and followed him from a distance. It wasn't very far. He went to a corner bar and walked in. I just knew he would do something like that. He wasn't the type to stay home on a Saturday night and clearly was single, so I had a pretty good idea of what his night would entail.

"Got the pill?" I asked Raven as we got within a few storefronts of the place.

"Of course, I'm no amateur." She grinned at me. "I'll be out within an hour, that's my prediction. Go find a motel, Jazzy. I'll text you when it's done."

And she disappeared. It was getting dark and a little chilly, and a motel sounded nice. I found one nearby and called an Uber. It was just two minutes away, the joys of a big city, and I was settled into the motel in no time.

I had one more thing I needed to do the next day to complete my fictitious trip to Atlanta for evidence, so I couldn't change my hair just yet. I set the hair dye next to the sink, though. That would be coming soon.

Sitting on the edge of the bed, I nervously waited for Raven's text. It took a little longer than an hour but not much.

Done. He's going to be feeling like crap tomorrow. He won't be leaving his bathroom, let alone his house. And you're right, what a jerk. He wanted me to sleep with him tonight. Total flirt and loser.

You're amazing. Thank you. One final favor. I need to take a few pictures around town to show that I've been here, but they have to be from behind. Can you help me tomorrow? Some sort of tourist place?

Centennial Olympic Park would be good. I can meet you there at noon. ALL the tourists go there, for what reason I don't know. It's just a stupid park

with Olympic rings and a few
fountains but it's definitely
Atlanta.

I hearted the message and said I would talk to her again the next day.

CHAPTER 42

Jasmine

The Sunday After the Flight

Sunday morning started with a text from Robert. The guy was relentless.

Inquiring minds want to know,
how was the first night with
Trent?? Do tell all, please.

The text had one of those little faces that looks like it's pondering something.

I still had to make him think things were off to a great start, but I also needed to establish that Trent was inside all day. He was, thanks to the pill Raven had given him, but I wanted the police to believe he was indoors having a hot romance with Stephanie, so I wrote:

So far, so good. He wants
us to stay in all day today to
get to know each other.

Robert replied with some hearts.

Va, va, voom!

My plan was working perfectly. At this point he still thought his friend was in love.

An hour later, a text popped up from someone new named Diana.

Ready to meet up? I'll be there in an hour.

Who was this, and where was Stephanie supposed to meet her? Well, no matter. I would have to hold her off like the others.

Sorry, I have to push it back. Something came up. I'm out of town for a week.

What are you talking about? You're kidding, right?

Not kidding. Contact me in a week.

My phone started ringing. Over and over. Diana's name. *No thanks, sister.* I just kept ignoring it until she finally stopped calling.

The rest of the day was all about laying groundwork for further text evidence. I started by scouting Trent's neighborhood. Knowing he was going to be inside sick all day gave me the freedom to wander the area known as Peachtree Village. There was a nearby coffee shop named Peaches and Cream. Was everything in Atlanta named Peach something? I ordered two lattes and set them up on a table near a window, taking several artsy photos to make it look as if two people were having coffee together. The drinks came in brightly colored mugs with pictures of big peaches on the side, making them all the more distinctive.

Next I looked up Trent's TV station and took an Uber there, snapping a picture of the outside with the NBC logo. Then I stopped at a convenience store and bought the tackiest mug I could find, one with GREETINGS FROM HOT-LANTA printed on it, taking a picture to text to Robert as further evidence that Stephanie was texting him and she was here.

Finally, I met up with Raven at Centennial Olympic Park and had her take photos of me from behind my head, with the fountains in the background so that anyone who knew Atlanta would know the place. My hair looked like Steph's—same color, same basic cut, and I had used her curling iron to give my flatter locks a little pop to better resemble hers. I wore her cream-colored coat and hat too.

Those chores being done, I could finally change my hair, and I did so that evening back in the motel, dyeing it jet-black and cutting it as short as I could. *Goodbye for real, Stephanie*, I thought as the final wisps went down the drain. I didn't need to be her anymore.

Admiring myself in the motel mirror, I turned left and right. The cut looked good on me, my lighter skin contrasted with the blackest of black hair. The new look called for bright red lipstick, in my opinion, and buying a vibrant red color would also serve as a final vanquishing of Allison and the memory of her shade. I was putting her further into the rearview with every move on this trip.

Walking to the nearest CVS, I decided to treat myself, purchasing the most expensive brand they had. I deserved it. Adding more rubber gloves and alcohol wipes to my cart,

I passed the travel section and saw there was a cloth passport holder, the kind that goes around your neck. I grabbed it, along with some travel-size lotion and shampoo. Noticing a bin of temporary tattoos near the cash registers, I picked out several, thinking they would help transform me. I could put one on a collarbone, one on a wrist, just obvious places where someone identifying me would mention them. And to complete the disguise one final time, I put my John Lennon glasses back on. I looked like a punk rock chick instead of a news executive, and I loved it.

Using some of Steph's money, I rewarded myself with a shopping trip to the mall, buying clothes I liked in nicer fabrics than I had ever owned. Her credit cards from stores that ranged from Sephora to J.Jill to Macy's made me so happy, and I charged up a storm.

I also added a new duffel bag and rolling carry-on to my collection. Steph's suitcase would need to be disposed of near Trent's place. If anyone found it, they would think of it as further evidence he had done something wrong and that he had been the one to dispose of it. Now that I wasn't her anymore, I couldn't be seen traveling with it.

Finally, I hit some thrift stores. You could take the girl out of the trailer park but couldn't take the thrift shopping out of the girl, I thought, chuckling to myself, and came home laden with even more clothing, including a black knit hat and a ski mask. I would need those.

Treating myself to dinner at an Italian place near the motel, I had more wine, pasta, salad, and garlic bread than I had ever consumed before, going to bed with my belly warm and overstuffed. For the first time in my life, I felt like I had some disposable income, like I could do this without worrying about it. It was amazing, and I couldn't believe it had taken me decades to figure out a way to get this feeling. I was so used to living paycheck to paycheck and having everyone around me do the same.

Monday morning, I woke up to a missed text from Bruce.

Are you running late? Do you need me to start the meeting?

I had apparently guessed right that he was a coworker. I was contemplating what to do in response when I saw he was now calling Steph's phone. Not long after, another text from Bruce:

Everything OK? We're getting a little worried. People are asking about you. Aren't you supposed to be back today?

OK, Bruce was obviously another person I would have to deal with, to fend off, but also to drop a breadcrumb or two as well. Getting up to take a shower and get dressed, I thought about my response, then sat by the motel window overlooking the bland parking lot and typed what I hoped was a "leave me alone for a while" text:

Hi, sorry for the late notice. Something very unexpected happened at the conference and it required me to go to Atlanta. I will need to be off this entire week. Maybe more but I'll keep you posted. Thank you in advance.

That would further place me in Atlanta but not get him upset or raise suspicion like it might if I just said I was running off with a guy. Each person had to have their own breadcrumbs, ones that worked in the context of Steph's relationship with them. I still believed coworkers needed something different from friends like Robert. At least for now. A few minutes later, a response from Bruce.

This is really sudden news, Stephanie. Can you tell me more? I can run the newsroom but we have a lot on our plates this week and I'm off Thursday and Friday, remember? Did you want to reschedule the election meeting too?

I started typing, then stopped, then started again. I could sense his anger, but if Stephanie was the boss, then this guy had to be under her in some way. He would have to listen to her. I put on my best boss persona and wrote:

Don't worry, I'm fine. I know it's sudden but sometimes things pop up. Please reschedule the meeting.

A short time later, his reply:

OK. Do you have a second to talk on the phone? If you're going to be out all week there are some things we should touch base on.

Once again, I tried a few responses but deleted them. A thought came into my head: the voice cloning. I would send him a voice memo this time, rock-solid evidence that it was Stephanie responding. Going back to the program I had played with the night before, I typed this into the system and had Stephanie say it:

"No, I really don't have a moment. Please don't check in with me until next week. I will be very busy."

Then I sent it to Bruce. A minute passed with no response. I could feel his confusion and annoyance. Finally, he just hit the thumbs-up button. Great. He was out of my hair for a while.

A text from Anna came in to my phone:

Glenn is getting weird but
Raven is going to help out.

What a coincidence. I couldn't help but respond:

Really? She's helping me
with something too

Anna wrote back right away:

What is she helping with?

I had probably said too much. I didn't answer that one.

Someone named Dave Jenssen started calling and leaving Steph messages. From the tone of his voice, I gathered that he was her superior, but I didn't like his demands, very much like Glenn would sometimes talk to me. Dave kept insisting that Stephanie call him that instant to explain herself. I put my middle finger up at the phone and decided not to have any contact with him at all. He could stew in his own anger for a while.

Then there was Robert, the neighbor and cat-sitter. He was going to get the mother lode, the full onslaught of pictures from me that proved I was with Trent and could later be used by police. I sprinkled them throughout the day.

This is Trent's place. Check
it out on Zillow, it's gorgeous
inside

I put in the picture of the white stucco building and added Trent's exact address for extra evidence. Robert responded:

Ahh, the love nest. Very nice

A few hours later, I sent Robert the latte picture, the two mugs cozied near each other, conjuring up images of two people in love out for coffee.

Checking out the
local places in Trent's
neighborhood, Peachtree
Village. It's an area just full
of life

He responded:

L'chaim, l'chaim, to life!

I had no idea what that meant so I ignored it.

That afternoon, I sent two more pictures and the fake voice memo. The first picture was the one Raven took where I was looking out over Centennial Olympic Park, fountains dancing in front of me.

He's such a good tour guide, he's taking me all over the city

Then I got to work on the voice memo regarding the photo from the TV station. I wanted to plant the first seed of Trent being not exactly an entirely great guy, so I attached the picture from his station and the fake voice memo:

"Last stop: Trent's station! He's the boss here and he's very bossy with me—tells me exactly where we should go and what we should do and I just follow. Talk soon!"

The response came in.

Great to hear your voice. Have an amazing time. Fred is doing fine.

Yeeeessss. He believed it. I sent a final text with the picture of the tacky GREETINGS FROM HOT-LANTA mug about twenty minutes later.

Your gift from my trip

How fun! Thanks.

I smiled. Next came a text from someone named Lucy.

I hear you're out this week. Should I reschedule that

meeting with Mark R.? He'll be
very disappointed but I'm sure
he'll get over it

Another coworker. Sigh. I'd have to act like another meeting was being rescheduled. I waited about an hour and then wrote her back:

Yes, please reschedule with
Mark R.

Lucy responded:

Mark R. says to call him as
soon as you can, he misses you

That seemed odd. Was Stephanie having an affair with Mark R.? Why would Lucy say he missed her? I didn't know how to respond, so I ignored it, hoping Lucy would go away. Instead, a third text came from her:

Are you dissing Mark R.? You
know he'll turn into the Hulk

I wasn't going to answer that, so I ignored it as well. But that night I thought I should just treat Lucy like I had her other coworker, Bruce, and act like the boss I was. These people had to listen to me, right?

I am very busy this week, I
asked you to reschedule the
meeting. I should be back
next week

God, these people. *Leave me the fuck alone.* I could stay longer somewhere if I wanted to. That's what bosses do, what they have earned.

That night, Raven came to my motel room with the passport. Her digital guy had changed my hair, and it was almost a perfect match to what I had done myself. The passport looked real to me. She promised it would get me through a Mexican checkpoint.

"The best place to cross is anywhere you can walk," she counseled, sitting on the edge of my motel bed. "They get a lot more suspicious of cars. San Diego is good. You can take a light-rail right to the border and walk directly through to Tijuana. I've done it. There's usually only one Mexican guard, and they barely look at your passport. Trust me, they're happy to have people come into their country. Not like the US side, where they have a ton of checkpoints, drug-sniffing dogs, metal detectors, special flashlights and microscopes to make sure passports are real, the whole nine yards. Don't come back to the US, Jasmine. It's too dangerous."

"I won't," I promised. And I meant it. Opening the passport again, I was surprised to see the name: Erica Birchfield.

"Why Erica?" I asked.

"My guy does it like hurricanes. You were the fifth fake he's made this year, so you get an *E* name. As for last names, he has a software program that picks a random one."

"Got it," I said, handing her $3,000 of my hard-earned cash.

"Well," she sighed, "I don't suspect we'll see each other again for a bit. You shouldn't contact me or vice versa. But know that I'm with you. Do you remember that town from high school Spanish class? Maybe check it out. I'll even try to make it down there one day myself."

"Puerto Escondido!" I cried out with glee at the shared memory. "I remember it. I think I might try it. I mean, why not? It's as good as any place. I'll look for you. Thanks, Raven. You had my back on this and . . . on other stuff . . . You know what I mean, that one thing . . . the Halloween party . . . what I told you by the baseball field . . . I want you to know I appreciate it."

"Yeah . . ." She paused. "You know I never told anyone else about that, not even Anna. It's the truth, right? You weren't just pulling my leg?"

My chest and throat tightened, and I looked down. There was no need to lie to Raven. She was my friend. Plus, I was leaving the country.

"It's the truth," I said sadly. "You're the only one who knows. I've thought about it for twenty-seven years. I didn't mean to do it, I swear. It just happened. I kind of snapped."

"The bitch deserved it," she said. "I only wish I had gone to the party and helped you out. You know what was weird? A few years ago, I ran into Drake's brother at a bar when I was in Madison. He asked me if I knew anything about that party. Said his brother was innocent. Apparently, the family is still trying to figure it out all these decades later. I told him I didn't know a thing. Not that I would tell a Maple Hills person a damn word anyway. Bunch of silver spoon a-holes. Don't worry, Jazz, your secret is safe with me."

We hugged, and tears unexpectedly popped to my eyes. Female friendship felt so good, and now I was leaving it, going to a country where I had never been before. For a fleeting moment, I wondered if I should cancel this whole part of the plan, ask to stay with Raven in Atlanta and get to know her world, but I knew I needed an entirely fresh start. Although I had blocked Glenn from contacting me, the thought of him putting out an all-out search party or grabbing that hunting rifle on the wall still brought fear into my cells.

Mexico was my true freedom. Would I go all the way back to San Diego and actually cross there? Oh, the irony of it, returning to the scene of the crime to finish my escape. Maybe I would, maybe not. Maybe Texas would be better. It was closer to Atlanta.

First things first. I was going to keep sowing some seeds with Robert that things with Trent were getting bad. Then I would turn up the heat enough that Robert would call the police. I also needed to bury Steph's wallet and phone and my wallet in Trent's backyard one night, to make it look as if he had done so himself. Now that I was Erica, I didn't need my own wallet anymore. My phone I would dispose of somewhere nearby, but not in Trent's backyard. It had too many incriminating texts to Raven and too many things I had googled, like rigor mortis. I decided I would smash it somehow and put the pieces in a dumpster. I could get a burner phone, I was sure. The wallets and phones from me and from Steph needed to end here in Atlanta so that the police tracing them would see that their last ping was Trent's place, or near it.

I was entering the final phase of my escape plan, and everything was continuing to go well. The money withdrawn from Steph's accounts I figured the police would think was Trent convincing her to take money out and then pocketing it. More evidence, a motive for him to kill her. A divorced guy being pressed for child support by his ex. It all made sense. To add to the ruse, I went back to an ATM that night near Trent's place and withdrew $2,000 more from Steph's debit card. That covered some of my expenses with Raven and made it look as if Steph was taking out more money during her time with Trent.

I also planned to stop at a gardening store and buy a trowel. I would tell the person at the register that I just couldn't wait for gardening season.

Tuesday, I woke up very early ready to drop a few more texts on Robert—just more hints that Trent was becoming controlling and I was growing scared of him. I started with this:

I'm typing this while Trent is sleeping. I think I might come home earlier than expected. Remember how I said he was bossy? Well he actually yelled at me last night. It scared me. His anger came out of nowhere. He doesn't like it when I contact people from home. I'll call you when I can

Oh my god, are you OK? What's happening? Do you need help?

I waited, giving him time for a little bit of worry to escalate. His next two were filled with panic:

Steph, please answer

Followed a short time later with:

If you don't text me back soon, I'm calling 911

I couldn't let that happen juuust yet. Soon, but not yet. I texted back:

I'm OK. It's OK for now, he seems to have settled down this morning. I'm going to book a flight though. I'll be in touch

Come home now!!

He really cared about Stephanie. Wasn't that sweet? I wondered if he had a crush on her. I wished I had someone like that in my life. He wrote again.

Can I call you? Can I talk to you?

I replied by amping up the sinister nature.

No, not right now. I have to go. He's coming

I thought those words might seem like a scary movie moment, the monster approaching. It was perfect. I would lay more traps later.

A couple of hours later, after success at the garden store, I was still sitting in the motel room, cross-legged on the bed, googling border crossings when I had to deal with Stephanie's work people again on her phone. Lucy, the one who had written to me about Mark R., wrote again.

Susan and Frank called and need to speak with you. What should I tell them?

Must be more people Steph was supposed to meet with this week. She was a busy boss, that was for sure.

Tell them I'm out of town.

There was no response. Good. Hopefully she got the message. An hour later another text from Lucy. I sighed when I saw her name pop up again.

Your brother stopped by to invite you to lunch. Since you're out, he said he would call you to schedule a time.

Great, now a brother was going to be calling me. I typed back:

OK, thanks

I hoped all of these work people would just go away. I needed to focus on Robert. He was the one with the trail of evidence.

The typing bubbles from Lucy started going again, and I narrowed my eyes and heaved a deeper sigh. What else could she want?

I know you have a couple of brothers. This was the youngest one—I forgot his name, what is it again?

Well, shoot—what to do now? Should I make up a name? If she forgot his name, I might be able to get away with it. But what if she then compared notes with someone and found out it was wrong? I decided to pretend that I hadn't seen this text at all and ignore it.

Ten minutes later, another text:

Something with an A, right? I
just can't recall

Go away, I thought, and ignored the text. But just five minutes after that came a third:

Steph—are you OK?

I started chewing my almost nonexistent fingernails. Why was she asking me this?

Think, Jasmine, think. Think, Erica, think. My first question was whether to respond to Lucy. If I told her I was OK, she might press me for the brother's name. If I ignored it, she would likely get worried.

My eyes drifted to the fake passport sitting on the desk across the room.

I had my escape.

Maybe the time was now, like *right* now. I could accelerate my whole timeline before Lucy got really worried and called the police. Originally, I'd planned to draw out the clues with Robert further, but Lucy's texts were making me reevaluate that plan.

Grabbing for Steph's phone, I decided I would have to make Robert think she was in imminent danger at this very moment. It was the only way. I had already laid the foundation; now it was time to ramp it up. I crafted what I hoped was a terrifying note for any friend to read and hit send:

Robert—he hit me, he hit
me hard. I'm scared. I think
he's going to kill me

There was nothing at first. I wondered if it had gone through, but a few minutes later, Robert tried calling. Again and again. I ignored it, the better to make him think I was in deep trouble. His frantic text was next.

I called 911. They are on their
way. CALL ME

Grinning as it came in, I started packing up the motel room. This next phase might be a little accelerated from my original plan, but it was going fine, just fine. There was just one thing left to do, and I would do it that night. In the meantime, I would look up Greyhound buses back to San Diego. If Raven said it was the best place to walk across, that was good enough for me. I knew I couldn't risk flying to San Diego with a phony passport, US officials being so diligent. That passport would be saved for Mexico. I would buy a Greyhound ticket with cash and without an ID. People did that sort of thing all the time. It would be a long way, but I'd get there and get across the border.

There was a Greyhound leaving at five the next morning. That would work—I needed the overnight hours to plant Steph's stuff and mine in Trent's backyard; then I could hang out at the bus station while I waited.

Pulling out the temporary tattoos from CVS, I put a rose on my wrist and a snake on my collarbone, admiring how they added to the overall punk rock look. I organized all of my stuff and made my final list of to-dos on the motel pad of paper.

Another text came in from Robert:

Steph—what the hell is going
on? Police went by Trent's
house and no one was there.

Where are you?? I'm trying to
do everything I can think of. I'm
sick with worry.

Sorry, Robert, I thought. *I have to ignore this.*

It was time to drop another hint to Anna. So far she thought I was with a great guy named Trent McCarthy. She needed a clue that things weren't going so well. Picking up my own phone instead of Stephanie's, I texted:

This guy Trent is super sexy
but he has a temper. Don't
worry, I can handle myself.
Don't tell Glenn.

I hit send and waited. She wrote back almost right away.

Things have been crazy here.
Glenn is in the hospital.

Well, that was good news. He couldn't hurt me if he was there.

Glenn's in the hospital? I
promise I will send your
money soon. Thanks for
everything.

Yeah, robbery at the trailer if
you know what I mean. He got
beat up pretty badly. You're
good though? You don't need
anything else?

I'm good

After that exchange, I got to work on a fake voice message. The most important one: the 9-1-1 call I would need to place tonight that would bring police to arrest Trent after I planted all of the evidence.

I typed these words into the chat box for Stephanie to say:

"Please help me, my boyfriend is going to kill me. He already killed another woman named Jasmine. I'm at 4240 Horizon Lane in Atlanta. His name is Trent McCarthy. Please, please hurry."

When I played it back, it didn't have the urgency that such a call might normally have, but it did sound like her voice, so I would have to live with it. It was the best I could do.

To distract myself the rest of the day, I googled towns in Mexico, exchange rates, safe and unsafe places for Americans to go, how to beat Montezuma's revenge, and anything else I could think of about Mexico on my phone, the phone I would soon be destroying with a garden trowel.

I needed a burner phone, and I wanted to square up with Anna before I left the country. Walking to the motel front desk, I asked the clerk where I could buy a padded envelope and some stamps and where I could get a temporary phone, and he directed me to two places. At the post office, I took $500 in cash and slipped it in the envelope, then addressed it to her and paid for overnight postage. It felt good to send it off. Then I went to the second store and paid cash for a phone that would get me across the country. I figured I'd have to get another one in Mexico that worked with their cell system.

That night I had to wait until after midnight to sneak into Trent's backyard. I was wearing the black thrift store hat, wheeling Steph's carry-on with her laptop, robin's-egg blue purse, wallet, phone, and some jewelry in it, and carrying the ski mask, plus wearing all black clothing. The motel was close to his place, and it was a short walk.

When I got within sight of his condo, I looked around. Conscious of those doorbell Ring cam things, I slipped through the hedges of a neighbor's house, pulled on my ski mask, and crawled under bushes, dragging the suitcase behind me awkwardly until I was at the side of his building away from the eye of a camera he might have. Then I slowly shimmied and slithered my way around to the back, keeping my body pressed against the building the whole time.

The backyard was quiet and dark, and the lights in all of the condos were off, these people obviously being working professionals who had to get up in the morning. Using the trowel I had gotten at the garden store, I dug two holes in two different parts of the backyard as quickly as I could, then got ready for the final damning 9-1-1 call.

Putting our two phones next to each other, I dialed 9-1-1 on Steph's phone. As soon as the operator answered, I hit play on the fake voice memo on my phone, and Steph's voice rang out:

"Please help me, my boyfriend is going to kill me. He already killed another woman named Jasmine. I'm at 4240 Horizon Lane in Atlanta. His name is Trent McCarthy. Please, please hurry."

It was only a matter of minutes now.

Wiping Steph's phone with alcohol wipes in hopes of erasing any of my DNA, I hurriedly buried Steph's wallet, phone, and some of her jewelry in one area and my wallet in another in the dirt, covering both up.

Her phone would be further evidence for the police and would have the photos from around Atlanta on her photo reel, the texts with her family and friends on her text chain. My own wallet would match with my DNA from inside Trent's condo and make it look as if he had killed two women, thus getting Glenn off my trail. Whatever was going on with him, I knew he would be out of the hospital eventually. It was just the high-profile murder I needed to keep Glenn, my family, or anyone else from looking for me. If Trent could be framed as a womanizing murderer and I was a drifter, it was completely conceivable that we met somewhere and had a fling, and he then killed me too, keeping my underwear and Steph's as trophies for his work. I put her rolling bag with the laptop in it in one of the garbage cans in the back of the condo.

Done and panting with exertion, I took off the ski mask and walked away as quickly and casually as I could, hearing police sirens approaching. Making my way to the closest Walmart, I went around to the back and used the trowel to smash the GREETINGS FROM HOT-LANTA mug and my phone into smithereens, sprinkling half of them into the dumpster and dumping the other half at a garbage can down the street, just to be sure police couldn't find all of anything at once and put it back together. I ditched the trowel at a third garbage can.

After walking back to the motel and grabbing my two bags, it was time to check out. I had to walk all the way to the Greyhound station with no ability to call an Uber since my burner phone wasn't set up for it and there could be no trace of my credit card anymore, but I had so much adrenaline I needed the movement anyway.

I kept thinking over every detail again and again. Had I forgotten anything? Done anything that would trace police to me? I couldn't think of any loose details, and I finally began to relax. True freedom was waiting for me as soon as that bus would begin to pull away.

When I walked into the Greyhound depot at 2:55 a.m., the smell of urine was strong and there were a few loners and drunks milling about. Finding a bench off to the side, I tucked all of my belongings close to me and waited.

They called for boarding at 4:40 a.m. I was the first one in line, my fake passport in my new cloth holder right on my chest. Taking a seat in the back row, I set my stuff on the seat next to me so no one would join me. I needn't have worried. There were less than a dozen people on the bus.

It was still dark as we pulled away, the lights of the city whizzing past. I thought of Trent, likely being hauled away to jail, and I smiled. I thought of Stephanie and how she had to die to make this possible, and I felt a pang of remorse again, but I pushed it away. For the first time in my entire life—childhood all the way through adulthood—I was doing something on my time, just for me. And I had succeeded. I was hiding in plain sight, just as I had wanted to do. Memories of Allison and Stephanie seemed to be fading with each mile the bus drove from Atlanta.

It had taken me less than a week from the morning I woke up at Glenn's and snuck out. Less than a week and I had succeeded in upending my entire world. I had more money than I had ever had in one setting. I had new clothes and a fake passport and a destination. Glenn would soon think I was dead, my family too. I had a plan, a future that was all my own. And it hadn't been that hard. A little stealing, a few hair changes, a bunch of lies to various people. OK, yes, one murder. But here I was. As a major bonus, I'd sent a total jerk down the river for the murder of two women twenty-seven years after I had done the same to Drake for the death of Allison.

Not that I hadn't been scared at many points. It was terrifying that morning six days prior when I had to tiptoe out of the trailer with Glenn sleeping. I had been apprehensive about buying a ticket to San Diego, scared to sneak into Stephanie's hotel room, to put that pillow over her face, to dispose of her body, to go into Trent's room and plant evidence, to follow Trent and frame him, to dig the holes in his backyard as my final damning evidence to put him away.

I figured between the DNA in Trent's suitcase, the two pairs of underwear with his semen in his breast pocket, the paper trail I had left for Robert and others via texts, the voice memos and photos, the money withdrawn from Steph's accounts, the 9-1-1 call, and Steph's and my personal items buried in the backyard, he was cooked.

After all, Steph had said she was flying to Atlanta with him, and there was evidence of her paying with a credit card for a ticket and showing up to board the plane. Heck, even if you watched a video of passengers going through security, you would see her (me) walking through, and she (me) had made it through security with no issues. I had even cocked my head slightly as she did when I greeted the TSA security officers just so the footage would be believable.

There was evidence she had been at his condo from the texts and photos. Trent had no alibi thanks to Raven slipping a little something-something into his drink. He had been inside sick for two days, so he couldn't claim he wasn't doing what Steph's texts said he was doing. She had told Robert on Sunday that she and Trent stayed in all day; then she told Robert on Monday they were sightseeing.

As for me, there was the text exchange I had with Anna. That should be enough to place me with this guy and show that he had a temper. That would make it seem believable to Glenn and everyone else.

How was I this fucking good? I leaned my head against the

window of the bus and felt a huge smile coming on as I congratulated myself. I had outsmarted everybody. I was a mastermind. It was all just sweet justice, and as my eyelids began to feel heavy and close, I said a final goodbye to men like Glenn and Trent and Drake. They could all fuck themselves.

I was in charge now.

CHAPTER 43

Jasmine

Three Weeks Later

Crossing the border at Tijuana had not been a problem—Raven was 100 percent right. Mexico seemed eager to have me, and the lone female security guard only gave my passport a cursory glance, even as my heart threatened to burst out of my chest for fear of what would happen if she detained me.

Once across the walking bridge into Tijuana, I wanted to get away from the Baja peninsula quickly—too many Americans—so I caught the first bus south and just kept going until I got to the place I somehow always knew I was destined to be: Puerto Escondido.

The aging bus sputtered into the station just as the sun was starting to set. I walked a few blocks to the beach, bags still in hand. Birds were circling and singing overhead; a warm breeze kept me at just the right temperature. I watched the sun slowly melt into the horizon, and I was hooked. I would never leave.

The village was exactly what I had pictured from high school and more. Out of the way, still with fishermen leaving on boats every morning, but touristy too. It was casual and fun as heck, not as overrun with Americans as other Mexican hotspots. Bars and restaurants dotted the boardwalk and beach, nearly all of them with SE BUSCA AYUDA (help wanted) signs.

The first place I walked up to hired me on the spot. I couldn't tell anyone how much money I actually had with me—still over $10,000 of Stephanie's—or I'd be the next dead American tourist, so I lived in a cheap motel, went to work as a waitress, bought another phone, and started refreshing my Spanish. I even got a tattoo—real this time—of a compass. It reminded me to go where the wind blew.

It had been hard to keep up with news about myself and the murder. One, because the news was entirely in Spanish, and two, because I didn't want to be obvious every time something came on about the high-profile case back in America. I also had a phone that wasn't very high quality, and service was spotty. From what I could gather through the weeks, investigators had somehow figured out that an imposter was at the conference (I had no idea how they deduced that), and that the person had then gone back to Atlanta. They thought it was likely to be me, but also said they believed Trent had then killed me in a dispute over Stephanie's money.

Ha! Let them run with that story. They hadn't found my body yet, but they were sure it was coming at some point. Meanwhile, Trent rotted in jail. It made me smile.

The *only* fly in the ointment was that some guy with a poodle and a purple cape held his own press conference, dog in hand, to say he saw Stephanie and a woman in a tight top sitting on a bench near Trent's apartment talking to each other the night Trent got back from the conference. He claimed he had secretly taken a picture of the women from down the street because he had a gut feeling we were not from that area and it would be important.

I remembered seeing the man in purple eye us as I went to

hand Raven her money, right at the moment when she hissed at me not to do it there. Now this guy wanted to have his moment in the sun and share this little tidbit. But nothing seemed to have come of it, so I didn't worry. Besides, an actress from LA was now being reported as missing, and news stations were covering that. I was moving out of the limelight.

As I went about my days in this new paradise, I looked for Raven in crowds and on the beach, just in case, but there had been nothing yet. Meanwhile, everything was so cheap down here, from food to clothes, it made me drool. I finally felt like a wealthy woman, and I loved every second of it.

On my way to work I would pass a small beach shack painted a brilliant turquoise blue. One sparkling sunny morning, an EN VENTA (for sale) sign was on it and I noticed two men inside doing some plastering. Gingerly, I walked up the wooden front steps and poked my head in, calling, "¡Buenos días!"

"Buenos días, señorita," one of the men said, and then added when he saw me, "¿Puedo ayudarle?" (Can I help you?)

"¿Me permite ver?" (Would you allow me to look around?)

"Sí," said the younger guy, looking at me eagerly. Even with my dark hair, I knew I looked different from most of the Mexican women down here. My skin was a pearly white, my eyes light.

They went back to plastering, chattering to each other in Spanish and stealing glances at me. I walked around, trailing my fingertips against walls and banisters, peering into a cozy bedroom and an office, imagining myself sitting on the porch gazing out over the sun and sand with a cup of warm, rich coffee. The place was delightful, and I could already see myself filling it with Mexican pottery and rugs, the bright colors so inviting to the eye.

A sea breeze swept past me as I stood at the window, and I

knew that this was my future home. Quickly, I walked back to the workers.

"¿Cuánto cuesto?" (How much does it cost?) I asked.

"Trescientos treinta y siete mil" (337,000), said the younger man.

I sucked in my breath.

"Pesos," he added, and I exhaled, doing the math. I had already learned to make fast calculations as a waitress. That was less than $19,000 US. It was absolutely doable! I could put a down payment on it and start collecting furniture! My eyes glistened.

"¿Americana?" the older man asked.

I hesitated. Should I lie? Yes, I should. The better to put some distance between myself and any questions.

"Canadiense. Soy de Toronto. Muy frío." (Canadian. I am from Toronto. Very cold.) He smiled and I waved goodbye, visions of the cottage growing in my mind. I was having a blast mentally decorating it already.

At work a few nights later, a TV was on over the bar area, tuned to CNN International but with the volume down. Tourists and locals sat at the square tiki bar, brightly colored lamps waving in the breeze above their heads. Music pulsed from our sound system. Everyone was drinking and talking and having a generally amazing time. I loved this place. It was exactly what I had dreamed of when I left Glenn, exactly what I had hoped for when I followed Stephanie.

Now I had the power, the money, the freedom to make my own decisions. No man in my life, no ties to anything or anyone. Just serving up pitchers of margaritas and bowls of chips with the best guacamole I had ever had, along with fajitas, burritos, enchiladas, and anything else our creative cooks whipped up.

No one bothered me down here. I felt safer and happier than I think I ever had before. Each morning, I would go for a long walk on the beach, stopping to pick up shells, which I kept on the dresser in my motel room. Maybe I would put them together into some sort of collage for the new cottage. I was imagining I could put that down payment on the place within a week or two.

And then . . .

I looked up at the TV. There was a picture of Raven.

With the volume down and the subtitles on, all I saw were flashes of some Spanish words I knew and some I did not.

Trying to look busy wiping down shot glasses but flitting my eyes back and forth frantically to the TV, I saw enough to know that Raven had been arrested in a passport bust the feds were calling the "Hurricane Passport Ring" in Atlanta. My eyes squinted to read more as the subtitles came flying across the screen.

It looked like Raven had worked out some sort of plea deal by telling police she had gotten me, currently one of the most notorious women in America, a passport to use at Tijuana to cross the border.

The blood drained from my whole being, and I dropped a shot glass, hearing it shatter on the floor. Kneeling hurriedly, I grabbed to pick it up without looking, and a broken shard of glass punctured my finger.

"Shit," I said and looked down at the finger. No one at the bar area seemed to notice, though. Salsa music continued pumping, and a few drunk tourists were up dancing.

Sticking my finger into my mouth and tasting the metallic tang of blood, I looked at the TV again. A picture of my fake passport was being shown on-screen along with my fake name:

Erica Birchfield. Oh no, oh holy hell. This couldn't be happening. My eyes darted to the name tag pinned to my shirt: ERICA.

How could Raven do this? How could she rat me out? She told me she had my back. She took my money. We had known each other for decades. We were friends. Anger spiraled into my whole chest. I felt like a dragon that could literally spit fire.

Looking at the TV again . . . there was now a picture of Allison on the screen, taken hours before her death. She was wearing the black catsuit with rhinestones, whiskers perfect, her hair shiny as a mink.

One of Allison's friends must have taken the picture. How did it get on the news? The only thing I could think of was that Drake's brother gave it to Raven when he asked her for any tips she might have, and Raven gave it to the police when she turned me in. Raven had never mentioned the photo when she told me about seeing Drake's brother in the bar. Another layer of betrayal.

But suddenly . . .

It got worse.

On-screen next was a picture of *me* from our high school yearbook. The video switched back to the announcer, and she began talking. The Spanish subtitles on the screen started to swim in front of my eyes so quickly that I couldn't digest them. I couldn't process what was happening. The room swayed.

Raven. Did. This. To. Me. She. Told. Them. She. Ratted. Me. Out.

Nausea overtook me.

The words Raven had said as we sat on the bench by Trent's house came storming back:

I do what I have to do to make money . . . and to keep out of jail. Been there once. I will do anything not to go back, and I do mean anything. I'd turn in my own mother if I had to. It ain't easy to make a living, but I find ways. Just gotta stay one step ahead of the feds, you know?

She sold me out to the feds to keep herself out of jail. Told them everything. We had been RAJE: Raven, Anna, Jasmine. Now *rage* was all I felt.

Calm down, Jasmine. Allison's death was twenty-seven years ago. There's not one shred of evidence against you, I counseled myself.

But as for Stephanie's murder? This was very, very bad for me. If Raven shared all of the text messages I had sent her, plus the story of her spiking Trent's drink and faking pictures at Centennial Olympic Park and the phony passport, I would be in deep trouble.

I had to get out of here, had to change my hair and my name again, to flee as fast as I could.

Where could I go? The passport was no good now. I couldn't even cross farther south into Guatemala without it likely being flagged. I was stuck in Mexico as a fugitive, a wanted woman, my picture with a black pixie haircut all over the news. It was only a matter of time.

Unless . . .

I looked over at the drunk tourists dancing, all oblivious to their purses sitting back at the tables off to the sides. A woman about my height caught my eye, arms flailing overhead as she moved. She had short hair like me, but platinum blond and in a different spiky style. It would take a mountain of hair dye, but I could turn black hair into blond if I tried hard enough. If I had her ID, I could do a lot of things, even more with her credit cards.

I knew where she had been sitting because I had served her earlier. I began to drift toward that spot and to her purse, which remained on the table. I kept my eyes on her, but she was oblivious, dancing away. If I could just grab her items . . . But no, this would never work. She would notice things were missing, right?

Unless . . .

No, Jasmine, I scolded myself.

You can't. You are done with that.

But you're next to an ocean, the other part of me thought. *And there's a luggage store in the shopping district. And a pillow on this woman's bed in her hotel.* Her key card was likely in her purse. Tourists went missing in Mexico on a very regular basis; people would suspect a drug deal gone wrong or a spiked drink from a shifty male bartender, not little old me.

I conjured up the image of a giant suitcase, of shoving her into the ocean, taking her stuff and escaping again. My fingers grazed her purse and tiptoed their way to the zipper, which I began to slide open. She danced on, throwing her head back and laughing.

But just as my hand began descending to the promised land of her wallet, I felt a hard tap on my shoulder.

Somehow, I knew it wasn't just the bar manager needing something. I turned slowly, my stomach a swamp pit.

There stood two men and a woman.

The men were unfamiliar.

But the woman . . .

It hit me with such electric force that I felt as if I were taking a bath and someone had thrown in a plugged-in hair dryer.

CHAPTER 44

Stephanie

Puerto Escondido, Mexico

Jasmine let out a piercing scream and took off running, pushing through the dancing tourists as a woman with spiky blond hair yelled: "Hey! Watch out!"

Officer Healy and Officer Rodriguez bolted after Jasmine, all three a blur of arms and legs. I chased after them as best I could.

Officer Healy reached Jasmine first and wrapped her in a tackle. They went down in a bundle. She began screaming and writhing around.

Panting, I pulled to a stop next to them.

"The jig is up, Jasmine. I'm with San Diego PD. We're working with Mexican authorities," said Officer Healy, pinning her to the ground.

"Whaaat? What are you talking about?" she croaked, twisting her head wildly to look at me. Officer Healy followed her gaze.

"Recognize her, do you? I think you might remember Stephanie Monroe."

Jasmine's eyes filled with horror and disbelief. I could only imagine what it must be like to see a woman alive who you thought was dead. I wanted to speak, but my breathing was still ragged from running, so I put my hands on my knees, gasping for air while glaring at her, hatred burning in my whole being.

Officer Healy had his knee embedded on Jasmine's back and spoke again.

"You thought you got away with Allison's murder in high school and Stephanie's murder until now, didn't you? You even faked your own murder. And somehow you framed Drake and Trent along the way."

"I don't know what you're talking about. You have the wrong person," she cried out, eyes darting wildly between me and Officer Rodriguez.

"Do we?" He pushed down harder on her back and twisted one arm behind her. She winced. "Then why'd you run?"

"I'm not a murderer. I'm a regular person, just a waitress."

"Just a waitress, huh?" asked Officer Healy. "You did a pretty good job impersonating a news director in San Diego, Jasmine. Your time is up. Give it up. Do it for Diana. Do it for Allison. Don't you owe them at least that?"

"Who's . . . Diana?" She sputtered as a trickle of mascara started making its way down one cheek.

Finally, I had steadied my breath enough to speak.

"Diana was an actress."

"An actress?" Her eyes were wild. "What do you mean?"

I sighed. It all seemed like a bizarre dream now, how I had concocted this idea for a little weekend fun to scratch my rebellious itch, how it came to me the day Lucy had shown me the website: Find My Doppelganger. We both laughed as she pointed out how you could put in a picture of yourself and watch it spit out an actor or actress from its database whose facial features and skin tone closely resembled yours. For an extra fee, you could send them a picture and sample of your hair, and they would clone it for a high-end wig, so professionally done it wouldn't come off and a person could shower or sleep in it.

I played with the site a few times, just for kicks, late at night when I had trouble sleeping, and I thought of the absurd idea of using it one day. When my boss, Dave, told me I was going to Southern California for a conference, this one with people I had never met, and it was so close to Tijuana, where I wanted to explore, it just seemed like a crazy thing to try. It was the sort of adventure I hadn't allowed myself to have since DePaul, a true "carpe diem" moment. I imagined sharing the story with Robert afterward, the shocked look on his face, the awe in his voice, but first I needed to accomplish this trip. Telling someone beforehand would have cracked my courage. Just a few nights in Mexico, that was all I wanted. No one would get hurt; no one would know. It was fun.

Diana could have been my sister, we were so close in looks, and I was shocked at the further resemblance when I used the "transfer my hair" option to swap her hair for mine. I paid the premium for the high-end wig.

We met at the hotel and exchanged phones so that she could make sure everyone back home thought I was at the conference by sending pictures to my Facebook, Instagram, Threads, and Twitter accounts. For added insurance of my whereabouts, if anyone tried "Find My iPhone," for any reason, it would ping in San Diego. We traded all of our clothing except underwear and bras, and we thankfully wore the same size shoes. I gave Diana the passwords to both my laptop and phone on a Post-it note that I stuck on the laptop screen. When I told Diana that I had to take notes at the conference for Dave, she told me not to worry, she was an excellent note-taker, the best in her acting classes, and she would write down everything in a Google Doc I had waiting for her on the laptop. We pored over the conference schedule. I noted the one session I wanted to have especially great notes on, mental health, as it was so important to me, Dave, and our HR team back in Madison. The National Press Foundation was spending a lot of money to bring in the best experts in the country, and Dave was counting on me for my takeaways. Diana told me mental health was her own highest priority, and she would be a sponge.

With a suitcase full of her shorts, T-shirts, and sundresses, and my passport in hand, I took off happily to the Baja peninsula to peruse beach cottages and think about whether I wanted to actually move. At night after house hunting, I would drink a Dos Equis on the beach and walk up and down looking for shells. It was a perfect weekend escape, just what I needed, and I even found a few places I loved. I felt like my old college self, and more genuinely me than I had been in a while.

Diana promised to alert me right away if anything was amiss. When I didn't hear from her, naturally I assumed all was well. She was supposed to text Robert that I was extending the trip by one day just to give me a bit more time on the beach and to let all the other conference attendees go home Saturday before I returned to the hotel for the swap. I was planning to fly back to Madison Sunday in time for work Monday. Diana and I were supposed to meet to switch back phones, wallets, and clothes, but when I texted her, she said she was out of town for a week and then stopped responding.

I panicked, calling her over and over and then racing to the hotel in La Jolla, but she was nowhere to be found. In a frantic haze, I drove to LA, but no one answered at her address. I contacted the Find My Doppelganger website for help, but they pointed out that I had signed a waiver absolving them of any responsibility. I hadn't even read what I had signed. It was ten pages long, and I had just clicked "Acknowledge" and added my electronic signature.

Still in LA, I was trying to figure out my next move when national news hit about me, some guy named Trent McCarthy, and a woman named Jasmine Littleton in Atlanta. I was so confused. I remembered a woman named Jasmine from my flight to Denver. Was this the same person?

Petrified with indecision, I did nothing but curl into the fetal position at my hotel for days. Going public would mean exposing my lies, but I realized I had to . . . for Diana. She was an innocent person, a struggling actress. She was getting ready for a revival of *The Golden Girls*, but had some time before rehearsals and just wanted to make a little money.

So I went back to San Diego and walked into the police station closest to the hotel, asking to speak with a detective. Soon I was sobbing and confessing everything. They asked me to keep it quiet until they could find out what happened to Diana, allowing me only to contact a handful of close family members and friends. They didn't want knowledge of my existence to hamper the investigation or to get back to someone who had potentially done something criminal. When they finally cracked the case and asked me to come along on the arrest for identification purposes, I knew I owed Diana's family at least that.

Now Officer Rodriguez turned to me:

"Is this her? The woman from the plane?"

I looked at her again. The hair was different, short and black, and she had tattoos I didn't remember, but the face was undoubtedly Jasmine's.

"Yes," I said. Her eyes and mine locked. I narrowed mine. She did the same. A rage rose into my throat and I yelled out, "What the hell did Diana or I ever do to you? You met me on a plane and stalked me. You stole my money. What's wrong with you? You're a pathetic excuse for a human being."

She didn't reply, but turned her head to look down the sidewalk. Following her gaze, I could see a turquoise cottage with a FOR SALE sign in Spanish.

"Is that what this was all about? A beach cottage?" I asked. "How ironic. We both wanted the same thing. You know what? We could have been friends in another life if you weren't a psychopath."

Officer Healy jumped in again.

"That's probably enough, Stephanie. We know you're angry." Then he addressed Jasmine directly. "Raven told us we would find you in this town. In fact, she told us everything."

"Whaaat??" Jasmine cried. Her body began to shake violently. "But . . . how did you find Raven?"

"You want to know? I'll tell you how it *all* happened," Officer Healy said. "First we got a tip from someone at your table at the conference in San Diego that certain things didn't make sense and that it wasn't actually Stephanie in attendance. We looked up airline records and saw that you sat in the same row as Stephanie on the way to Denver, and we learned you subsequently bought a ticket to San Diego at the Denver airport and rented a minivan with a wheelchair lift in San Diego. After that, you seemed to fall off the grid. There was no record of you until your wallet was found at Trent's. So how did you get to Atlanta? There was security footage of someone who looked like Stephanie—same clothes, same hair—going through the San Diego airport on the way to Atlanta, but we soon learned from the real Stephanie that she never left Southern California. It all started to add up, but the thing that really did you in was the guy in purple taking your picture with Raven in Trent's neighborhood. With enhanced photo technology, we knew it was you, not Stephanie. Then your ex-boyfriend called Madison police to say some high school friend might have been in on this with you. He had an address and everything. All we had to do was track down Raven. That's when we found out she was dealing drugs and helping a passport ring. Raven was looking at fifteen to twenty years in federal prison, and I'll tell you what—she turned on you so fast it would make your head spin."

"Noooo . . ." Jasmine moaned. Her body went from agitated to limp as the realization of the predicament she was in seemed to overtake her. She added softly: "The cardboard box . . . the birthday card . . . I should have burned it all . . . the bastards are going to win, aren't they?"

"Who are the bastards?" I asked, venom still boiling over in my voice. To me, she was the bastard.

Jasmine paused, gulping air for a few moments before speaking.

"Glenn . . . Trent . . . Drake . . . my mother . . . my brother and sister . . . the Fun Bunch . . . all of them, they're winning. And you, you too," she said, staring daggers at me.

"What the *hell* did I *ever* do to you?" I pressed again, my agitation growing. "I was nice to you on the plane. I listened to your stories, I answered your questions."

"OK, I think that's about enough," Officer Healy said, trying to cool the tension.

"You had the perfect life," Jasmine said. "That was enough. You just had to be Little Miss Perfect, didn't you?"

"That is just not true. You don't know a thing about me. And by the way, the bastards you talked about. Guess what? They didn't kill anyone," I fired at her. "And you did."

She was silent for a few moments, but then a sob escaped her throat and she whispered, "I guess my mom was right."

"About what?" I couldn't help but ask. Officer Healy shot me a warning glance, and I knew he would cut us off again soon. Jasmine paused before speaking softly one more time.

"I *am* too much like my dad. My mom said I never should have been born. The world would have been better off without me."

I said nothing. I couldn't really argue that point, and I didn't have one ounce of a desire to comfort her.

"Where's the body?" Officer Rodriguez jumped in. "Where's Diana?"

Jasmine just shook her head.

"We'll find her," Officer Healy said. "You obviously got that wheelchair lift for a reason. Video from Walmart shows you buying a giant suitcase and hair dye. We know you took her somewhere. It's only a matter of time, and we'll bring her back for a proper funeral. She deserves that."

"Trent killed her. You'll see. His key card and handkerchief are there," she said.

"Where?" asked Officer Healy, but she only shook her head again.

"Time for the handcuffs, Jasmine," Officer Rodriguez said.

"Nooo . . ." she moaned again, but we all ignored her.

Jasmine looked toward the beach shack one more time. She sniffled as the first cuff went on her left wrist. When the second one clicked on her right wrist, I heard her whisper:

"Goodbye, sweet cottage."

Then she shut her eyes.

What Jasmine didn't know was that I had said my own goodbye recently. After lying about my whereabouts, I had resigned from Channel 3 before Dave had a chance to decide whether to fire me. I knew it was a tough decision he was wrestling with, as he cared about me, but I made his choice easy: I needed to preserve what little dignity I had. There was no way I could return to the newsroom given that everyone knew I was a liar and a sneak. Bruce was named the interim news director while they searched for my replacement.

Turning to look at the ocean, I thought about my future, so unknown now. I had no idea what I would do for a job, none. Only one thing was for sure: I planned to start an acting scholarship in Diana's name with some savings I had. It was the least I could do. Jasmine had stolen a lot of my money, but she didn't know about my money market accounts or retirement savings.

Gazing at the darkness of the ocean, I whispered:

"I'm so, so sorry, Diana. I would do anything to rewind time."

EPILOGUE

Stephanie

Five Months Later

How does one go about writing a press release announcing flavored milk? That was my dilemma. The Midwest Dairy Association had a new flavor—mint caramel—that was being unveiled at the Wisconsin State Fair, and I had been assigned to write the release. It was still odd to me to be on the other side of the public relations machine. Instead of receiving hundreds of press releases each day, I was sending them, hoping to catch the eye of a news manager who would assign a reporter or a photojournalist to do a story about whatever it was we were pushing.

Sighing, I tried to think of a punchy way to sell the milk story to local TV stations. "Moooo-ving on Up: New Milk Coming to the State Fair!" was my current headline, but I wasn't convinced it was the winner. Leaning back in my chair, I was looking at the ceiling to think when my desk phone rang.

"Stephanie? There's a Mr. McCarthy here to see you," Julia, the receptionist, said.

Mr. McCarthy? Who was that? My mind tried to flip to various people I had been meeting with recently on different projects. Our little PR firm could be hired by just about anyone to help spread their word. Maybe Mr. McCarthy was with the Wienermobile, another account we had just secured. The giant hot-dog-shaped vehicle would drive around the state during summer months, encouraging people to buy Oscar Mayer products. Sighing, I stood up, thinking of ways I might need to market a hot dog on wheels as well as flavored milk.

This was the only job I could find after leaving Channel 3. I was the woman who had lied to her station, and I was still blackballed in news circles. Even our local community college wouldn't hire me to teach writing, citing their ethics code. So I'd landed here, in a strip mall between a Taco Bell and a party supply store. Our building looked more like a tax-prep place than a PR firm; we had cubicles, not offices. But it paid the bills and kept me close to Robert and within a four-hour drive of Evan. My reunion with friends and family had been incredible, but I was still trying to make amends with the people I loved.

Walking to our tiny lobby, I saw a tall guy with slicked-back hair leaning against one wall.

"Well, well, if it isn't the *real* Stephanie Monroe . . . and in the flesh," he said with a grin, stepping forward and looking me up and down. I couldn't help but notice how white his teeth were. "Trent McCarthy. I trust that name rings a bell for you."

Holy crap, this was the guy Jasmine had framed.

My mind scrambled. What was he doing *here*, in Madison? I'd heard he was let out of jail, innocent of all charges, but his station in Atlanta refused to take him back, saying he had violated their code of conduct in other ways.

"Hello . . ." I said hesitantly. "Nice to meet you. Can I help you with something?"

"You sure can, let's sit down and talk," he said. "I already asked your receptionist here . . . Julia . . . lovely name . . . if there are any available conference rooms, and she told me there were, so let's hit it."

He winked at Julia, who blushed. Putting his hand on my elbow, he began to steer me as if he were leading the way instead of the other way around. I shook him off. We walked to the conference room, and I sat down as far across the table from him as I could get.

"You know you're even prettier than the fake Stephanie! It's too bad we didn't really meet at the conference," he said, and I could feel my skin begin to crawl. I had read plenty of things about the way he acted toward "me" in San Diego and the way he was with women in general.

"Why are you here?" I asked, wanting to cut to the chase.

"Because I have the best idea in the world. I know you're going to love it. Get ready for this . . . I think we need to go in on a partnership."

"I'm sorry, what?" I asked, trying to maintain a calm face.

"A partnership. Listen, Steph, you got screwed out of this whole deal, and so did I. And now you're working here, and I can't find a job. It's bullshit. So I decided we should write a book together and make a million bucks each. What a story we have to tell, right? I was thinking you could be the writer, and I'll tell you everything that happened at the conference and after. That psycho bitch Jasmine tried to pull one over on me. And she tried to *kill* you. People will want to read our story. We'll go 50–50. I flew up to meet you in person and figured we could get started right away."

He leaned back in his chair and put his hands behind his head, beaming. I was so shocked that I couldn't even form words, and I just stared at him. Writing a book was the last thing I wanted to do. Writing one with him would be worse. And then there was his grand proposal: 50–50 when I would be the one doing all of the writing.

I found my voice and tried to be polite but firm. "Thank you for thinking of me, Trent, but I will pass. I have no interest in retelling this story."

"You're kidding, right?" he asked, taking his hands off his head and sitting up straight in his chair.

"I'm not kidding, I want to move on. I don't want to relive what happened. You go ahead and write one if you'd like."

"It wouldn't be the same without *you*," he said. "Two former news directors who got the short end of the stick but came back swinging. It's an American tale of redemption. People will love it. Come on, Steph."

It bothered me that he had called me "Steph" twice already as if we were old friends. I could feel my jaw tensing.

"I need to go back to work now," I said. "Thank you for the offer, but my final answer is no."

His eyes narrowed, and one of his hands balled into a fist.

"So I came all this way for nothing?"

"It appears that way. I didn't ask you to fly to Madison."

"Tell me why you won't do this, Stephanie Monroe. You don't need the money? I don't believe that with you working in a shithole like this. What are you writing—press releases about some new toilet paper brand? This can't be what you want in life, and it sure as hell isn't going to be the kind of place I land either. We have an escape route: a book. And I think we'd be fun partners. I'm in if you're in."

My insides were burning. This guy was repulsive.

"I'm not in. Julia will see you to the door," I said, standing up. His face was turning red, and he started thumping his balled fist on the table.

"But why, Steph, why? Tell me why you won't do this with me." His voice was a mix of desperation and anger.

If he wanted one more reason, he was going to get it. I put my hands on the table, leaning forward as I gave him a long, hard stare.

"Because you're a bastard, and bastards can't win."

ACKNOWLEDGMENTS

It's not often that you thank a stranger in your acknowledgments, but if not for the random woman sitting next to me on a plane, this book would likely not exist. Our conversation on the way to Denver got me thinking about these types of encounters in life.

My agents, Meg Ruley and Logan Harper of the Jane Rotrosen Agency, were brilliant in every step of the process, from early edits to taking it out to the world. Rebecca Scherer and Christina Hogrebe from JRA also offered invaluable input.

Jen Enderlin at St. Martin's Press was a dream editor. Her suggestions were gold, her marketing prowess unmatched, and she brought this entire project across the finish line with aplomb. At St. Martin's, I would also like to thank Brant Janeway, Christina Lopez, Erica Martirano, Katie Bassel, Kejana Ayala, Lisa Senz, and the folks at Macmillan Audio. I am indebted to copyeditor Mary Beth Constant for her excellent work and keen eye. The number of times I said "good catch" is surely in the double digits.

My husband, Paul, allowed me to slip away to my favorite writing spot time and again and patiently listened when I would read chapters aloud. His suggestions always strengthened the book and his enthusiasm for my writing lifted my heart. My two sons, Jake and Charlie, are my soul. They have no idea how much they mean to me.

I dedicated this book to my mother, Judy. She started her career at a New York City publishing house before becoming an English and English as a Second Language teacher. Her passion for libraries, reading, grammar, newspapers, and current events spurred me to become a journalist and a writer. My stepdad, Howard, entered my life at a critical time and quickly became a wonderful father figure. He too champions my work.

I wrote this book while working as a television news director, and I am indebted to my general manager, Anne Brown, and our company, Weigel Broadcasting, for their support.

Finally, to you, for taking time out of your life to open this book. I hope you enjoyed it. I certainly had a blast crafting it. As a debut novelist, I am humbled by everyone who had a hand in bringing this tale to fruition. More than anything, I am grateful. The ten-year-old girl who walked home from school every day making up stories in her head is looking at herself many decades later, and she is thankful.

ABOUT THE AUTHOR

Henry Jorgenson

Jessie Garcia is an award-winning journalist who has risen through the ranks in television news, first as a sports anchor/reporter, then to newsroom management. She is the news director at the CBS affiliate in Milwaukee. Jessie is the author of award-winning nonfiction books, and her documentary *Leaps and Bounds: The Men Who Changed Track and Field* was featured in over a dozen film festivals. She also taught journalism at four universities. A native of Madison, Wisconsin, Jessie has two grown sons and resides in Milwaukee with her husband, dog, and cat.